"A marriage proposal?"

"Is that what you think? Marriage? To you?" She gulped a breath, stifling her laughter. "That would be akin to not being married at all. You're never around. You hardly speak. You certainly won't touch—"

The rest of her words were cut off by his mouth. She cried out, but the sound was lost, consumed in those ravaging lips.

It was nothing like the quick, chaste kiss Bloodsworth gave her upon the completion of their wedding vows.

He nibbled on her bottom lip sweetly. When he stroked the bruised flesh with one swipe of his tongue, everything inside her shook alert, awake and alive and hungry . . .

By Sophie Jordan

How to Lose a Bride in One Night
Lessons from a Scandalous Bride
Wicked in Your Arms
Wicked Nights with a Lover
In Scandal They Wed
Sins of a Wicked Duke
Surrender to Me
One Night with You
Too Wicked to Tame
Once upon a Wedding Night

Sophie Jordan

How to Lose a Bride in One Night

Forgotten Princesses

AVON
An Imprint of HarperCollins*Publishers*

This is a work of fiction. Names, characters, places, and incidents are products of the author's imagination or are used fictitiously and are not to be construed as real. Any resemblance to actual events, locales, organizations, or persons, living or dead, is entirely coincidental.

AVON BOOKS
An Imprint of HarperCollins*Publishers*
10 East 53rd Street
New York, New York 10022-5299

ISBN 978-0-06-203301-7
www.avonromance.com

First Avon Books mass market printing: August 2013

Printed in the U.S.A.

10 9 8 7 6 5 4 3 2 1

For Shana Galen, who helped plant the seed for this story.
Who knew a book of folk tales would be so inspiring?

How to Lose a Bride in One Night

Chapter One

It wasn't every day a woman lost her virginity.

This was the only justification Annalise could give herself for the way her hands trembled. Ordinary wedding day nerves and nothing more. Any bride would suffer it. Especially a bride like her. Plain. Crippled. Muddied lineage.

A little over a year ago she could barely afford a new pair of winter boots. By all accounts, a day such as this should never have occurred. And yet here she stood in a lavish gown of gold charmeuse trimmed in the finest Brussels lace, her hair swept up in emerald-studded combs. She had certainly never allowed herself the dream of a happily ever after such as this. Not before her father had found her, claimed her, and insisted she deserved only the finest things in life—namely her own knight in shining armor.

She buried her gloved hands into the voluminous skirts of her bridal gown as she crossed the vast expanse of lawn and reminded herself that she deserved happiness as much as the next girl.

It had showered earlier in the day, leaving the grass damp and yielding beneath her feet. Her jewel-studded slippers were soon soaked, the cold wetness seeping into her stockings and numbing her toes. Her husband walked a few feet in front of her, an assortment of young bucks on either side of him, all decked out in a vivid assortment of cravats and jackets, their boots polished to a high gleam. His closest friends, all young men from the finest families, garbed in finery the likes of which she had never touched as a seamstress's apprentice a mere year ago.

The irony was not lost on her. Peerage such as these had not even seen fit to grace the confines of Madame Brouchard's humble shop, and yet here she was. Among them.

One of them.

Her gaze fixed on her husband's back. As though sensing her stare, he looked over his shoulder at her. A slow smile curved his lips, and her heart tripped as it always did when he looked at her.

Husband. The word reverberated through her mind before sinking like a stone in her stomach, where it sat uncomfortably alongside the kippers and champagne from their wedding feast. Her thumb rolled against the band on her ring finger. She glanced down at the giant yellow diamond in disbelief. It was an enormous monstrosity that had been in the Bloodsworth family for generations. And now it was hers. She was a bona fide duchess. Married to a duke. And not just any duke. A young handsome man only seventh in line from the Crown.

He looked over his shoulder at her again and winked, grinning that endearing smile that had charmed her from their very first meeting. And he was besotted with *her,* too. Unbelievable but true. Her cheeks heated and she was certain she was as red-faced as any schoolgirl ensnared in the gaze of a member of the opposite gender.

Really, she was no callow maid. She had seen much of the world before Jack plucked her from obscurity. She should comport herself better. Especially now. As a duchess ought to.

A glance behind her revealed the massive stone-faced edifice of the new home she would now reign over. Dozens of windows lined the five-storied mausoleum, all dark eyes staring out at her in the fading day. The family seat of the Duke of Bloodsworth. And the Duchess of Bloodsworth—*her.*

Family and friends surrounded her as they made their way to the dock. Even that structure was bedecked with flowers and ribbons for the happy occasion. She glanced around her at the merry faces. Perhaps not friends, she amended. At least not hers. Lord Bloodsworth was exceedingly popular. The same could not be said for Annalise.

Her year in London had not afforded her many friendships. As the bastard daughter of Jack Hadley, her father's deep pockets might have won her entry into the finest ballrooms, but it did not win her esteem within the *ton.*

Once it became clear she had gained the young duke's favor, the ladies were quick to cast her withering looks. One such lady glared at her now. The beautiful Lady Joanna. A true English rose with her golden hair and sea-blue eyes. The duke had been paying her suit when he met Annalise. Everyone had been convinced he would offer for her. When Annalise had dared to ask him why he chose her over Joanna, his reply only deepened her regard for him.

You, Annalise, are a rare gem. I could not stomach being wed to a female who cannot engage me in discourse. It is my greatest fortune that I can see you better than these other fools.

"Nervous?" Marguerite, one of her half sisters, fell into step beside her. Her skirts swished softly on the night, mingling with the hum of conversation and soft laughter surrounding them.

Annalise tore her gaze from the sour-faced Joanna and offered a smile that belied the tremor in her voice. "Not at all."

"It's fine, you know," Grier added from her other side. "If you are."

Of her three half sisters, Annalise knew Grier the least. She'd only just arrived from Maldania a fortnight ago in order to meet Annalise and attend her wedding. The shock of marrying a duke was nearly as astonishing as learning that her half sister was a princess.

Until a year ago, Annalise had been an orphan, inhabiting a rented room in Yorkshire with two other shop girls employed by Madame Brouchard. Jack Hadley's man had found her. Evidently, Annalise's mother, dead these last six years, had once been Jack's paramour, and Annalise was in fact the bastard daughter of one the wealthiest men in England. All her life, she knew nothing of her father. Her mother never spoke of him and only scowled when Annalise mentioned him.

It was a fairy tale come true. Her father riding in on his white horse to save her from a life of drudgery. And the fairy tale only continued once she reached London and met the duke. After a whirlwind courtship, he'd proposed. It didn't matter to him that she was illegitimate. Or a cripple. Or plain as a wool sock.

Oh, she was no fool. She knew her dowry played a significant part in his interest, but he had assured her that he'd come to care for her as well—that they would have a marriage in the truest sense. That they had found love together. Butterflies fluttered in her stomach.

"I am a bit nervous," she admitted, wobbling when the foot of her lame leg hit a patch of uneven ground. Grier's arm tightened around her, stopping her from falling. It was a nuisance, but she had grown accustomed to this limitation of her body. She'd lived with the disability long enough. At fourteen she fell from a tree and broke her leg. Unfortunately, her limb never healed properly.

"Very normal," Marguerite asserted. "But anyone can see your handsome duke is clearly besotted with you. I'm certain he'll be a most solicitous husband."

Grier nodded. "For certain. Do you not agree, Cleo? You are the newlywed among us, after all."

Annalise glanced at her other sister—the first she had met upon moving to London. Cleo walked beside Grier, her lips pressed into a straight line that was unlike her usual smiling self. Especially since she'd married her Scotsman. She was rarely without smiles now. Only today she had been oddly solemn. All throughout the wedding ceremony and during brunch, she sat in pensive silence, even as her husband offered up a congratulatory toast.

"Cleo," Grier prodded.

Cleo blinked as if her thoughts were somewhere else. "Of course. I'm certain His Grace will be most gentle and understanding with you."

Grier shook her head and looked back at Annalise. "It will be lovely."

"Have more champagne," Marguerite suggested. "that shall relax your nerves."

Grier nodded in agreement.

Cleo continued to stare ahead. Almost as though she was attending a funeral and not a wedding.

They reached the dock and the chatter grew to a surge all around them. The wedding barge swayed softly on the current. Bloodsworth approached her and claimed her hand. *Richard.* After he had proposed, he insisted she call him by his Christian name, but it still felt strange. She wondered when it would become natural. When would she think of him as Richard and not Bloodsworth or simply *the duke*?

Bringing her hand to his lips, he pressed a moist

kiss to her knuckles, his smiling gaze brushing over her briefly before addressing the wedding party.

"Thank you all for your delightful company on this most glorious of occasions." His free hand moved naturally, gracefully, as he spoke.

She'd noticed that about him right away—his inherent grace, the smooth elegance of his hands. Not like her own—thankfully snug within a pair of gloves so he couldn't feel the rough, chapped palms, testament to her life of toil.

Applause broke out, perhaps none louder than Jack. Her father had finally gotten his wish. His daughter had married a duke—about as close to a British prince as he would ever get. Bloodsworth might not be an actual prince like Grier's husband, but he was British-born and close enough. Jack could hope for no better. Certainly she had never hoped for as much. It still felt a bit unreal, like something that was happening to someone else.

Annalise blinked, realizing Bloodsworth was still talking and he must have uttered something amusing because everyone laughed. The ladies tittered behind their artful fans and gloved hands. He winked down at Annalise. Her heart pounded as wildly as a snared rabbit as he leaned down to press a swift kiss to her lips. It was only their second kiss, the first having been less than five hours ago in the Bloodsworth family chapel.

Heat crept up her checks at the hoots of approval from the gentlemen. The ladies showed more restraint, giggling softly.

"Come, Your Grace." He gave her fingers a comforting squeeze. She started. If he wasn't looking at her she wouldn't know he was addressing her. Would she ever become accustomed to it? "Ready to begin our new life?"

Our new life. She smiled, reveling in the sound of that. She finally had a future. And someone to share it with. That was all she had ever wanted. Acceptance. Belonging. *Love.*

"Yes, Your Grace," she murmured.

Nodding in approval, he led her toward the edge of the dock where a ramp extended from the grassy knoll up to the barge. She was too busy studying his face, caught up in the remarkable fact that he was her husband. That she was his and he was hers. She did not lift her lame leg high enough. It caught on the edge of the ramp and she went tumbling. Her right knee hit the wood before he managed to get his arms around her and halt her descent. Sharp pain shot up her leg.

"I—I am so sorry," she stammered, brushing away the multitude of hands that were suddenly there. Aside of her own husband, her sisters' husbands were there to assist her . . . making her feel even a greater fool. Oh, they meant well, but the pity on their faces only reminded her of the feelings of inadequacy she had harbored all her life. Ever since she took that fateful fall.

"I'm fine," she insisted, face flaming, waving their hands away while still clinging to Bloodsworth. She sent him a small, embarrassed smile.

"Come." He patted her hand reassuringly where it rested on his arm.

She faced forward and tried to calm the hammering of her pulse. Even worse than the hammering pulse at her neck was the trembling that coursed through her. Wedding night nerves. Perfectly normal, according to her sisters.

Only this trembling was the result of something else. Her stomach tightened and knotted.

In her mind, she saw it again—the look of contempt that had crossed her husband's face when she stumbled. For a fraction of a moment the scornful expression was there. Just a flash, but she saw it nonetheless. The expression was not new. Others had looked at her with disgust in her life.

Just never him.

Chapter Two

The barge rolled slightly beneath her as she sat at the small dressing table and stared upon her reflection in the gilded mirror. Her large brown eyes gazed back at her—too big, in her opinion. They were certainly nothing like Lady Joanna's stormy blue ones. She immediately reprimanded herself for the comparison. Bloodsworth had not chosen Lady Joanna. He had picked her, Annalise, for his bride.

They had cast off some time ago and Bloodsworth left her so she could prepare herself. *Prepare herself.* For some reason the words made her feel like a goose before Christmas dinner. She shook the thought aside and considered herself critically, hoping Bloodsworth—*Richard*—would approve.

Sighing, she fussed with one of the ribbons at her throat. She supposed the nightgown was satisfactory. By no means seductive, it was still the prettiest thing she had ever worn to bed. The fabric was the finest lawn—virginal white with several delicate, pale blue ribbons braided through the neckline and tied off in a bow at the center of her chest.

She glanced to the cabin door, wondering where her husband had disappeared to. There couldn't be too many places to hide on the barge. That look on his face rose up in her mind, and she gnawed at the corner of her lip. She closed her eyes in a tight blink and told herself to think no more of it. She had likely imagined it—projected it upon him because of her own embarrassment for losing her footing.

Rising, she moved to the window and gazed out at the river. A soft current rippled the black surface. The moon gleamed down, leaving a ribbon of glowing white on the undulating water.

The door opened behind her, and she turned, the hem of her nightgown whispering at her ankles as her bare feet rotated on the floorboards. Bloodsworth—*Richard*—stood there, leaning one shoulder into the doorjamb, a glass of port in his hand. He gazed at her thoughtfully, wearing that boyish smile she adored.

She tried not to fidget beneath his perusal.

"Frightened?" he queried, taking a sip.

She shook her head. Perhaps too quickly. "A bit," she allowed, returning his smile with a tremulous one of her own.

He pushed off the door and closed it after him with a soft and final click.

Suddenly she was aware of how alone they were. Her throat thickened and she fought to swallow. She had never been alone with a man before. The air throbbed with a strained silence around them—as though they were sealed inside a tomb, secreted away from the world.

She knew there were two members of his staff on board. His valet, to see to their needs and someone steering the vessel abovedeck, but it felt as though they were utterly alone, cast adrift in a vast sea. When he first suggested the wedding be held at his family estate followed by a night aboard their very own wedding barge, she had thought the idea romantic and thoughtful. It had only confirmed her belief that she was the luckiest of girls.

Only now, on this barge, in this cabin, floating down a dark river, she wished they had married in St. James with all the pomp and ceremony of any peer's wedding. She longed to hear the steady pulse of Town bustling outside her window. She missed the gentle cacophony lulling her to sleep. Somehow there was comfort . . . *safety* in the busy clatter.

He advanced on her. She held her breath, releasing it in a soft whoosh when he stepped past her to gaze out at the river.

"Beautiful night."

She turned to follow his gaze out the window. "Yes. It's been an altogether lovely day. A lovely wedding."

She felt his gaze return to her face. She held her poise, her hands clasped together before her.

"It was, was it not?" he mused. "A memory to keep. Something to . . . cherish."

If his comment struck her as strange, she didn't reveal it. If an even odder sense of disquiet grew in her belly, she did not reveal that, either.

"Tired?" he asked.

She nodded, and then stopped, having no wish for him to think her too wearied and resistant to the notion of sharing a bed with him.

Her gaze skimmed over him. She knew the sight of him well by now—had memorized his tall slimness, his slightly sloping shoulders, the narrow waist. For nigh on a year he had been the embodiment of all her dreams.

He set his glass down and motioned to the bed with an elegant sweep of his hand. "Shall we?"

Her pulse leapt against her throat. She nodded perhaps too briskly. With her heart beating like a drum in her chest, she moved to the bed and sat upon its edge, folding her hands in her lap. At sight of her rough, chapped fingers, she winced, wishing she could hide them within gloves. Perhaps they would soften with time and be the sort of hands more fitting of a duchess.

He approached the bed. She stared steadfastly at his legs, too nervous to look up and meet his gaze.

With one finger he lifted her chin. His gaze held hers, and he was looking at her in that considering way he sometimes did. It wasn't unkind or disapproving. It was speculative. As though she was something alien, something not quite decipherable. Not unusual, she supposed. He probably never imagined himself marrying the likes of her.

"Lie back on the bed," he instructed evenly.

She hesitated at his command, at the flatness of his voice, relaxing only when he smiled. "Don't fret. We are married now, are we not?"

She nodded and scooted back on the bed. Her heart pounded like a wild bird, fighting to burst free of her chest, of this room.

Her nervousness grew into something else as he crawled above her on the bed, his thighs settling on either side of her hips. His eyes pinned her in place, and fear stirred in her heart. She batted it back. He was her husband. Handsome. Charming. A duke. She had waited her whole life for him. There was no reason to fear him. None at all.

His eyes grew darker as they gazed down at her. Deep and dark. She blinked and looked away, looking back only when he said her name.

"Annalise. Look at me." He loomed over her, his hands coming to rest on either side of her head, trapping the long strands of her hair beneath his palms.

She wet her lips. "Yes."

He brought his face closer, his mouth a hair's breadth from hers. The brandy on his breath wafted over lips. "Are you ready?"

She inhaled a sharp breath. *No.*

"Y-Yes," she managed to get out, knowing it was her duty to comply. It was *right*. The correct thing to do. Even if some vague instinct shouted at her to get up, to squeeze out from under him and flee. She nodded. He chose her. Above all others. Even the dazzling Lady Joanna. He cared for her.

His smile deepened, a familiar dimple appearing in his cheek, softening him into that boyishly handsome man she had met so many months ago.

He traced his finger down her cheek. "I'm sorry. This may hurt a bit."

She nodded jerkily. "I—I know." She had heard

as much from others. Her mother explained it once in somewhat vague terms, but she had understood. And then there had been the other shop girls who worked for Madame Brouchard. They were far more experienced than she. They had always shared stories of their exploits.

His head cocked to the side, his dark eyes glinting. "Do you?"

"I've been told as much, yes . . . but afterward it won't hurt again."

He angled his head, studying her with a sharpness that made her think of the hawks that had hunted the mice in the field behind the manor home of Mrs. Danvers, her mother's employer. "No. I suppose it won't. You shall never feel pain again beyond this initial discomfort. That is some comfort, at least. Cling to that, my dear."

His hand moved so quickly then that she could not calculate his intent.

There was a flash of white, a blur of the pillow coming toward her, but she could not comprehend its purpose.

Until it was too late.

Until the soft, luxuriant fabric slapped down on her face, plunging her into a world of relentless dark and pain.

Her neck snapped back as he pushed down. *Hard*. Bearing her head and shoulders deep into the bed. She felt the bruising pressure of his two hands on her face, one at her cheek and another at her chin.

She opened her mouth but couldn't cry out. Couldn't scream. Couldn't breathe.

The smooth cotton filled her mouth, covering her tongue, muffling her sounds. Wild, panicked half-words and fractured thoughts.

No . . . Please . . . Don't . . . Why. . .

Her hands searched, flailed all around her, grabbing at the pillow, clenching its softness in aching-tight fingers, desperate to rip the offending object from her face.

No good. He held tight and pushed, pushed, *pushed.*

Her legs kicked. Even her lame leg lashed out, her heel beating uselessly on the bed, fighting against the crushing weight of him. *Her husband.* Killing her . . .

Fear closed around her. *Oh, God. I'm dying.*

A desperate burning withered her lungs. She struggled against him, against her death. Her hands found his arms, his neck, his face. She clawed, scratched, scored his flesh until she felt his blood wet her nails. His curse dimly registered. She was rewarded with a sharp explosion of knuckles to her ribs. She gasped on a mouthful of linen. No air. No air anywhere.

A smooth blanket of calm settled over her, edging out the sharp sting of panic. Even the pain in her shriveling lungs abated.

Fighting wouldn't stop him. It wouldn't save her. She was too weak.

Faces flashed through her mind, her mother, the children in her village, Mrs. Danvers, the shop girls she lived with. Their eyes watched her, floating above her where Bloodsworth pinned her to the bed. Their eyes surveyed her as they had in life. Scornful. Judging. She could hear their voices.

Useless cripple. Weak.

She stilled. Utterly. Her hands fell limply at her sides, heavy as lead. Her chapped fingers opened, unfurling like the softest of petals. Fighting only proved to him she still lived. Only made him keep killing her.

Perhaps if she held herself still he would think he had succeeded. That he had successfully murdered her.

And perhaps he had. She could feel nothing anymore. A dark fog rolled in, dimming her awareness, eating at her thoughts, devouring the last of her.

All there was left. All there would ever be.

Chapter Three

Consciousness pulled at her. Eyes still closed, Annalise floated, flying, arms suspended at her sides.

A heavy, pulling throb in her head and a sharp sting in her ribs pawed at her—urging her to dive back into the comfort of oblivion. But something else nagged at her, urging her to wake up. A memory. Something she shouldn't forget. It sank its teeth through the fog of her thoughts, hunting her.

Everything came back in a rush then. She stopped herself just short of opening her eyes. She tensed and then quickly forced the tension back out, purging it from every limb as she concentrated on lying perfectly still. *On not opening her eyes.*

A soft breeze swam over her. The hem of her nightgown fluttered at her calves and she knew she was outside. Still near the water. She could hear the waves lapping the sides of the barge.

Cool hands held her. He was taking her somewhere. She knew without opening her eyes that it was Bloodsworth. Her husband. *Her murderer.* He thought he had killed her back in their cabin. Smothered her with a pillow. So where was he taking her now?

It was safe to assume he would finish his gruesome task once he realized she was still alive. She hung limply in his arms, not daring to so much as lift her chest to breathe. Her life depended on his belief that he held a corpse.

He came to a halt. It felt windier, standing in one place—wherever that was—no longer swaying with his movements. He adjusted her in his arms with the barest grunt. The moments stretched. The silence deafening. It took everything in her to play dead, to feign that she wasn't aware of his body holding her so closely, of the hands gripping her—the same ones that had held a pillow over her face just moments ago.

Then she was lowered unceremoniously, dropped to the hard deck. Her head hit with a hard thump, her neck snapping back sharply, but she schooled her features into a blank mask and bit the inside of her cheek to keep from crying out. The wind buffeted her, playing with the hem of her night rail.

His voice rolled over her, his tones as crisp and familiar as ever. "Well, we can't forget this, can we?"

He seized her hand, grabbing her ring finger tightly. His fingers pulled on the wedding band he had slid on only hours before. His grip was hard and merciless, twisting her finger in an unnatural direction in his effort to reclaim his family heirloom. "Don't want to give it up, do you, wife?"

She prayed the ring would just slide free and rid her of this agony. At last it slid off her finger.

The soles of Bloodsworth's boots scraped over the deck. She sensed him standing above her. His voice rang out in satisfaction. "There we go. Saved you from that nasty bit of rubbish."

She envisioned him standing over her and addressing his precious family ring. She was "that nasty bit of rubbish." How could she have ever thought he cared for her? She should have known her bridal settlement was the only thing that attracted his suit. And perhaps she had known that, but she thought he at least *liked* her. Enough to keep her around. Enough not to *kill* her.

His arms came around her again. He hefted her up with a grunt. "Little cow, I'm thinking you'll sink straight to the bottom. Farewell, *wife*." The last word was uttered with such scathing scorn she marveled that he had stomached marrying her at all. The entire ceremony must have revolted him.

And then she was falling through air.

Plunging deep into the abyss. Water rushed up all around her, enveloping her. She gasped at the sudden cold, swallowing a mouthful of briny water for the effort.

She swam to the surface, breaking free with a ragged gasp. Dragging a deep breath into her aching lungs, she tossed her head left and right against the swiftly moving waters, trying to clear the tangle of hair from her eyes.

The view had been deceptive from her window. The river had looked calm. Peaceful. But now a captive of its freezing depths, the current sucked at her, carrying her away from her wedding barge.

She squinted against the dark night, marking the dark looming shape of the barge, a hulking beast hunched over the waters that crept slowly away from her.

She detected Bloodsworth's dark figure at the railing, his face a shadowy smudge on the night. She watched as he turned and disappeared back into the bowels of the barge, free of a wife. Free of her.

Swallowing back her terror, she kicked, grateful at least that she could swim. The shore didn't look too far. Struggling to ignore the incessant ache in her ribs where Bloodsworth had struck her, she worked her arms and legs, only to discover that the shore was much farther than it looked, and the current was determined to keep her from it.

Choking, she strained to keep her head above the slapping waves. Her strong leg worked three times as hard and yet it wasn't enough. Her exhaustion grew, dragging her down. The current slapped at her face, continuing to pull at her, tugging her along. She went under again and again, popping back up only to suck in a wet breath.

Jagged shapes emerged in the water, first only a few and then more, increasing in frequency. Rocks. She jerked to avoid them, but there were too many. Her foot scraped something sharp and jagged. She cried out and choked on water.

Suddenly pain slammed into her lame leg, spinning her. She quickly became confused, no longer sure what direction was up. Lancing pain shot up her limb, settling deep into her bone, reverberating to every nerve in her body.

She tried to kick her way to the surface, but one strong leg wasn't enough to help her. Agony screamed through her lame leg, telling her something was wrong. Dreadfully wrong. She couldn't force it to move.

Gray edged at her vision, closing in. She couldn't do it anymore. Couldn't fight. Bloodsworth had succeeded after all.

She wasn't going to make it out of this river alive.

Owen squinted against the afternoon's gray sky, swaying loosely in his saddle as his mount meandered along the road. Never mind that it was overcast. The day was too bright for him. The consequences of last night's binge with a bottle of brandy still bore its effects. Thousands of tiny hammers beat inside his head.

He scratched at his bristly jaw, unable to recall the last time he had shaved. Perhaps a week ago. He hadn't cared enough even when he had arrived home into the loving embrace of his family. Not that he had stayed longer than a day. It took him all of five minutes in the company of Jamie and Paget to realize he couldn't stomach either one of them.

His brother and bride were nauseatingly happy, and he was not fit company for happy people. It had nothing to do with the fact that his older brother had wed his own childhood sweetheart. Discovering Jamie and Paget happily wed had not overly concerned him. Not as it would have four years ago when he was besotted with Paget. When he possessed a heart. When he was more than the shell of a man he was now.

He felt only relief to know that Paget had moved on—that she wasn't waiting for him. There was no disappointing her. Because *what* he was, *who* he had become . . . there was no coming back from that.

The Owen they once knew was dead. Lost halfway around the world.

His mount quickened its pace, and he knew he was approaching the river. Reaching its banks, he dismounted and led the horse to water, holding the reins loosely in his hand as it drank.

He scanned his surroundings, his gaze missing nothing on land or water. He might be in the land of his birth, a mere day's ride from London, but a part of him would always be back in India scouting for rebels. Ready to kill. A talent he had perfected these past few years. It turned out he was extraordinarily good at killing.

His gaze stopped, arresting on something several yards downriver. Everything inside him tightened with familiar alertness, his time as a soldier rushing to the surface.

Ever wary, he moved closer. At first he thought it nothing more than a mound of fabric, discarded and washed ashore. Even soiled, the material was startling white alongside the muddy bank. But then he detected the shape of a body beneath the sopping wet fabric.

A female body.

She lay facedown, a limp arm stretched above her head. One leg stretched out, the pale foot and calf disappearing into the ink of water. He took a slow look around, well aware that a trap could wait anywhere. She could be the bait some nefarious brigands left to lure unsuspecting travelers to a foul end.

The still and silent woods met his sweeping stare, the gentle slap of water the only sound. He pushed the ghosts from his head, burying the cries of dead men deep as he turned his attention back to the woman. He cautiously approached. Crouching, he carefully touched her shoulder and rolled her onto her back.

She was young. Her face ashen. Eyes closed, her lashes fanned out against her cheeks in dark crescents that looked almost obscene against her waxy, colorless skin.

He pressed his fingertips to her throat. Icy cold to the touch, her pulse hiccupped, the smallest, barely-there flutter. Soft as a moth's wings. Not good.

He leaned closer, listening for her breath. The air escaped her bloodless lips in tiny, hard-fought rasps. He compressed his lips.

His gaze skimmed her, assessing. Scratches, cuts, and bruises marred her pale skin. The hem of her gown was streaked in faint pink tinges of blood. He tugged the gown up, checking for injuries, wincing at the sight of her leg. From the odd shape, it was clearly broken. A deep gash on her foot probably needed stitching as well. Owen glanced to the river and back at her, marveling that she was alive. Given her injuries, he couldn't quite fathom how she had not drowned.

Staring at her for a long moment, he brushed some of the brown hair from her forehead. "How'd you get in that river, hmm?"

His mind quickly worked, plotting the best way to find her help. He had spent the last five years attacking *sepoys*, assassinating them at the behest of his commanders. He was about taking lives, not saving.

They were a day's ride from his family home—not that he wanted to return there again. The next village was a half day ride south. He'd planned on spending the night there before continuing on to London.

Sighing, he glanced around them again, suddenly wishing someone else would happen upon them. Someone better equipped to care for a female who didn't look as though she would live out the day.

"Come, little one," he murmured, slipping his arms beneath her, one beneath her legs and the other at her back, taking care not to jostle her leg more than necessary.

Contrary to his words, she was no fragile bit of crystal. She was generously curved in his arms, and yet his six-foot-plus frame ate up the distance toward his horse as if she weighed nothing at all. After grueling conditions in India, she was only a slight burden.

Remounting with her in his arms was a tricky task, but he managed it, laying her carefully across his lap. With her legs dangled off to one side, he grasped the reins and prodded his mount to move. Her head lolled against his chest, her face settling against his well-worn jacket. Almost trustingly, it seemed. Absurd, of course. She was unconscious.

Disconcerted, he blinked down at her. It was impossible to recall the last time a woman had fallen asleep in his arms. There'd been women in his life, in his bed, but no one that he actually *slept* with. No one he had held in his arms once he satisfied his body's need for them.

Looking up again, he urged his mount into a

faster clip, eager to reach the next town and rid himself of this newfound burden. So that he could be on his way. Just him and the demons of his past.

The female in his arms stiffened with a sharp gasp.

Startled, he looked down to find himself staring into a pair of brown eyes. Framed in lush lashes, the eyes were no ordinary brown. They were velvety . . . brown rimmed in the darkest black. They shined, as if lit from within. She stared directly at him, the fear there unmistakable.

His hand reached down to cup her face, trying to offer some comfort. "Don't be frightened. I mean you no harm."

Nothing in her wild, searching gaze indicated she understood or even heard him. Those eyes looked right through him, as though she were somewhere else entirely, caught up in a living nightmare. Her breath fell faster in sharp little pants.

"Easy," he soothed, not really knowing what sort of words he should say. He wasn't accustomed to doling out comfort or reassurances. He pressed a hand awkwardly over her forehead and made a hushing sound. The kind his old nanny used to make whenever he'd hurt himself as a child.

Perhaps it worked. Or perhaps she was just out of her head with pain.

Her eyelids drifted shut. After a long moment he looked back up at the road and urged his mount faster, suddenly determined that she *would* live out the day.

Chapter Four

An hour into the trek, and he knew the damsel in distress he'd rescued from the banks of the river was in the gravest danger. She burned with fever. Heat radiated off her and roasted him through his clothes. He rode his mount hard now. Digging in his heels, he gave Jasper his lead, less concerned for her comfort. Jostling the woman's leg was now secondary to getting her into the hands of someone who could ease her fever.

He doubted they would reach the village in time. He glanced around, debating stopping somewhere. But then he was plagued with what it was he himself could do. What could he offer her? He wasn't equipped to care for her along a roadside.

He wondered if he should take one of the more

obscure paths leading off the main road in search of a farm or cottage. He cursed beneath his breath and spared her a quick glance. Her face was even more colorless, if possible—the shadows beneath her eyes twin bruises. He'd seen men look this badly before. Moments before they took their last breath. Comrades, men he fought alongside. And sometimes, naturally, they had been enemies. Men whose lives he'd been charged with ending.

He shook off the memories. She was not them. Nor would she become one of them either. Not if he had any control over the matter.

You've never had any control over the matter, a dark, insidious little voice whispered inside his head. He dismissed the voice. Saving this girl's life had somehow become important to him. Something he had to do. Maybe this once he could help. Maybe this one could live. And perhaps he could be the reason. It was hardly his area of expertise, but he was determined to try.

Ahead, he spied a rider. Several, in fact. At least four horsemen emerged, followed by two slow-moving wagons. Trailing the wagons were another three riders. He eyed their colorful attire. Females drove the wagons, their dark hair loose down their backs, their heads covered by bright kerchiefs.

Gypsies. He's seen his share here and abroad. Realizing they might be his best hope, he spurred his mount. Holding up a hand, he called out a greeting.

The horsemen riding in front quickly formed a wall, shielding the wagons. "Move aside," one of the men quickly demanded in a thick accent.

"We need help." He nodded to the female in his arms, lifting her higher for them to see. "She's hurt."

The men exchanged glances before the older one spoke. "Not our concern."

"Please. I found her beside the river . . ." He looked down at the girl. "There must be one among you who can help her . . ." He knew Gypsies looked after themselves. They wouldn't have a physician in their midst, but someone among them must be savvy in the healing arts.

"Move out of the way."

Owen did not miss how one of the younger men slid a long look from his leader back to the idling wagons.

Owen pointed to the wagons. "One of your people is a healer perhaps? Please. We haven't much time. She's very ill. I can pay . . ." His voice faded as the Gypsy pulled an ancient looking pistol out from his leather vest and aimed it directly at him.

Owen smiled at the irony. To die here . . . after making it out of India alive.

The leader frowned. Clearly he expected a different reaction from a man facing the end of his pistol. It had been years since Owen cared one way or another about his living or dying. Back in India there were days when he would gladly have accepted death.

"If you must shoot me, will you then tend to her? Can I have your word on that?"

The leader's swarthy skin flushed a splotchy red. He pulled back the hammer. "You are one foolish Englishman."

"Luca!" The sharp command carried from one of the wagons.

The leader looked back over his shoulder. The curtain behind the driver parted a slit to reveal a fraction of a woman's face. Old and wrinkled, brown as the cracked earth of a desert. Her night dark eyes settled on Owen for a long moment, measuring him where he sat atop his mount.

At last she snapped, "Find somewhere to camp, Luca. Bring the Englishman and the girl."

"But Mama—" Luca begin.

"Do as I say." Her face disappeared as the curtain dropped back in place.

Luca turned a scowl on Owen. "Follow." He bit out the single word, but his flashing gaze conveyed just how much he resented the directive. He slid his pistol into his thick, leather studded belt, keeping the weapon in plain sight. No doubt to serve as a warning.

Owen followed the group as they continued down the road, turning off an obscure path. Brush and branches encroached on all sides. When the path finally opened wide enough to position the wagons side by side, they halted. Several more bodies climbed down from the wagons. Mostly women. A few children. They eyed him with speculation and a general distrust, although none looked at him with quite the iciness that Luca did.

The back door of a wagon opened and the same woman who had addressed Luca emerged. Everyone stilled and watched her as she took the three narrow wood steps down to the ground with far more agility than he expected for one so ancient looking, with her wizened face and crooked, gnarled hands.

She approached Owen in several quick strides, then peered up at him, scanning the girl in his arms. "Come. Down with her. I thought you wished to hurry? You wish her to die up there on that horse?"

Shaking his head, he dismounted. Standing before the older woman, he saw in an instant that she was no taller than a child. She only came to the middle of his chest, her shoulders and upper back deeply hunkered. He imagined it had been some years since she could walk fully upright.

Eyeing the bundle in his arms, she lifted those gnarled hands to the girl and announced, "I am Mirela." Her fingers prodded and squeezed. When she came to the broken leg, she made a disapproving cluck of her tongue. Peering beneath the ragged gown at the leg itself, her expression grew grimmer. Shaking her head, her hands moved to cup the girl's face. She made a hissing sound at this contact with her skin.

"Too hot," she pronounced. "Quickly. Bring her inside."

"Mama," Luca objected, stepping in her path.

She glared up at her son, not appearing the least intimidated by the giant.

Another woman stepped closer, dark and lovely with eyes an eerie whiskey color. "Mama, these are outsiders. You always say that we must keep to our own."

Mirela wagged a twisted finger. "You don't need to fling my words at me, Nadia. I know what I say. And I also understand what I mean." Her dark eyes narrowed meaningfully on her son, clearly implying that he did not.

Nadia shook her head, tossing her thick mane of glossy black hair around her slim shoulders. "Then why?"

Owen waited, quite certain that Mirela held the final power among the tribe. "He said he has money." She snapped her fingers toward him, the sound startling and sharp on the air. Her dark eyes pinned him. "You have money, yes?"

Still not speaking, Owen nodded, even realizing as he did that this group could simply overpower him and take the money without helping the girl. It was a risk he had to take.

"We need money, and this girl . . ." She swept her gaze over his charge. "I can fix her. Perhaps." She shrugged. "We will see, no?"

With that less than heartening assertion, she turned and waved a hand for Owen to follow. "Nadia," she called over her shoulder. "Come. You help me."

Owen heard the younger woman sigh, but she fell into step behind him.

He ducked inside the wagon. Mirela directed him with an imperious finger to set the girl upon a bed.

"She has a name?" she asked as she bent over her.

He shrugged.

"You do not know?" Nadia looked him over, the suspicion in her eerie golden gaze all the brighter.

"I found her."

Mirela made a noncommittal sound as she set about removing his damsel's damp nightgown. Owen quickly turned.

"Why you look away?" Mirela demanded over the sound of ripping fabric.

"To protect her . . ." He groped for the word for a moment. " . . . virtue." It was not a word that had crossed his thoughts in a good many years.

Nadia passed his line of vision, the ruined nightgown in her hands. A faint smirk curved her lips as though he had amused her.

"You should have no such concerns," the old woman said matter-of-factly behind him. "She belongs to you now. You may look your fill."

A frown pulled at his lips.

"You don't think so. You found her. You saved her life. She is yours now."

His frown deepened, the notion beyond troubling. He didn't want anyone to *belong* to him. "Perhaps in your culture."

"It is not culture. It is a law of nature. If she lives, it will be because of you. You are bound. Now turn around."

Convinced that no one ever disobeyed this woman, he turned, relieved to see the girl covered in a blanket. Her leg was exposed. In the lamp-lit confines of the wagon, he could better assess the damage. It was undeniably broken, the bone pushing oddly against her pale skin.

Nadia returned and together they quickly cleaned her, carefully rinsing off her leg, as well as the cuts and abrasions riddling so many of her limbs.

With a look of intense concentration, Mirela then ran her knotted hands up and down the length of the broken leg. It obviously hurt. Even in her feverish state, the girl winced and squirmed.

He sent a questioning look to Nadia. Mirela did not miss it.

"We need to set this properly if she has a hope to walk normally," Mirela answered, as if he had asked her. "You." She nodded at him. "Come up here by her shoulders."

Owen rounded the bed. Following the old woman's instructions, he slid his arms beneath the girl's arms and watched as Mirela moved to stand alongside her broken leg.

She and Nadia exchanged several words in a language he could not interpret. Nadia grasped the bare foot of the broken leg, gripping it tightly in two hands.

Mirela looked at him. "When I say pull, you jerk her back by the shoulders." Her dark eyes glittered at him from her lined face. "Very hard. Understand?"

He nodded.

Mirela's hand fluttered over the broken limb. "Now! Pull!"

He and Nadia yanked in unison. Mirela's hands

worked on her thigh, seizing and pushing down hard. Her gnarled hands worked the wrecked limb like she was molding and forming dough.

The girl arched, a deep, anguished moan spilling free.

"There we go." Mirela nodded to Nadia and Owen. "You may release her."

Letting go of the girl's foot, Nadia moved away to return with bandages. She handed them to Mirela. The older woman accepted them, speaking again in that language.

Nodding, Nadia left the wagon.

Mirela looked at him. "If she survives the fever, she should walk again."

He sighed, unaware until that moment that he had been holding his breath. For this girl. A stranger. He felt vaguely unsettled over the realization. "Thank you," he murmured.

She stared at him hard for a long moment, and he was hard pressed not to look away beneath that probing stare. "And what of you? What ails you?"

Ails him? "Nothing."

She snorted. "I know people . . . men. Your kind, Romani, it matters not. Poison can leak into any man's heart. If it is not purged it is just as lethal as any dagger."

He could only stare at her for a long moment before finding his voice. "I am not . . . poisoned."

Shaking her head, she returned her attention to her patient. "Say what you will. At any rate, I haven't the power to heal what sickens you."

All business once again, Mirela dismissed him with a sniff. "Look here," she instructed, lifting the first half of the thin blanket that covered the girl's torso, exposing the softly sloping belly to the air. Skin pale as milk. Pulling the blanket a fraction higher, she uncovered the nasty bruise spanning her ribs. The flesh there was the deepest purple, almost black, and edged in red.

"Here. This." She pointed at the bruise. "The river did not do this to her."

He considered the bruise. "It could have been rocks . . ." He motioned to her leg. "She broke her leg—"

She snorted as her fingers gently tested the bruised area. "I've seen what a man's fist can do. A man did this." Nodding in certainty, she removed her fingers and covered the girl back up with the blanket. "Just bruised, though. Not broken. There's that at least."

Straightening, she rose and moved to an ornately carved cupboard. The elaborate etchings in the wood brought to mind craftsmanship he'd seen in India. She slid open a drawer and selected a pouch. Her eyes made contact with his as she took her place beside the bed again. Opening the pouch, she sprinkled a dark powder into her hands. It sparkled and gleamed like coal dust against the lined and wrinkled flesh of her palms.

Her lips moved then, her voice so soft he had to lean in to hear, but then he realized she wasn't speaking to him. Nor was she speaking in any language that he could understand. She turned her hands over, letting the substance rain down on the girl's injured leg.

The odd words continued to flow out of her in a strange litany, almost chantlike. Her hands moved as well, coating the injured leg lightly in the medicine. He watched the bizarre display, the swift movement of her fingers, certain he was witnessing something outside the ordinary. Certainly none of the physicians to tend him and his comrades back in India had ever sprinkled sparkling black dust and chanted in a strange tongue.

His gaze moved to the girl's face. He recalled those eyes that split second they had opened. The wide pools of brown so brilliant, so bright and deep with pain and fear . . . and something else. A horror that only she knew . . . only she could see.

He recognized it. Had felt it himself. Had seen it in others. In friends. In enemy rebels moments before he extinguished their lives.

As the old Gypsy chanted her liquid words and treated the girl's leg, the tension ebbed from the girl's face. The pain that had been etched deep into every line and hollow evaporated like smoke on the wind.

"What did you do?" he whispered.

Mirela smiled. "Just something to help with the healing . . . it will hasten things along."

He shook his head, tempted to rub at his eyes . . . as though he had not just witnessed some bit of magic, or some trick of poor vision.

She moved away from the bed. "Care for some food?"

He snapped his attention back to her.

"Come." She waved him from the wagon. "She will be fine. Nadia will return to wrap and splint the leg. You can sit with her after you eat. When was the last good meal you had?" Her gaze raked his tall frame critically.

"What if she wakes?" The moment he asked the question, he winced. He should not be so invested in the welfare of a stranger . . . a girl who might not yet survive.

"She will sleep long and hard until the fever breaks and that will be no time soon. Come. Eat."

With one final glance for the nameless girl in the bed, he followed the old woman from the wagon.

Chapter Five

Annalise fought through the fog of pain. She felt like she was swimming in it, drowning in a hot onslaught of agony. Her every nerve vibrated, the agony sharp and twisting. A keening moan spilled from her lips, pulled from somewhere deep inside her.

She shifted. Sudden, white-hot pain flared to life in her crippled leg. Her eyes shot open with a gasp. Her hand flailed, reaching for her thigh where the pain burned deep.

"Ssh. Easy there."

A face filled her line of vision. Panic washed over her as she recalled everything that had happened to her. *The duke had tried to kill her. Her husband!*

And now there was this voice. This man. In the dim room, she could not make out much of his features. She only knew that it wasn't Bloodsworth. This man's voice was different. Deeper. Gravelly. The knowledge immediately quelled her panic. She squinted, struggling to peer at him through the gloom. Even in the weak lighting, she could make out that his hair was not as dark as the duke's.

She swallowed against her parched mouth, struggling to form words. "My leg," she rasped, her fingers stretching, reaching.

"It's broken, but we've set and splint it. No fear. It will mend."

Broken? Her head lolled to the side and a hot tear slid from the corner of her eye and vanished into the pillow. She'd broken her leg before. It had never healed properly. She doubted his assurances. Would she even be able to walk this time?

"What's your name?" he asked.

She moistened her dry lips. "Anna—" She stopped herself from saying the rest. Her name wasn't that common. There could be news of her drowning. Clumsy, crippled Annalise, the newly minted Duchess of Bloodsworth, fell off her wedding barge. *Such a poor, hapless girl.* She was certain the duke would present the image of grieving husband to perfection. She, better than anyone, knew how well he could act.

"Anna," she repeated.

She pressed her lips as though her name might slip past against her will. She would guard her identity. Doing so might be the only thing to keep her alive. The last thing she wanted was her husband showing up to finish the deed. Her throat tightened as the image of his face filled her head. His words echoed inside her ears. *Little cow, I'm thinking you'll sink straight to the bottom.*

A whimper rose to her lips. She swallowed it back, vowing that she would never be afraid again. He would never hurt her. No one would.

"Anna," the stranger whispered. "Do you know what happened?"

"I don't remember," she lied. She shook her head, shifting on the bed. Pain lanced her leg and traveled up though her hip. She gasped.

"Here." He pressed a cup to her lips. "Drink." She swallowed, coughing against the bitter liquid. Clearly not the water she first thought he was offering her.

"What is that rot?" she choked.

"Water laced with some herbs to ease your discomfort. Mirela has been giving it to you to help with the pain."

"Who is Mirela?"

"A Gypsy. I found you and brought you here. She's been caring for you." He fell silent, and she heard his slight movements as he took her cup and set it down somewhere close. "Do you know how you ended up on that riverbank?"

A reasonable question. He would want to alert her family that she was alive and well—return her to their care.

She shook her head, grateful for the dim lighting that he could not see her face. No doubt she looked as panicked as she felt. "Sorry. I don't know what happened."

He sighed softly and contrary to her earlier wish, she would have liked to see his face, to ascertain whether he believed her. Madame Brouchard's other apprentices had always called her a horrible liar. They knew, of course, because they loved to tease her and ask her terribly awkward questions that she wouldn't dare answer truthfully.

Have you ever been kissed, Annalise?

Annalise, tell us, do you not find Mr. Newman the most handsome fellow . . . I'm sure you wouldn't mind a kiss stolen from him.

She winced at the memory. How those girls would laugh now to see her broken and rejected in the worst way imaginable by her own husband.

Shaking off such thoughts, she moistened her dry, cracked lips. "Who are you?"

He did not immediately answer her. She sensed his body shift, as if moving farther away from her.

"My name is Owen. Owen Crawford."

Owen. A nice, strong name. The type of name that belonged to a man who rescued young ladies from near-death.

"How long have I been here?" She glanced around the shadowed space, sensing it was small. And where is *here*? She bit back the question. One at a time. She already felt tired again, her lids heavy over her eyes.

"Almost a week."

A week!

At her sharp inhalation, he explained quickly in that deep voice that was coming to soothe her. "You were feverish. We didn't know if you were going to survive."

Her mind raced. Were they even looking for her? Everyone must assume her dead by now. That realization actually made her breathe easier. The tension ebbed from her body. If Bloodsworth thought she was dead, why correct the misapprehension? Her family would not miss her. She had known them for only a short while. Jack had ignored her for the entirety of her life until recently, when he decided he wanted a blue blood for a son-in-law. She'd not put her trust in him again. She'd trust no one but herself ever again.

"Th-Thank you." It was impossible to keep her eyes open. The pull of sleep was too much. "Still . . . tired."

"Get some rest. We can talk more later."

She managed a nod before her eyelids drifted shut again, the deep rumble of his voice a faraway echo through her head.

Her lips moved. Words fell without deliberation, "Will you . . . stay . . ."

Another long pause. In the hazy fog of her thoughts, she began to wonder if he was even beside her anymore.

At last his voice came, as distant as thunder on a sweeping Yorkshire plain. "I'm not going anywhere. I'll be here when you wake."

"She awake?"

Owen turned to where Mirela stood in the doorway. Afternoon light flooded around her small frame, suffusing the interior of the wagon. The caravan had stopped briefly for lunch. They should be arriving in Pedmont, a village outside London later today. Apparently it was Pedmont's annual fair. Mirela and her kinsmen supported themselves by traveling from fair to fair and offering up their talents.

He nodded. "For a moment, yes."

"She spoke?"

He nodded, his gaze returning to Anna's face, the features soft and relaxed in sleep.

"Good. Tomorrow we will have her move about some."

"Her name is Anna," he volunteered.

Mirela nodded, hardly seeming to process this as she moved back out the door.

"Thank you," he called after her, well aware that the girl—Anna—would probably have died if not for Mirela's care. For all her gruff ways, Mirela had been ever attentive, nursing her through her fever, tending to her leg and barking commands at him.

Standing, he ducked his head to avoid hitting the ceiling, he watched Mirela as she waved a hand in dismissal, moving to rejoin her family lunching beneath a tree outside. He usually stayed in the wagon with Anna or rode his mount behind the wagons when the tight space became too oppressive for him. Luca eyed him resentfully from beside his mother.

A reminder that this was only temporary. He was an outsider, tolerated but not accepted. Which was well and fine with him. He didn't want to belong here. He didn't belong anywhere.

Once Anna could move, they would leave.

They.

Dragging a hand through his hair, he turned to stare back down at the girl. It wouldn't be *they* for long. Once she was awake and could communicate at any length, she would tell him where her people were and he would safely deliver her into their care.

Then it would be just him again. As it should be.

Less pain greeted her the second time she awoke. She sat up cautiously, her hand brushing the thin fabric of her nightgown. Well, not *her* nightgown. Someone else's nightgown.

The tight space was even darker than the last time, but she knew she hadn't changed location. The same musty, herbed aroma permeated the air.

She listened to the silence for a moment, reassuring herself that she was all alone. She felt herself, her hands patting down her body carefully, testing for injuries. Her palms encountered her splinted leg. Dread filled her chest as she recalled the last time she broke her leg. In the beginning she thought the aching limp would go away. It never had. Again she wondered if she would even be able to walk this time.

The burn of tears prickled her eyes. Following her accident, self-pity had threatened to overwhelm her. There were so many times it took every ounce of her will to face the world. The day she had climbed that tree haunted her. At night, in the bed she had shared with her mother, she would close her eyes and play it over and over in her mind. Only in her wishful imaginings, she refused the dare issued by Mrs. Danvers's obnoxious son, and never climbed that tree. She never fell.

Now she had broken it again. Regret swept through her. Tears stung her eyes. She squeezed them tight until the burn abated.

If only she hadn't believed in Jack's fairy-tale promises and married the duke.

If only she hadn't allowed Bloodsworth to throw her into that river.

Inhaling sharply, her fingers clenched tightly around the wooden splints on her leg. She shook her head in the dark. *No.* No more pity. She wouldn't pity herself ever again. Even if she couldn't walk. She was finished letting things happen *to* her. She would make her own fate from now on.

"Anna?"

She jerked, swallowing back a scream.

"It's me."

And instantly she knew. She recognized the deep voice of her rescuer. She drew in a shuddery breath. He was somewhere to her left. Below her. Presumably on the floor. "Mr. Crawford?"

"Are you in pain?" he asked.

"No." Her breath came out whisper-soft. "What are you doing?"

"Sleeping."

Evidently not. Not if he had heard her slight movements. "On the . . . floor?" In the dark? In such proximity to her bed? Her skin shivered.

"I've slept on this pallet since we joined Mirela and her family."

She realized she still had no clue where she was. She had just vowed to never be a victim again, but she wasn't exactly in a position of strength. She was completely at the mercy of this man. An altogether untenable situation. One she would change as soon as possible.

"Where are we?"

There was a slight shifting, and she imagined he was scooting closer to her bed—this unknown, faceless man with his deep voice. Goose bumps broke out across her flesh.

"We're outside a village. Pedmont. How are you feeling?"

"Sore," she replied.

"You're very lucky. Mirela is a healer. I don't think a physician could have cared for you better."

"Lucky." The word escaped her like an epithet. Nothing about her life felt lucky. True, she could be dead, but her fate still hung in doubt. She couldn't surface and reveal herself. The duke would finish what he started on their wedding barge.

"Yes. When I first found you, I did not expect you to live. You were barely breathing."

She stared into the dark, in the direction of his voice, trying to see something of him, even just a hint of shadow. The outline of his shape would be reassuring. The last man she'd been alone with had attempted to smother her, after all. And although Owen Crawford wasn't Bloodsworth—he had in fact rescued her—she didn't feel entirely secure. Perhaps she never would again. Perhaps she would always be this—a wary creature of distrust, always on the verge of bolting.

Only she was bed-bound. She wasn't bolting anywhere. Her fist knotted into the blanket at the unwelcome thought.

Although not for long, she quickly vowed to herself. Somehow, some way, she would regain her strength. She'd be stronger than ever before. Smarter. Her thoughts shied away from the fear that she was perhaps *worse* than before. That her leg was completely and irrevocably lame. She would not dwell on the possibility.

"Yes. I am." She nodded with decisiveness, as though he could see her in the lightless space. "Lucky, indeed." She was alive. She had escaped her murderer. She had another chance.

"Can I get you anything? Are you hungry?"

She pressed a hand to her belly, noting that it wasn't quite as curved as usual. If she'd slept for an entire week, she didn't imagine she'd eaten that much. Even now the notion of food made her stomach rebel. She wasn't ready for that.

"I'm thirsty."

There was a scuffling against the floor and a swift yellow flare. She squinted, holding a hand over her eyes, blinking, adjusting to the sudden lamplight.

He was there, offering her a cup. Her gaze moved over the long stretch of his arm, appreciating the taut and flexing tendons and muscle beneath his sun-kissed skin. Her breath escaped in a short, quick burst. He wore no shirt. No jacket. No vest or cravat. Her mouth dried. She couldn't recall ever seeing so much of a man's chest before. Did they all look like this? So broad and dense with muscle?

She tore her gaze away and looked up. Fixed her stare to his face. Only that was worse. He was handsome. Beautiful in a harsh, menacing sort of way. In an instant she knew this was a dangerous man. She had never thought such a thing by looking at Bloodsworth, but looking at this man, she knew.

His deep-set eyes were a piercing dark blue. They drilled into her, watching her keenly. "Go ahead. Drink." He nodded at the cup. The movement dipped his dark blond hair lower over his forehead.

She resisted the impulse to hide from his scrutiny—where could she go, after all?

She took the cup from him, careful not to touch his fingers with her own. She meant to only sip, but the moment the water touched her tongue she was gulping it down. She handed the cup back to him. "More, please."

He moved back to a small tray on a scuffed, ancient-looking sideboard and poured water from a pitcher. "Just a little more. Don't want you getting sick."

She took the cup and drank greedily again, eyeing him above the rim. He watched her in turn, not looking away.

Lowering the cup, she wiped the water from her mouth with the back of her hand, not caring how unladylike she must appear. She'd been the perfect lady before—or tried to be, at any rate—exemplifying only the best manners, aping her betters, and look where that had gotten her.

"I suppose I owe you a thank-you." The moment the words escaped she realized they sounding grudging.

He held her stare for a long moment with his deep-eyes gaze, not responding. Taking the cup, he finally turned from her. "You owe me nothing. I found you. Was I to leave you there to die?" His words were terse and she was struck with the suspicion that this was not a man accustomed to making polite conversation.

"Not everyone would have bothered with me." Indeed not. Her faith in mankind was dismally low at the moment. Inhaling a deep breath, she repeated, "Thank you." This time she sounded sincere.

He shrugged one well-formed shoulder and his lean, muscled torso once again became a point of fascination. She had never seen a man built like him before. She forced her gaze from the ridged plane of his stomach and examined the room. After a moment she frowned. It was not like any room she'd ever seen. It was all wood, crammed with cupboards and chests.

"What is this place?"

"We're in Mirela's wagon. You'll meet her in the morning when she comes to poke and prod at you again. Sadly, you'll be awake for it this time."

Like a magnet, he drew her gaze again. She watched as he effortlessly sank down onto the pallet beside her bed, one arm propped over his knee.

"They've given us use of this wagon? That's very kind of them."

"Oh, they're not entirely altruistic."

"What do you mean?"

Those dark blue eyes stared steadily at her. "Nothing is free in this world. Everything has its price." Truer words had never been said. Hadn't Jack, in effect, bought a duke for her?

"You're paying them?"

"They need to survive, too."

She considered this before replying. "People do what they have to." Just like she would. She would do what she must to make sure she never became *that* girl again. The one cast into the river. She wouldn't be naive and stupid again.

His head tipped to the side. As though he didn't expect her to say that.

She continued gazing at him evenly. "And what shall be your price for helping me, then?"

He stared until she grew uncomfortable. She resisted the urge to fidget.

"You said nothing is free in this world. I simply wondered what manner of recompense you expected."

He spoke at last. "I did not mean myself."

"Oh." She stared at him, wondering about this man. He held himself tensely, clearly uneasy with their exchange, and she began to suspect that it wasn't just her but conversation, *people* in general, that discomfited him.

He looked away, the flesh along his jaw tensing in a way that hinted at his lack of comfort.

She moistened her lips. "Where does Mirela sleep?" she asked, changing the subject.

"Outside with the others. I'm sure you'll meet them, too. They've been curious about you."

"Curious?"

"Yes. You've only shared your name with us, after all."

"I only know your name," she rejoined.

He stared at her for a long moment, his vaguely menacing features measuring her in silence. "If I didn't know any better," he began slowly, "I would think you're being evasive with me on purpose."

"Not at all." She absently brushed her fingers against her temple. He was practically accusing her of hiding something—which would be accurate.

"You still can't remember how you got into the river?" he pressed.

She lowered her fingers from her temple and held his stare a moment before shaking her head. "No. I don't remember . . ." Her voice faded as an idea seized her.

It was so simple. An escape from admitting the shameful truth that her own husband would rather kill her than keep her as his wife. And there was the very real concern that if Owen Crawford knew her identity he would turn her over to her husband. What did she know of him? He rescued her, true, but he might not believe her husband did this to her. A murderous duke—it was far-fetched even to her ears. Bloodsworth was a powerful man, seventh in line for the throne. He might think she belonged with her husband and insist on returning her to his clutches. Fear clawed at her throat at that prospect. No, she could not risk telling anyone who she was.

"Anything? Your family? Friends?"

She grimaced, wondering how plausible he found her lie. "I . . . no, nothing. It's all nothing. Just blank."

After a long moment in which he studied her, he sighed softly. "I'm sure it will come back to you. In time."

She wished she couldn't, in fact, remember. How wonderful would it be to have no memory of that night?

"Get some sleep for now. Mirela says you need rest the most."

Nodding, she let her head fall back down on the pillow. Rest wasn't all she needed, but for now she would settle for that. She would rest, heal, regain her strength.

And then she would figure out what came next.

Chapter Six

Mirela lifted the tray from Annalise's lap with a satisfied grunt. "You ate almost everything this morning, I see."

Annalise patted her stomach. "I tried. Still don't quite have my appetite back."

"Eh, give it some time. You're a good stone less than when he first dragged you in here." Mirela nodded a head toward the wagon door as if he stood out there somewhere. *Owen*. The man she knew so little about. Except that he had saved her.

It had been almost a week since she woke in the middle of the night to find Owen Crawford sleeping beside her bed. A week since they'd spoken and she claimed memory loss. Since then, he'd kept his distance and talked not at all. He continued to sleep in the wagon with her every night, only entering the confines *after* she had fallen asleep. And he was always gone before she awoke.

"Who is he?" she asked Mirela, realizing if she wanted to know anything about the elusive man, the old woman might be her best source.

Mirela looked up at her sharply. "You ask me? He's the one who brought you here."

"I was out of my head with fever—"

"And you've been awake for several days now. Why don't you ask him your questions?" She waved a hand in the air. "You are his now. I told him as much. It is right that you know who he is."

Her cheeks burned with scalding heat. "I am not *his*!" What utter rot. "You did not tell him *that*, did you?"

The elderly woman nodded as if it were of no account and not a mortifying revelation. "Not that he put much store by it."

"Of course he didn't! It's utter nonsense." Annalise pressed a hand to her burning face.

"He saved your life. Without him, you would be dead." She held her hands out in front of her and laced her fingers together, interlocking them. "Your lives are woven together now. Threads in a tapestry."

Annalise stared at those gnarled hands, the locked fingers. A heaviness built in her chest. It was not true. The woman possessed antiquated principles. She owed Mr. Crawford her gratitude. Nothing more. He certainly wanted no long-standing connection between them. He scarcely spoke to her.

If she was bound to anyone, tragically, it was Bloodsworth. As much as she was loath to admit it, in the eyes of the law and before God she had bound herself to the evil man. Immediately, she felt his weight bearing down on her, smelled his brandy-laden breath . . . heard the echo of his words. *Little cow, I'm thinking you'll sink straight to the bottom.*

She sucked in a deep breath. Her fist knotted in the blanket covering her lap as if she could crush the reminder in her grip. Her breakfast of porridge and milk threaten to rise up on her.

She belonged to no man. Not her social-climbing father who wanted nothing more than to wed her to the highest bidder—she saw that now. Not her husband. And not some stranger who scraped her up off the banks of the river. She was her own independent woman and would be solely that from now on. She would recover, heal, and carve a new life for herself somewhere far from all of them.

Mirela watched her with interest, one gray eyebrow lifted in silent inquiry. Annalise, shaking her head slightly, forced a tremulous smile and turned her attention to the portrait of a long-ago family member set within the cupboard.

She held silent as Mirela went about gathering the wet linens used for her sponge bath earlier in the day. After a few moments she found her voice to ask, "When do you think I can get out of this bed?"

"Hmm. Perhaps another four . . . five weeks."

She felt her eyes bulge in her face. "Five weeks?"

"You broke your leg . . ."

"Last time I didn't stay in bed nearly so long." She had already confessed to the childhood memory of breaking her leg when she fell from a tree. She thought that could be important for Mirela to know as she went about nursing her. After all, just because she remembered something that happened to her at fourteen did not mean she could remember the traumatic event from a week ago.

"And you had a limp, no?"

Annalise nodded again.

"That is why. You did not give it time to heal properly." Mirela looked at her in accusation. As if she was to blame for her limp.

Not that she'd had much of a choice in the matter. Mrs. Danvers demanded her up and moving about within a week, helping her mother with the smaller children in the nursery. Her mother's employer did not care one whit about allowing her time to recuperate.

Mirela lifted the bowl of soapy water. "This time, we will let it heal." She stabbed one gnarled finger toward Annalise. "You will not move from that bed."

Her face flushed both hot and cold as the reality of her life for the next five weeks settled over her.

She would remain in this bed, in this wagon, with a strange man sleeping a foot away from her every night? It wasn't to be borne.

A path of sunlight tunneled into the wagon as Mirela opened the door and descended the steps. Annalise leaned forward, eager and aching for its warmth, for the vast openness of the outdoors. Just as quickly the light was gone. The door shut with a click and she was all alone in a space that felt like it was shrinking by the moment. She slumped back in the bed, quite convinced she would go stark raving mad stuck here for several more weeks.

Owen looked up from where he stacked an armful of kindling he had gathered from the nearby woods. Mirela stood in front of him, the rare afternoon sunlight glinting off her many brilliant gold necklaces.

"Mirela," he greeted, marveling how this elderly, slow-moving woman managed to move with such stealth. He never heard her approach.

"What do you think you are doing?"

He glanced down at the kindling and bit off the sarcastic reply rising to his lips. "Helping . . ." He let the word hang, more question than statement. From the irritated way she glared at him, he did not think she approved of his activity.

Several of the men had gone into the village to speak with townsmen regarding tomorrow's fair, and Owen had taken it upon himself to gather the day's kindling. It was something to do rather than sit idle and wonder what precisely he was doing here with a band of Gypsies and an invalid female.

She pointed to the wagon. "That girl needs some attention."

He stared from the wagon to the old woman.

"I don't understand. Are you no longer capable of caring for—"

"I'm not talking of tending her injuries. I speak of her spirit. She is restless, lonely."

He stared, unsure how to respond to *that*. He was not a companion for hire. "I'm certain you or one of the other women would be better equipped—"

"Nonsense. She trusts you. You rescued her."

"That hardly makes me fit company." He'd

taken measures to give Anna her privacy. Rising before she woke and retiring after she slept. Even though she claimed memory loss, she had clearly been through an ordeal, and he had no intention of making her uneasy with his hovering presence. Or perhaps he didn't want to make himself too comfortable. Either way, he kept his distance.

Mirela pointed to the wagon. "She's been in that bed two weeks now and you dawdle out here . . ." She waved wildly. " . . . playing with your sticks."

He blinked. "What am I to do?" He was still here. He hadn't left. He was obliged to stay with the woman. At least until they learned her identity and he knew where she belonged. No doubt she had a family waiting for her somewhere, sick with worry. Maybe even a husband. Perhaps she had been traveling with family and was set upon by brigands.

He glanced back at the wagon as though he could see within to its confines, to Anna lying there on the bed. For all he knew, the damage to her leg, the bruise to her ribs, had not been the only injury done to her person. His chest pulled and tightened uncomfortably at the notion. Regaining her memory might be the worst trauma to befall her yet.

Mirela's agitated voice reclaimed his attention.

"Talk to her. Keep her company. Carry her outside so that she might get some fresh air."

Carry her?

He recoiled at the idea of holding her again . . . touching her.

Since she regained consciousness, he was achingly aware of her as a female. She might be bedridden, but that didn't stop him from studying her as she slept. Creeping into the wagon at night with only a taper to guide him, the dark fan of lashes on her cheeks fascinated him.

He could not understand why. She was no beauty in the classic standard, but there was something about her. She occupied far too much of his thoughts. In his head, alongside his dark and disturbing recollections, his ugly memories . . . that was no place for her to be. She was injured, vulnerable. He shouldn't be thinking of her as a man thought of a woman. Even after everything he went through in India, he had clung to his own code, some semblance of honor to get himself through it all, to keep himself sane. When he set forth a rule, he would not break it.

He would not touch her.

In order to uphold that promise to himself, he couldn't imagine carrying her around for fresh air a very good idea. "I don't think that would be proper."

Mirela laughed. "Proper? You sound like such an Englishman . . . all staunch and dignified, but we know you are not that, don't we?" She tapped the corner of her eye. "We know. I see you."

He stiffened, wondering what it was she thought she saw in him. "I will not carry her. She's fine as she is. She stays in bed."

Turning, he strode back into the woods under the pretense of fetching more kindling. He did not emerge for several hours.

That night, Annalise heard him enter the wagon. She held herself still, feigning sleep with her eyes closed, debating how best to approach him. As he did not show himself during the day, if she wanted words with him, this was the only way.

She heard him lower himself to the cot, the rustle of his clothing as he removed his jacket. One boot hit the floor with a soft thud, then the next. She heard a puff of breath and suspected that he just blew out a candle.

Moistening her lips, she spoke into the dark. "How long are we going to stay here?" The moment the question escaped her, she winced. *We.* When had she decided their fates were entwined? Was this because of the foolish words Mirela had rattled off to her?

There was a long pause and she imagined the

strong lines of his face contemplating her question. "And where is it that we should go?" His deep voice floated over her. There was no ring of surprise that she was awake, and she wondered if he had known. She recalled his dark blue eyes, so deep and intense. It was as though they missed nothing. Maybe they could even see to her through the dark.

She hastily sought a reply, regretting her rash words.

"Have you regained your memory?" he asked.

"No." Silence stretched for several moments before she spoke again. "There is a fair," she announced, turning and staring in the direction of his voice.

"Yes. There is."

"I should like to see it."

"You cannot walk," he reminded her.

She blew out a gust of breath. "Could I perhaps be . . . carried? Pushed on a cart? Anything? I can't stay in this wagon for weeks."

Silence met her request.

She balled her hands at her sides. "Do you hear me?"

"Yes." He sighed as if it took everything to utter the single word.

She fumed. Talking to him was like pulling one's teeth.

"The fair?" she prodded.

He did not respond. Clearly he had no wish for her company.

"Why are you even here? Why haven't you just left?"

He shifted. She thought she identified the outline of him, sitting up beside the bed.

"I found you. You are my responsibility—"

"Oh, indeed?" She snorted lightly. "So you're a man driven by duty and honor?" She knew she should sound more gracious, thankful even. If he wasn't that sort of man, she would likely be dead.

His voice stroked the air, low and deep. "You say that like it's such a bad thing."

It wasn't, of course. If not for him, she would doubt such men existed at all anymore. On the heels of her trauma, however, she was still skeptical. "Forgive me. I'm bad-tempered from being cooped up in this wagon." She took a deep bracing breath, sliding her hands down her face in a slow drag. "Some fresh air for even a short time would improve my mood considerably." She stared at his shadowy shape, wincing at the plea in her voice.

His silence seemed to indicate that her words were lost on him.

She tried a different tactic. "The fresh air might even be good for me—speed my recovery." She plucked at her blanket with her fingers, focusing on a patch of loose threads. "I've heard that, you know. Well in spirit is well in body."

Nothing. He didn't even stir, and she began to wonder if he had fallen asleep.

She propped herself up on an elbow. "Mr. Crawford? Are you listening?"

Annalise strained for a sound of him below her.

"Mr. Crawford?"

Finally he answered her, "Good night, Anna."

A slight rustling told her he was settling back down, ignoring her request. No promise to let her out of this wagon. No hope from moving from its increasingly oppressive space.

His dismissal was clear.

Inhaling thinly through her nose, she vowed that she would find a way to alleviate the stretch of monotonous, mind-numbing hours stuck in this bed. Without his help.

Chapter Seven

"You there, Englishman. Come. Help us carry these." Nadia nodded to one of the chests laden with colorful shawls, scarves, and blankets, all wares to be sold at the fair.

He glanced back at the wagon, feeling that inexorable pull—no matter how he tried to deny it. Fortunately for him, Anna had been asleep when he left just before dawn.

He was being unreasonable, he supposed, refusing her request for a bit of fresh air. There was just something about her. She made him uncomfortable. Those velvet eyes . . . they seemed to drink him up. The notion of being in close proximity to her, carrying her against his chest—he couldn't bring himself to agree to such a thing.

The village was already abuzz with activity.

Nadia and three other women led him through the growing press of people to their area of the fair. The men were already there, practicing their dagger throwing skills with enthusiasm. Everyone was garbed flamboyantly in vibrant colors. If their dark coloring didn't alert the world of their Romani roots, then their wardrobe did.

"You can set that down there," one of the women said, directing him beneath the striped tent they had erected.

A crowd of children had gathered around the tent, watching in loud approval. He smiled as one of the young Gypsy boys tossed daggers back in forth with his younger brother, a lad of no more than nine years. It was a wonder he didn't slice off a finger.

Shaking his head, his gaze scanned the rest of the fair. Somewhere nearby a hawker loudly offered roasted chestnuts. The aroma of hot sticky buns filled the air, making his stomach growl. A faint smile brushed his lips as he recalled he and his brothers stuffing themselves sick with sticky buns at their own village fair. Well, it was mostly Brand and himself. Jamie had been too dignified for that.

Paget had been there, too. Eating more than her share. Too much for a girl of her slight frame. He had no idea where she put it, but she matched him bite for bite. She'd always been there. A permanent fixture of his boyhood. Now she belonged to Jamie.

A wave of longing swept through him. Not because he wanted Paget for himself. God, no. He'd released the thought of them, together, from his mind long ago. His first year in India ruined him for any respectable woman. He was glad she and Jamie had found each other. He simply wished for carefree days again.

Days like the ones he spent at his mother's home in London, quiet evenings reading alongside her in the library or helping her in the garden. His grandfather had spent his final years there. Owen could still recall his large, callused hand rumpling the hair on his head as he played with his toy soldiers before the fireplace. If he closed his eyes, he could still hear the old Scot's brogue. *That's my fine lad.*

Shaking off the nostalgic thoughts, he continued to scan the merrymaking, feeling more isolated than ever. He didn't belong here any more than he had in India. His mouth flattened in a grim line. Perhaps he was more at home among battle cries, wielding a pistol or a rifle or plunging his blade into an enemy than here. A sad testament to the man he had become.

Although he knew he could never recapture

the innocence from his youth again, he longed to return to his mother's town house in London and find the peace and contentment he had once known there.

Suddenly, something caught his eye. A brown-haired head bobbing amid the fairgoers. The afternoon sunlight cast the hair into burnished mahogany. His gut twisted in annoyance. He knew that hair. A contrast to the other occasions he'd viewed it—a sopping wet mess or cloaked in the dim confines of a wagon. But he knew it. *Anna.*

What was she doing out of bed? Bewildered, he tracked her in the crowd. Even dressed in a deep red gown with a single blue ribbon pulling back the top half of her hair from her face, she looked fresh and clean. And in Luca's arms.

He scowled. Before he could consider his actions, he was moving across the fair, elbowing past hawkers dangling their wares before him.

He trained his gaze on her, eyeing with disapproval the way she laughed at something Luca said as he pointed into a pen full of pigs waiting to be auctioned.

He stopped beside the ramshackle pen. "Anna," he greeted tersely.

She turned her head at the sound of his voice. "Oh, hello, Mr. Crawford. Fine day for a fair, is it not?"

He ground his teeth, certain he heard snideness in her comment. "What are you doing up and about from bed?"

"Mirela said it was perfectly safe as long as I was carried. Luca here graciously offered to let me see some of the fair and get a bit of fresh air."

Owen eyed the brute's hands on her. One of his large paws cupped her beneath the legs, holding her carefully at her splinted leg. The other was wrapped around her back.

"If you insist on leaving your bed—"

"Mirela said it would be fine." Her bright brown eyes sparked defiantly.

He ignored her interruption. "You should be in a cart and not carried about. You could still jostle your leg."

"I'm in good hands with Luca." She smiled at Owen as if he were a child and she the tolerant parent. The little minx. She knew he was annoyed, and she was enjoying it.

Luca adjusted her in his arms, and his hands moved a little too much against her back for Owen's liking. His own hands opened and closed at his sides.

Anna stared at him patiently, those amazing eyes of hers blinking with innocence.

Luca looked bored. "Come. The pie eating contest is about to start."

Owen watched as they strolled away, Anna's head bobbing among the villagers as she was carried.

"The sunlight will do her some good." Once again, Mirela appeared at his side with no warning. He looked down at her, a surge of resentment flaring inside him.

"That's what I hear."

A mocking smile curved her wrinkled lips. "Should have taken her about the fair yourself."

He crossed his arms, losing sight of Luca and Anna as they became lost in the throng of people waiting for the pie eating spectacle.

"I have no wish to carry her around the fair."

Mirela gave a low, cackling laugh and walked away, leaving him standing by himself.

Annalise laughed with delight as a scrawny boy of no more than ten years was declared the winner of the contest and presented a ribbon. His mother appeared, wiping pie from his face fondly with her apron, looking every bit as proud as the boy himself.

Luca's voice rumbled beside her ear. "What would you like to see next, Anna?"

She glanced around, eyeing the happy chaos, in the guise of deciding where to go next, but it was just a ruse. She was really looking for Owen.

He'd looked decidedly unhappy to see her up and about, which only puzzled her. Why should he care if someone else was kind enough to escort her around the fair? It was no imposition on him.

Then she saw him, pushing a cart in her direction, a decidedly resolute look in his eyes, his handsome features implacable.

He stopped the cart before them. Releasing the handles, he rounded the cart and walked toward her. "In you go."

Annalise blinked and looked from the cart to Owen.

At her hesitation, he sighed and gestured at it. "This is far safer for your leg than being carried about."

She opened her mouth to insist she was fine, but before she had the chance, Luca was lowering her to the blanket-lined cart. She pressed her lips shut, feeling very much like a child. An *invalid.* A bitter taste filled her mouth. Granted, a broken leg inhibited her and made asserting her independence somewhat of a challenge, but this . . . being deposited in a cart with no thought to her wishes, no care for what she wanted, it rankled.

Crossing her arms, she glared up at Owen. "I'm not going back to the wagon if that's what you're thinking." She looked at Luca again, ready to suggest they move along to admire the display of horseflesh up for auction.

Suddenly the cart was moving. She was being rolled away and leaving Luca behind.

She heard Owen's voice call out above her, "I'll take her from here, thank you."

Annalise tossed a glance over her shoulder. Luca was already walking away, shrugging his shoulders.

The colors of the fair whirled past her as she was rolled over the grounds. It appeared as though they were leaving. She bit her lip to stop an angry retort.

With every second that passed, her face grew hotter. Arms crossed over her chest, she hugged herself tightly.

A young girl stepped in front of the cart, myriad ribbons woven in her lovely hair. "Would the lady like her hair plaited?" She motioned to a trio of young girls working deft fingers through the hair of bright-cheeked women.

She huffed, certain Owen was scoffing at the offer above her.

His deep voice floated down to her. "Would you?"

Startled, she looked up and found herself ensnared in the blue of his eyes. *Did he mean it?* She nodded hastily, fearful that he would change his mind and take her back to the wagon.

"Follow me," the young girl trilled enthusiastically before Annalise could form a response.

Owen obeyed. Grabbing a fistful of ribbons, the young girl faced Annalise and hesitated, unsure how to attack her hair from her position in the cart.

"Come, this way." Owen moved around so the girl could stand at the end of the cart. He stood awkwardly beside it, surrounded by women in the process of having their hair plaited. Annalise suppressed a smile and lowered her gaze as the girl's fingers worked quickly, weaving a coronet of plaits around her head with various colored ribbons. The vibrant ends dangled in her face until the girl finished and gathered them up.

Moving to the front of the cart, the girl admired her work. "There. Beautiful, is she not?" Annalise looked at Owen for assent, her cheerful smile slipping when she caught sight of his brooding expression.

With a muttered, indecipherable reply, he fished a coin from inside his jacket pocket and paid the girl. A moment later he was pushing her along again, moving quickly through the fair. She frowned and crossed her arms, guessing that now he would return her to the wagon where she could resume her examination of the ceiling.

"Are you hungry?" he asked, his voice rising to be heard over a nearby orchestra.

She craned her neck around to look at him, wondering if she had misunderstood him.

He stared straight ahead, his gaze not dipping to look at her.

She moistened her lips. "I could eat . . ."

He finally glanced down, his lips unsmiling, his expression unreadable. Everything about him seemed to indicate that he was only tolerating her. He stopped before a hawker selling meat pasties. Another hawker quickly appeared, proffering lemonade. Owen set the meat pasties in the cart and handed her the carafe of lemonade to hold.

She settled the carafe carefully on her lap as he pushed them from the center of the village toward the outskirts of the community—but not, she noticed, in the direction of the Gypsy camp. Her shoulders eased. That's all that really mattered to her at the moment. He wasn't taking her back to that dreadful wagon. For whatever reason, he was granting her more time out of doors. Even if it was to be spent in his stilted company. She would take her delights where she found them. Perhaps that's what nearly dying did to a soul—made you appreciate the small pleasures.

As he pushed them through a small opening in a shallow stone wall, she tilted her face up to the sun, letting its warm rays brush over her skin. Even before she'd been forced into bed, the weather had been dismal. This sunlight was a refreshing change.

He steered the cart beneath a tree.

"This looks a fine spot," she murmured, admiring the spray of delicate buds dotting the ground. "It will be spring soon and all this will be in bloom."

He took one of the blankets from the cart and spread it out on the grass.

"You've come prepared," she added, wondering how long she would have to carry the conversation alone.

He slid her a look beneath his lashes as he spread out the final corners. "You need to eat."

She propped an elbow on the edge of the cart, her lips quirking. "Don't fret, Mr. Crawford. I wasn't accusing you of being thoughtful. I would not dream of making such a suggestion."

He sent her a derisive look but didn't respond as he reached for the food and carafe and settled them on the blanket.

"I mean I realize you're thoughtful and generous enough to save my life, of course," she hastily explained. "I would never be so remiss to forget such a fact, but you're just not . . ." Her voice faded as she stared at his stoic profile rather helplessly.

"You're not the garrulous sort, are you? Certainly no—" Her voice cut off into a squeak as he leaned over the cart and slid his arms beneath her.

He carefully lifted her from the cart, bearing her with ease. His body was all lean lines against her, his chest a hard wall. Her gaze crawled back up to his face. She blinked in consternation at his ever aloof expression.

"Who can talk with you around?" he murmured.

She gasped as he set her down in the middle of the blanket, then arranged her skirts over her legs. She wore no shoe on the broken leg. A thick woolen stocking covered the foot, peeking out from beneath her hem.

"Are you saying I don't give you the opportunity to speak?" She lifted her chin and crossed her arms. "Very well. I shall leave it to you to carry on the conversation. I will follow your lead, Mr. Crawford."

Without comment, he unwrapped a meat pie and handed it to her. She watched as he did the same for himself. He took a large bite, indifferent that she watched him. Indifferent to the stretch of silence.

She took a nibbling bite, the quiet hovering between them. Even the sounds of the fair were too distant to hear anymore. She glanced from him to her meat pastie several times, waiting, expecting for him to say *something*. Nothing profound. Simply . . . something. She accepted the lemonade when he offered it, savoring the cool tartness on her tongue.

After several more minutes of silence, she dropped the pastie back into the wrapper. "This is just silly."

He smiled slowly and something unfurled in her stomach at the sight of that smile. Triumphant as it was, there was a hint of the devil to it that made her pulse quicken.

"Oh, and now you think you've won?" Annoyance swam hotly through her blood—perhaps mostly at herself for breaking down and talking first.

His shrug only irritated her further.

"After we finish lunch, will you return me to the fair?"

His smile faded and she knew that had not been his intention.

"I was enjoying myself," she added, as if that would somehow make a difference to him.

"This is the first time you've been out of bed since you woke," he said. "You don't want to overtax yourself."

"I've either been carried or in a cart. I'm hardly overtaxing myself." At the arch of his eyebrow, she snapped, "I don't require your permission, you know."

He nodded to the cart. "Unless you plan to snap your fingers and make the cart move, you actually do."

"You're not the only one capable of pushing a cart."

"No one else is at the camp. Who will you prevail upon? I doubt Mirela and the others will return before evening."

She beat a fist against her lap. "You are cruel. If you don't want to escort me, I don't know why you won't permit Luca—"

"Has it occurred to you that you're keeping him from work? They depend on their efforts at fairs like this to keep them clothed and fed. It's rather inconsiderate to monopolize Luca."

At this, her shoulders slumped with deflation. She hadn't considered she was somehow taking advantage of Mirela's hospitality. "I see. I did not realize . . ." She wrapped her pastie back up in the paper. "I'm ready."

"You haven't finished eating."

"I'm quite full."

"That can hardly be the case. You need to regain your strength." His gaze skimmed her. "You're wasting away."

She stopped herself just short of throwing

her wrapped-up pastie at him. "There you are again . . . lavishing me with your charm." She motioned to herself. "I'm hardly wasting away. I had quite a bit of cushion on me before I fell in the river."

"Did you?" His gaze sharpened on her, and she realized her error.

"I—yes, at least I feel that much is true."

He leaned closer. "What else do you 'feel'?"

She reached for her lemonade and took another long sip, looking anywhere but at him as her mind feverishly worked, desperate to come up with a viable response.

Lowering the lemonade, she lifted her gaze to him.

He stared back expectantly, his handsome face ever impassive—not a hint of emotion seeping through. "What else do you remember?"

"Nothing." Beneath his probing gaze, she felt compelled to elaborate. "Nothing *yet*. I'm certain I will. I'm certain . . ." Once she could stand on her feet again and take herself away, she could claim a sudden full recovery of memory.

She couldn't risk telling him her identity until then. Couldn't risk him returning her to her husband. Annalise's throat tightened at the prospect of coming face-to-face with Bloodsworth again. Especially in her weakened condition.

Squaring her shoulders, she held his gaze, commanding herself not to look away. That would be as good as admitting she was lying.

"I look forward to it," he murmured. There was just enough of something in his voice—skepticism perhaps—that she arched an eyebrow at him as he took a final bite of his lunch.

She watched as he leaned back on his elbows and gazed up at the branches swaying above them. She followed his gaze, feeling some of her tension ease away as she enjoyed the afternoon. He must have believed her. He certainly wouldn't relax beside her on a blanket if he believed her to be a liar.

"You know," she began, "I don't know anything about you, Mr. Crawford. Aside from the fact that you rescue drowned females. Where are you from?"

Where are you going? What life is it that I'm keeping you from? She resisted the urge to bombard him with these questions. He certainly wouldn't be so forthcoming to tell her his entire history in one sitting. Not as brusque as he was.

"I grew up not far from here." He exhaled. "A village called Winninghamshire. I just left there."

"You don't live there?"

"No. I was . . . visiting. My parents are gone, but I have a brother left there. And his wife."

There was something in his voice. Something

he was leaving out. Was it the loss of his parents? Grief for them?

"And where do you travel now?"

"I have a residence in London."

She studied his profile. A residence in London, but no mention of a profession. He must be a gentleman. Somehow she suspected as much, although he possessed none of the haughty airs of the gentlemen of the *ton* she'd met over the last year. His clothing was of fine quality but not the height of fashion. His hair was in need of a good trim. The sun-streaked dark blond locks brushed the collar of his brown jacket. It was a pleasure to study him. She recalled that brief smile she had seen. In that moment he had truly been irresistible.

"Well, what have we here?"

Owen launched himself into a sitting position before she even fully turned her gaze to the pair of men approaching where they reclined.

She tensed at the sight of them. They looked like they hadn't washed in the better part of a year. Their hair was scruffy, matted at the roots, shorn at the ends as if by a knife. The taller of the pair stood at the helm, adjusting his impossibly soiled neck cloth. "Looks like little lovebirds on a picnic." His grin showed furry, rotting teeth. He looked from his friend back to Owen and Annalise.

Owen rose to his feet in one easy motion. "Move on your way."

"Oh, this is a private affair? My apologies." The man looked to his companion. "Freddy, I think we're imposing."

Freddy nodded with exaggerated movements.

And yet neither of the ruffians made a move to leave. Instead they continued to smile, seemingly harmless. Only there was an undercurrent of menace in the way they stood shoulder-to-shoulder, almost as though they were deliberately forming a wall.

"Oh. What did the young lady do to her leg?" Freddy inquired, noting the end of the splint peeking out from her hem. Her fingers slid there self-consciously, tugging on her hem as if she could hide the vulnerability from them.

Unease skated over her skin, reminiscent of another night not long ago when Bloodsworth had toyed with her moments before he slammed a pillow over her face. Anger followed on the heels of her unease . . . anger that the arrival of these two should bring her back to that place again and make her feel like the old Annalise.

Owen stepped around her, blocking her from their view. "None of your concern."

Her hands moved over the blanket, seeking something, anything she could use to defend herself. Her fingers bumped the half-full carafe of lemonade. She circled the neck with her fingers and held it close.

"Oh, wants her to himself, does he, Peter?" Freddy elbowed his taller companion.

Peter stepped to the side, his eyes looking beyond Owen to Annalise with interest. She fidgeted beneath his gaze, her fingers flexing around the carafe. She'd never seen a man look at her in such a lascivious manner. She felt the urge to snatch the extra blanket and cover herself.

But that still wouldn't hide her face. Suddenly she regretted the ribbons and artfully arranged hair. She felt like a silly girl . . . and that made her feel somehow more vulnerable.

"Can't blame him. She is a picture." Peter attempted to sidestep Owen.

Not only did Owen move to block him, but he set a hand to the ruffian's shoulder.

Peter knocked it aside with a snarl. Freddy moved then. She gave a small squeak and scooted back as he tackled Owen to the blanket.

She dragged herself out of the way of their thrashing bodies. The carafe slipped, spilling lemonade. She fumbled for it as they fought—a tangled blur of limbs beside her. Dimly, she heard Peter shouting encouragement.

Crying for help, Annalise looked around wildly, seeing no one else in that stretch of countryside. Securing her grip on the glass carafe, she lifted it over her head, waiting for the opportunity to bring it down.

Then the two bodies went still. Locked, but utterly still.

She stopped shouting, stopped breathing. Her gaze fixed on Owen, one arm wrapped around Freddy's throat. His free hand pressed the tip of a knife to his cheek, indenting the flesh.

She gawked. She had not known he even possessed a knife. Certainly she had not seen it anywhere on his person. His sun-streaked hair was wild about his head, brushing the sharp planes of his face, falling low over his brow. His dark blue eyes appeared even darker, glittering like a night sea, full of an emotion she had never observed in him before. Not that she *ever* saw emotion from him.

Peter sputtered obscenities. "Let him go, you bastard!"

"And why would I do that?" Owen spoke as calmly as he looked, easily holding Freddy in check. "Considering what you were planning for us?" The knife pressed closer, blood pooling around the tip and dripping down Freddy's cheek. "That wouldn't be very wise of me."

Freddy's face was purpling now, his lips fighting for words, arriving only at a squeaked "Please."

"We weren't going to do nothing. Promise." Peter held his hands up as though to show how harmless he really was.

"Lying curs," Owen said in that coldly even voice. "You were going to rob us and do whatever other sordid whim struck you. Why should I let you go to just do it again? To carry on and hurt others?"

Annalise couldn't look away. She knew she should tell him to stop, to let them go, but she couldn't. Owen's words resonated deeply within her. What if the duke had been hurting others, innocents, for years? No one would have dared stop him—a powerful lord. She vaguely realized she was nodding, silently encouraging Owen to stop these two.

Then Owen was looking at her. Those dark blue eyes trained on her, all that carefully restrained emotion focused on her. Watching her. Seeing *her.*

And something changed in his face then. A subtle altering. Some of the hard-edged tension ebbed from his features. That fire in his eyes faded, like coals banked.

His eyes still on her, he said to Freddy, "I'm going to release you. If you or your friend make any sudden movements . . . if you come at either me or the girl, I will show you just how good I am with a knife. I've left a long line of corpses that can attest to just how excellent my aim is."

" 'Course, 'course, yes, thank you," Freddy babbled in his arms.

"We understand," Peter agreed.

After some moments Owen slid his gaze from her and released his captive. He moved to stand before her as the unsavory pair scurried off, resembling wild animals. They scampered away as fast as their legs could carry them, looking over their shoulders several times as though to assure themselves that Owen was indeed letting them retreat and not making good on his threat.

A beat of silence held before she found her voice again. She moistened her lips and stared up at him. He still watched the men flee, the long lines of his body rigid and tense, like a spring ready to snap. "That was impressive."

He turned and looked down at her, his eyes once again an impenetrable blue.

She moistened her lips, realizing her pulse still raced in her neck even though they were out of danger.

And then it dawned on her that they had never been in danger. Not truly. Not with this man—this stranger who apparently knew how to fight and wield a knife with deadly skill. He had always been in control. She scanned him from head to foot, admiring him . . . this man who could handle himself in any situation. She doubted he'd ever been a victim . . . ever tasted the sharp, coppery flood of fear in his mouth.

He said nothing in response to her compliment, merely stared at her with that maddening impassivity.

"How did you—" She stopped, swallowing back words as sudden hope blossomed in her heart. It didn't matter how he knew how to handle himself in dangerous situations, only that he did. Only that he could.

Chapter Eight

"Impressive?" Owen echoed as he looked down at her.

"Yes." She nodded doggedly. She waved her hand in a small circle. "What you just did . . . how you protected yourself." She paused and moistened her lips. "I wish that I could be like you."

His expression cracked as he looked down at her, and she knew she had astounded him with her words. A frown pulled at his well-carved lips. "You don't want to be anything like me." He moved then, gathering up their things and setting them in the cart.

"Why not? To do what you just did? To be so capable? You're a hero. You saved me. Twice now, I suspect. To be able to do the things you do . . . that would be . . ." She paused, groping for the words to convey just how tremendous, just how relieved and at peace she would feel to be that strong, that in control.

He shook his head as he bent to lift her in his arms.

She squeezed his shoulder as he moved her toward the cart, her fingers digging into the muscle and sinew beneath the jacket. She tried to finish her earlier words, "That would be— "

"No," he bit out, depositing her.

She searched his face, trying to catch his gaze as he draped the blanket over her lap. "No?" He wouldn't even let her praise him? "Why aren't you proud—"

"Please. Stop."

"Maybe if I could comport myself as you just did I could have prevented this from happening . . ." She waved at her body.

He stared hard at her. "You remember what happened to you?"

She inhaled and fought to hold his gaze as the lie tripped off her tongue, "No, but Mirela told me that the bruise on my ribs was from someone hitting me. I don't think I fell into that river by accident." She paused for breath, arching an eyebrow. "Do you?"

He held her gaze a moment before looking away, staring off into the horizon where the two ruffians had disappeared. "No. I don't think it was an accident."

She leaned forward, reaching over the edge of the cart to seize his arm. She curled her fingers into his forearm. "Then you should understand."

He glanced down and stared at her hand on his arm.

She continued, "I can't even walk—"

"In a few more weeks you can get out of bed," he reminded her.

"But I'll never be like you." She felt herself smile and knew it was rueful. Sad even.

He angled his head, surveying her with a bemused expression. "But you'd want that?"

She looked down and plucked at the colorful fringe on the blanket, nodding and feeling foolish admitting such a thing.

"I can teach you that."

Her head snapped up at his softly worded declaration. "What?"

He was moving around the cart with his usual swift, easy strides to take up the handles again. "I can teach you," he repeated, the words crisp, succinct.

Her heart pounded in her chest. Her hand trembled on her lap. Had she misunderstood? Did he just offer to teach her to be more like him?

"What . . . how . . . what do you mean precisely?"

"I can show you how to be more self-possessed,

more aware. You don't have to be an easy target, Anna."

"Yes," she breathed, awed and eager at the possibility. Questions whirled in her head. Would they remain with Mirela and the others until she could walk again?

"Leave it to me. I'll handle the arrangements," he said as though he could read her spinning thoughts. He stared straight ahead, no longer looking at her.

She scooted until her back rested against the wall of the cart and settled in for the ride back to camp, not even minding that he was returning her to the dreaded wagon with its dreaded bed. Imminent boredom didn't matter anymore. Not with hope looming in her future.

Owen strolled through the camp, searching for Mirela. Night had fallen and most everyone had returned from the village by now. He spotted her near the fire, ladling from a pot set over the crackling nest of flames.

"Hungry?" she inquired when he approached.

"We'll be leaving in the morning. I'd like to borrow one wagon and one of your men to take us into Town. Naturally, I'll pay you for your time and services . . ."

She stopped and stared at him. "Decided to

keep her, have you?" She cackled then. It was the only word to describe her laughter.

He scowled. His forehead drew tight and he resisted the urge to rub there and ease the sudden tension he felt. "No, of course not."

Her eyebrows winged high, twin gray birds. "Oh? Not yet then?"

"Not ever," he quickly snapped. "I merely think she'll be more comfortable recuperating in Town." And he'd had enough sleeping on the floor of a wagon. He wanted a bed. "I appreciate all you've done for us—"

She waved a hand in dismissal. "You've paid for it. No thanks needed."

"At any rate, she would likely have perished without you."

Mirela was already turning away. "Luca can take you where you wish to go in the morning."

He watched the bent old woman walk away, wondering at her conviction that he and Anna were somehow linked. Absurd. It was the stuff superstitious old Gypsy women believed in.

He winced again as he recalled the promise he made her. What possessed him? It was her eyes. He had seen something in them. It was the same thing he had seen when she first opened her eyes atop his mount. The same haunting fear was there, glazing that velvety brown.

He supposed offering to help her didn't exactly promote the notion that they were unattached—two strangers whose paths were only briefly intersecting. In his mind, he saw that bruise on her ribs, the cuts and scrapes covering her body, the wheeze of her breath, barely there, scarcely alive.

His hands tightened into fists at his sides. She wasn't a soldier. This wasn't a war, and yet someone had brutalized her. Something out there terrified her. Whether she remembered or not—and he suspected she remembered more than she revealed—she needed to armor herself.

And he couldn't deny her the chance to help herself. Not staring into those eyes that seemed to reach inside him and pull at what was left of his soul.

He'd help her heal, teach her to be strong.

Her words from earlier washed over him. *You're a hero.*

He sucked a breath inside his suddenly shrinking lungs, reminding himself that she would soon be gone. Before she discovered just how far from a hero he really was.

Chapter Nine

It was pouring by the time they arrived at his town house. Not in the most fashionable neighborhood, the two-storied, white-stone-faced edifice peered down at him through sheets of rain like a long-lost relation.

Something eased inside his chest at sight of it. The house was a feast for hungry eyes. His mother's family had resided here whenever they visited from Scotland. He recalled her telling him that his father had proposed to her in the back gardens beneath the crab apple tree.

He'd thought the story fanciful then, even as a lad, but it had not stopped him from asking her to tell him the story again and again. He shook off the memory of his mother and pounded on the front door, holding his jacket over his head in an effort to ward off the rain. The door opened to a groom he did not recognize.

The young man blinked at him like he did not quite know what to do with the drenched man on the doorstep so late in the evening. His eyes only widened further when he spotted the hulking wagon behind. With its ornate markings, it obviously belonged to Gypsies.

Before he could announce himself, Mrs. Kirkpatrick appeared behind him, holding a lamp. "My lord," she cried out when she saw him.

Grateful that she recognized him, Owen pushed inside the foyer. Standing in an evergrowing puddle, he was about to request an umbrella to fetch Anna from the wagon when Luca was suddenly there. Carrying Anna, he'd tossed a blanket over her head to shield her from the weather.

Inside the shadowy foyer, Luca pulled the blanket from her face. She blinked her brown eyes, eyeing her new surroundings. Several wisps of hair floated loose around her face.

"Where should I put her?" Luca asked in his deep accent.

Mrs. Kirkpatrick gaped, her lips working, clearly trying to form words that would not offend while obviously curious about what was happening.

"Mrs. Kirkpatrick," Owen said, "please see to it that the young lady is made comfortable in the master chamber."

She nodded, even as her lips thinned in disapproval, the lines at either side of her mouth drawing tightly. Clearly she was making her own conclusions.

Unwilling to let her labor under the misapprehension that Anna was his mistress, he added, "She's suffering from a broken leg. You will need to assist her as long as she is our guest here." His mind shied away from just how long that would be.

"I see . . . yes, my lord. Of course."

"My lord?" Anna looked from him to his housekeeper, her velvety eyes impossibly big. "You're . . ."

Mrs. Kilpatrick pulled back her shoulders and surveyed Anna as though she were mad. "He's the Earl of McDowell." Her voice dripped with censure that this hapless girl did not know.

"You are?" Anna's long lashes blinked over her eyes.

He gave a curt nod. Through odd circumstance—since he was a youngest son of an English earl and not in line for a title—he'd inherited an earldom through his Scottish grandfather.

With a wearied breath, he turned to the groom

and motioned outside. "See that my mount is taken to the stable and my things are brought to one of the guest chambers."

With a swift nod, the man dashed out the door into the rain.

Luca looked Owen over appraisingly, no doubt wondering if he should have demanded more money from an earl.

Owen stepped forward. "I'll take her from here."

Luca hesitated only a moment before shrugging and handing Anna over. Owen flexed his hands carefully on the soft slope of her thigh as he took her. With his other hand he cupped her arm. She was pleasantly warm. The musty aroma of the damp blanket mingled with the fresh, clean smell of her hair. He felt her gaze on the side of his face without looking at her and knew she was watching him, measuring him with the new knowledge that he was an earl. For some reason he did not sense relief or awe—all likely sentiments. Especially from a young lady in her precarious situation. He felt only trepidation coming off her in waves.

Luca nodded to each of them in farewell before turning and striding back out into the rain.

Mrs. Kirkpatrick motioned to the stairs. "We can have Edmond carry her up, my lord."

"Unnecessary. I recall the way well enough." And he was not quite confident Edmond would handle her with the care necessary for her leg.

He took the steps, hearing Mrs. Kirkpatrick scurrying below, snapping orders.

Anna's hand rested lightly on his shoulder, barely touching, as though fearing too much contact. He felt the hand there nonetheless, the imprint of each slight finger against his shoulder, searing through the fabric of his jacket.

He stopped at the door to his chamber. "Can you open it, please?"

She reached down to turn the latch. He shoved it open with his boot and carried her to the chaise lounge near the balcony doors. He set her down carefully before turning to the bed that dominated one side of the room, and felt her gaze on him as he pulled back the counterpane

He stopped for a moment, unsure of himself. Which only served to annoy him. He wasn't a green lad, uncomfortable around females. Nor should he feel uncomfortable beneath his own roof. But here he stood, wondering how he had ended up in circumstances where he was totally responsible for a girl he'd only known a fortnight—and for one week of that time she had been out of her head with fever. Indeed, he knew her not at all.

She watched him across the dark room, her

eyes glowing like a timid creature peering out of the woods.

"Mrs. Kirkpatrick will be here momentarily," he murmured. "She'll see you settled . . . bring you something to eat. Tell her if you require anything. She will care for your needs."

He started for the door, stopping in the threshold at the sound of her voice.

"When will I see you again?"

There must have been something in his manner that hinted at his eagerness to leave—to deposit her in the housekeeper's capable hands and go to ground. After all, when he left Jamie and Paget in Winninghamshire it had been with the express goal of doing that very thing. Burying himself in the comforting familiarity of his mother's town house.

All of that was before he found her. Before he had, in a moment of weakness, made that promise to her.

"When you're on your feet, we'll begin your . . ." He paused, not even knowing what to call it. What was it precisely he intended to do for her?

Prevent her from ending up broken and facedown on a riverbank again, a voice whispered across his mind.

Apparently she understood even as he failed to articulate himself. She nodded from where she sat in the shadows, sitting straight and prim, her legs stretched out over the chaise. "Yes," she quickly supplied. "Yes, I look forward to that."

I look forward to that. As if he was going to merely instruct her on the fine points of needlework.

With a nod, he bade her good-night, turning his back on the image of her, so small and alone on the other side of his vast chamber.

He heard her soft echo behind him, "Good night."

He departed the room, tying to ignore the notion that he should have remained.

It was the same dream.

Annalise woke shaking, lurching upright in the bed she had been sleeping in for the last week. The silken sheets puddled to her waist like a waterfall.

Panting, chest heaving, she stared straight ahead into the dark.

She could still see Bloodsworth's face, so lifelike in front of her. His whisper still floated in her ear. *Nasty bit of rubbish . . .*

Annalise swallowed past the lump in her throat and glanced around her darkened bedchamber. She knew it was Owen's chamber. Mrs. Kirkpatrick had said as much when she helped her settle in the first day. Even though it belonged to him, it bore none of his influence. No personal effects. A wardrobe and a few other simple pieces of masculine furniture. The bed was the most ornate piece in the room. A mammoth, canopied, mahogany four-post.

Filmy curtains fluttered at her balcony window, and her throat constricted as she realized those doors were open.

Her hands pressed down on the mattress on either side of her. If she could have walked, she would have risen, crossed the room and closed the doors. But she was trapped on the bed. Alone with her fear, that thing she loathed so much.

A small sound scratched the air. Her gaze swung around the room, searching for the source.

The pulse in her throat thumped impossibly harder, faster, as the latch to the bedchamber door slowly turned. It swung inward and Owen stood there, light flooding into the room behind him from the corridor. A relieved breath gusted out of her lips, replaced with a different kind of anxiety at the sight of him wearing only a dressing robe, open down the chest. Her mouth dried.

"Anna?"

She nodded for a moment before answering. "Yes."

"Are you well? I heard you call out."

Her hands twisted the silken sheets. "Did I disturb you? I'm sorry."

Annoyance flickered back to life inside her. He'd been avoiding her since they arrived. Now he cared to show himself?

"You needn't apologize. Nightmares aren't exactly something we can control."

Her breath eased from her lips. "You speak from experience?" She didn't know precisely where the question came from. She supposed from the desire that welled up inside her to know more about him. This earl that wasn't an earl. At least not like any earl she had ever met. What manner of earl kept the fact that he was an earl to himself? He was not like any of the noblemen her father had thrust upon her. He was deadly with a knife and rescued girls and consorted with Gypsies and eschewed Society and brought strangers into his home. He mystified her.

She wished the room were more well-lit so she might view him better. She craved a glimpse of him. Just to prove that he was as attractive as memory served. He'd been keeping his distance, leaving her to the care of Mrs. Kirkpatrick. Much as he had when they stayed with Mirela and her kinsmen.

She supposed she had not wanted for anything

in his neglect. With a staff of Mrs. Kirkpatrick, a cook, two maids, and two grooms, she was well attended. Mrs. Kirkpatrick had left a bell beside her should she ever need assistance. She rarely did.

Finally seeing him again filled her with a strange sense of hunger. She did not want him to go and leave her alone with her nightmares all over again. Desperate to keep him from leaving, she asked what had been weighing on her mind for weeks: "Where did you learn to fight like you did? With those two men?"

Silence met her question. She moistened her lips, wondering if it would always be this way. Would she have to pull speech from him like tugging a heavy bucket from a well?

Just when she was convinced he would ignore her, he replied. "I fought in India."

She inhaled a ragged breath to have this much from him. Finally. Some bit of himself.

Annalise recalled what the papers said about the rebellion, the horrible brutality the rebels inflicted on Europeans living in India and the equally brutal backlash against them.

"It was . . . difficult," he continued. "You had to do certain things to survive."

"Of course," she murmured in understanding. "It was war."

"No," he said, cutting her off quickly. "Certain things were expected, demanded, that went beyond war."

An awkward silence stretched between them before she once again filled it, hoping she did not sound terribly inane. "I'm certain you only did as you were commanded."

He laughed, and the sound was ugly and harsh. "Yes. I did as I was commanded. I was very good, exemplary even, at following commands."

She flattened her palms over the counterpane covering her thighs, knowing that complimenting him yet again on this was not the thing to do. Her leg tingled beneath her splint, desperate for a good scratch. She ignored it.

"I am excellent at killing." There was nothing in his voice as he uttered this, and yet she knew he was disgusted with himself.

He rose in one swift move, and she knew that it was with the same grace, the same quick stealth, that he attacked and took lives. She should be appalled, having just fled one killer to find herself in the company of another. And yet compassion swelled inside her chest because she knew this man was so much more, so much better, than the killer he described himself to be. He was heroic. Nothing demanded him to help her and yet he had. Everything he had done underscored that he valued life.

At her silence, he continued. "I've shocked you."

She lifted one shoulder. "Not so much."

"Horrified, then?"

"No."

His head angled to the side. "No?"

"No."

"You're a most peculiar female, Anna."

She smiled. "I cannot argue with that assessment."

"Aren't you the least bit concerned that you're currently residing beneath the roof of a seasoned killer?" His boots thudded across the floor as he moved toward her.

Her heart hammered faster at the knowledge that he wasn't leaving her. In fact, he was coming closer. He stopped at the foot of the bed. She stared at the lean shape of him, her gaze skimming the narrow waist, the peak of tantalizing, male flesh at his throat, the broad shoulders. Her face heated. The fleeting reminder came that she was still a virgin. Married but a virgin. Never even been kissed. Well, she refused to count those two pecks on the morning of her nuptials. And just as that fleeting idea crossed her mind the next thought came that she should *like* him to kiss her. She would like to taste his lips and the skin at his throat that always looked so warm and inviting.

Even when he was being taciturn and distant

that skin looked somehow warm and male and delicious. Her belly quivered with a sensation she had never experienced.

"I could do anything to you," he added, his deep voice hard and vaguely disapproving.

And while she should be concerned, even afraid, at the somewhat threatening comment, a frisson of excitement raced down her spine. *I could do anything to you. . .*

He was no Bloodsworth. He caused her no fear or unease.

The sudden image of him straddling her on this bed without the robe, just his bare body atop hers, leaning over her, his mouth coming toward her, seized her. Her palms prickled and tingled with the urge to touch—to *feel* him. To live and experience the lovemaking she had been denied on her wedding night.

A wicked thought entered her head. *Stuck in this bed for weeks, he could make her time here very diverting.*

Her cheeks went from warm to scalding. Apparently all her previous modesty had drowned in the river. Not a terrible thing, she acknowledged.

"I suppose I should be afraid." She took her bottom lip between her teeth for a moment. "If I didn't know that you're an honorable man."

He pulled back as if she had struck him. "You're a fool. I'm no hero, Anna."

Annoyance flared hotly in her chest. "Then why did you promise to help me?" she demanded sharply.

"I don't know. I've asked myself that question countless times since I've brought you here."

He had been thinking about her? Even though he distanced himself. Warm pleasure suffused her. "It's because I need help. And there is no one better than a man of your talents to teach me. Do you not agree, Mr. Crawford?"

At this, he held silent, but she could almost hear the wheels in his head spinning.

She took a quick breath. "Forgive me. I don't suppose I should call you that anymore. Should I, my *lord*?"

He walked around the bed, his movements slow and languid, a direct contradiction to her increasingly speeding heart. He stopped inches from where her left hand rested on the side of the bed. Her pinky finger twitched in reaction.

"Perhaps we should begin with your first lesson now?"

Her breath caught. Even though she knew he was referring to help train her in self-protection, a chill shivered across her skin. As dark as the room was, she felt his stare, the hot crawl of his gaze over her. She wore a prim nightgown buttoned to the throat, but she imagined he could see her through it. Shaking.

Only not with fear.

He leaned down, his palm landing beside her on the bed. Annalise glanced at that hand. Bigger than her own. The back of it lightly sprinkled with golden hairs. She resisted the urge to stroke the blunt-nailed, square-tipped fingers.

She looked back up. His face had moved in closer, and she resisted the urge to shrink back. Her chest tightened, the air trapped inside her lungs as his face stopped mere inches from her own.

"Yes?" she whispered hoarsely.

"Never let a man near you when he tells you he's especially good at killing."

Then he was gone, moving across the room. Her gaze followed him, her heart beating hard in her chest, his warning echoing inside her head.

"Too late," she murmured. She had let him near her, and she wouldn't pull away now even if she could.

She had let him near her, and the hope was already there, growing and spreading in her blood, that he would come closer again.

Chapter Ten

Owen didn't stop walking until he reached his room, a chamber that adjoined Anna's. He supposed Mrs. Kirkpatrick put him here because it was the second largest room in the house, but he couldn't help regretting the proximity to her. He could hear every sound, every thump through the walls. Every time she cried out from one of her many nightmares, he tensed.

Nor was the situation seemly. Mrs. Kirkpatrick must have decided he did not care about propriety, as he had brought the girl into his house in the first place. Or she merely thought there was no risk of anything inappropriate transpiring between him and a bedridden female. He would have agreed with the latter except that tonight she had looked beyond fetching in that absurdly prim nightgown, her big brown eyes glowing in the dark at him.

Her trust in him was utter and complete and baffling. She looked at him as though he were truly something good and heroic. Someone who could teach her to protect herself against everything evil in this world. Even as he tried to warn her that he might very well be the thing she most needed protection from.

He stared at the adjoining door as if he could see through the rich, polished wood, straining for a sound of her on the other side. He couldn't stomach the sound of her whimpers and cries and do nothing. He had decided to just watch her for a little while, to assure himself she was well, when she had awoken so abruptly. And then he'd talked to her. He inhaled a ragged breath. That had been a mistake.

Striding to his balcony doors, he braced his hands on the iron railing of the balcony and stared out at the night. Her presence didn't quite aid in his goal of solitude. He had thought he would return to Town and lose himself here. Wrap himself in the comfort of memories of better days.

His plan was simple, and it did not involve people. It did not involve her.

Except that he was here now and so was she. His fingers tightened on the railing as he reminded himself that the situation was temporary. Once she was on her feet, once she regained her memory, he could wash his hands of her. If she never remembered her past, then he'd grant her some funds and settle her wherever she wished to go. He had more than enough money and no one to share it with—now or ever. He would never marry. When he died, his title would pass back to some distant Scottish relation on his mother's side. He might as well help Anna with a fresh start. Perhaps the magnanimous gesture would clear some of the stain besmirching his black soul.

He winced at that unlikelihood. No good deed would ever be enough for that. He released a soft laugh. She thought him a hero. It was laughable. He had killed so many fathers. Brothers. Sons. He sucked in a deep breath. He simply needed to make certain he didn't act on any of the unwelcome urges he was experiencing around her. Simple indeed.

She was a female residing beneath his roof . . . her chamber adjoining his. He told himself it was nothing more than that. Proximity was the temptation . . . and the unwitting invitation he read in her eyes. He had not spent himself on a woman since returning to England. He should pop in at the brothel he and Jamie had visited before setting sail with their regiment.

Returning to his chamber, he contemplated doing just that. The hour wasn't too late for such diversion. Shrugging off his dressing robe, he slid back into bed, uninspired to make the effort. When it came down to it, he simply didn't want to badly enough.

That was the reason he told himself he didn't want to go. That reason alone.

Annalise sighed as the warm water enveloped her. Her muscles immediately eased and softened. Even the itchy ache in her leg felt better. She closed her eyes in a long blink, reveling in the sensation. Up until now she'd been bathing herself from a basin with a sponge. This was heaven.

"Nice?" Mrs. Kirkpatrick asked, her face intent as she sprinkled salts into the steaming water.

Annalise nodded, trying not to feel uncomfortable naked and exposed beneath her gaze. "Heavenly."

"Just one more week." The barest hint of a smile graced the housekeeper's lips. "Then you'll be on your feet."

"I cannot wait." Sitting up higher in the tub, she lightly stroked her leg in the water, hoping the bone there was healing as it should so that she could attempt to walk next week. *Please, God, let me still walk.* Her hands stilled over the thigh, hoping, praying with a fervency that burned through her soul that it would be no worse than before. That she would still be able to walk.

Tears burned her eyes as self-pity threatened to overwhelm her. No. She would not weep. Not when she didn't even know how bad it was. Besides, she wasn't that girl anymore—weak and given to self-pity. No matter how damaged her leg, she would learn to function.

"I'll be back shortly." Mrs. Kirkpatrick arranged the towel alongside the soaps, salts, and bell sitting on the small table she had dragged beside the copper tub.

Annalise looked up from her leg. "Thank you."

"Just ring the bell if you need assistance or when you're ready to get out." She nodded to the bell on the table and then departed, her gray, starched skirts scratching on the air as she left. The door thudded after her.

Alone now, she stared down at her body, much slimmer than it had been before she went over the side of her honeymoon barge. The weeklong fever had robbed her of some weight. Even after she woke, her appetite did not quite return in full. She could detect her hip bones now. Her waist appeared smaller, dipping before swelling out into her hips. She splayed a hand over her belly, noting how it didn't quite push against her palm any longer.

Careful not to bend her leg, Annalise dipped her head back into the warm water. Reaching for the soap, she made quick work washing the long strands into a deep lather until her scalp tingled. With a sigh, she arched her neck and rinsed the hair clean.

Leaning back in the tub, she used the sponge to wash her body, scrubbing her skin until it glistened pink. Finished, she wrung out the sponge and leaned back to relax in the tub again. Naturally, her thoughts drifted to him.

He'd stayed away since his late night visit to her chamber. The nightmares hadn't stopped. They still haunted her, but he did not show again when she woke with a cry on her lips. That bothered her most of all. The possibility that he had ceased to care.

She heard the occasional sound coming from his room, so she knew he hadn't taken up residence elsewhere. He simply chose to ignore her. As he had since the beginning. As though she was something contagious, a disease he must keep his distance from.

Initially, the realization hurt. She wondered if she had done or said something, but then she dismissed that notion. He'd rescued her, offered to help her, brought her here to his home and then proceeded to ignore her. Her thoughts of him grew less charitable with each passing day. *Wretch.*

If she didn't need him so much, if she had anywhere to go, she'd leave. And perhaps that was what he wanted. He'd certainly tried to scare her off . . . warning her that he was a killer. As if that would deter her. She needed a man like him, and she knew him to be honorable—even if he seemed to think otherwise.

She eyed the table beside her where the bell sat. The water was losing its heat. She supposed she should ring for Mrs. Kirkpatrick. She extended her arm, stretching as far she could and bumping the jar of salts, knocking it over against the bell. The bell toppled off the table with a clang, rolling a bit before stopping. Well out of her reach.

Her arm dropped over the tub's edge as she eyed the distant bell with malice. "Splendid." Now she would have to wait until the housekeeper remembered her.

Falling back in the tub, she relaxed in the water that was growing chillier by the moment. Minutes ticked by. Thinking the housekeeper might be nearby, she called out, "Hello! Mrs. Kirkpatrick! Hello?"

No response met her cry. She waited, hoping to hear the woman's firm tread. Nothing. After a few more moments she called out for her again.

Suddenly the door to the adjoining room swung open.

She gasped softly. He was dressed for the day in trousers and a jacket, his cravat askew as if tossed by the wind. Even his tanned cheeks looked wind-blown. Or perhaps his color was high from simply opening the door and finding her naked in the tub. Although she doubted it. He was not the sort of man to react with embarrassment when coming face-to-face with a naked woman.

Her skin tingled and her belly fluttered as she considered precisely what sort of man he was and what he might typically do when confronted with a naked female.

He didn't move from where he stood, and she knew he could likely see no more than her bare shoulders from his vantage . . . perhaps the top swells of her breasts. She also knew she should be mortified. The old Annalise would duck beneath the waterline as much as she could. She'd probably even demand that he leave the chamber in loud, screeching tones.

But not now. *This* Annalise—*Anna*—held herself still even as the heat crawled up her neck to her cheeks.

Most of her waking moments had been spent thinking about him. His hands, so strong and masculine. The handsome face, chiseled and tan from the sun. The dark blue eyes that stared at her with intensity. Even when she could read nothing of his thoughts, the eyes were always looking, probing, evaluating her in a way that made her feel noticed. *Seen*. Perhaps for the first time in her life. She wasn't poor crippled Annalise when he looked at her.

Across the room his eyes looked dark as a night ocean, black and fathomless deep. Her chest almost ached looking at him, so darkly handsome. Nothing like Bloodsworth's elegant beauty. She had thought the duke an angel the first time she spotted him. Considering the man she thought to be an angel tried to murder her, perhaps she would be safer with a man who looked more like he resided in Hades.

"Are you . . . hurt?" His deep voice echoed throughout the cavernous room.

"I'm fine. I was reaching for the bell."

His gaze flickered to the fallen bell and then shot back to her in an instant, almost like he couldn't look away.

"I'll fetch her for you." He started to turn.

"No." Her quick response tumbled from her lips before she could consider. "You can likely assist me with much more ease than Mrs. Kirkpatrick. She has been complaining of her back lately." A slight exaggeration perhaps. The woman had mentioned it only once when Annalise caught sight of her rubbing the base of her spine.

He hesitated.

She pulled the towel from the table and draped it over her, not caring that doing so brought the fabric into the water with her. Soaking wet, it afforded some shield to her body. It clung like a second skin to her curves, covering her breasts and stopping at her knees.

"If you please, could you lift me out to the bed?"

He hesitated for a moment.

She arched a brow. "If you are not up to it, perhaps you could call the groom . . ."

His features tightened, lips compressing. She resisted a smile as he moved across the room with hard strides, his boots thudding on the wood with precision.

He stopped beside the tub, and she felt his gaze everywhere. She glanced down at herself. The towel wasn't only a second skin, but it was practically translucent. The dark outline of her nipples was clearly visible, not to mention the shadow of hair at the juncture of her thighs.

Her hand swished lightly in the water beside her hip. A distant part of herself, that echo of the girl she once was, reeled with the shock of what was happening—what she was inviting to happen. She knew. She wasn't some dim girl who could not appreciate her actions or what they might lead to. She understood, and she welcomed it. What was she saving herself for? Certainly not a murderous husband. The reminder of him served to sting. That she could have been so trustworthy, so naive, made her angry.

Maybe she wanted this. Wanted him just because this was so apart from Richard and who she used to be. Owen was a world away from that.

Leaning down, he slid his arms beneath her in the water and lifted her high against his chest. Water rushed back down into the tub in a heavy downpour.

She looped an arm around his neck. Her other hand held the wet fabric of the towel to her chest. The clammy material sticking to her flesh wasn't the most comfortable sensation, but she ignored it, concentrating on him instead. Not a difficult task.

This close, she could see the darker line of blue, almost black, rimming his irises. "Sorry. I'm getting you wet."

Water pattered to the floor, puddling around them. He glanced to the screen. Obviously dismissing that as a possibility, he carried her to the bed and set her down on the edge.

She gingerly slid back so her leg was stretched out. "I'm soaking the bed." She plucked at the edges of the towel plastered to her.

He moved to the chaise and snatched the pashmina blanket. Returning, he extended it to her. "I'll take the towel. You can pat yourself dry with this."

Holding out the blanket for her to take when she was ready, he turned sideways, affording her some privacy, and she should have been relieved for that. Appreciative even. But she was beyond placing any value on her modesty or virtue around him. She didn't want him to turn away from her. She stared hard at his too beautiful profile, the slash of his eyebrows, several shades darker than his golden blond hair, the sharp cut of his square jaw.

Then the thought came that maybe he had no wish to see her naked. Maybe that was why he had been avoiding her. Perhaps she repulsed him—just as she had repulsed Richard. The possibility slid through her sourly, settling sickly into the pit of her stomach.

She desperately didn't want to think that. And yet if that was the truth, the new Annalise wouldn't run from it. Emboldened with that thought burning through her, she peeled back the towel from her body and let it hit the floor with a loud smack.

Air swept over her, chilling her flesh. Her nipples rose and hardened. She gazed at his profile, willing for him to look at her with something that was revulsion or even apathy. A deep hunger grew to a simmer in her blood as she willed him to look. For emotion to crack his implacable features. For him to react to her nakedness. To *her.* For him to feel the same attraction she felt for him.

Several more moments passed, stretching interminably until he glanced down at her, undoubtedly expecting her to be covered up by now, the pashmina blanket up to her chin. Anything except to be lying exposed on the bed like some kind of offering.

Her gaze locked with his. Her arms held her up from the waist, palms positioned flat down on the bed just behind her. She had no idea if it was a flattering pose. She didn't risk a look at herself—only him. He filled her vision, her world in that moment.

"Cover yourself."

The words could have stung if there wasn't a tremor in his voice. A slight wavering that belied the rejection.

She smiled slowly, hoping her action—or inaction—would be words enough.

He extended the blanket another half inch closer. She flicked it a glance, dismissing it, and looked back at him.

She didn't read revulsion in his gaze. There

wasn't that flash of disgust she caught sight of on Bloodsworth's face that last night. Of course, there wasn't anything in Owen's deep blue eyes. Just the usual fathomless dark. And yet his features looked strained, his jaw locked tight. A muscle feathered beneath the flesh of his cheek—a telltale sign that he wasn't unaffected. Instinct told her this was a good thing.

"Anna?" His voice was all exasperation. The blanket bobbed in his hand. "What are you doing?"

This time she spoke, her annoyance surfacing. "I would think that was obvious." She moistened her lips, letting her tongue trail her bottom lip just as she had seen other women do. The girls she apprenticed with had done that on more than one occasion when they wanted to entice a man. Certain male customers with plump pockets frequented the shop. They stopped in to purchase some frippery for their wives or sisters. Many a time she had found Agathe or Sally in the back, in the storeroom or in a closet, skirts hiked indecently while a man fondled their thighs.

She stared at him, trying to communicate with her heavy-lidded eyes: *Trying to seduce you*. Only it occurred to her that she wasn't doing it very well if he was prodding her to cover up.

He stepped forward, draping the blanket over

her, the backs of his fingers brushing her bare shoulders. Heat sparked on her skin at the contact, and from the way he quickly pulled back, she knew he must have felt it, too.

"I don't think this is a very good idea."

She leaned forward and seized his hand, her fingers circling around his wrist and holding fast, desperate to keep some form of physical contact between them. "And why not?"

His gaze drifted to her hand, lingering there for a moment before looking back to her face. "For one thing, you cannot even stand."

"I'll be on my feet next week. Besides . . . I don't need to stand."

He shook his head, his dark gold hair tossing in a way that forced the longing inside her to grow to an actual physical ache. "I'm not in the habit of taking advantage of injured young women in my care."

"Then a week from now you'll have no qualms?" She cocked her head, enjoying herself a tad too much. "Your honor could be appeased then?"

"I did not say that. Have you also forgotten you have not fully recovered your memory? How do you know you're even unattached? What if you are married?"

The question hit its mark. She schooled her

features to reveal nothing of the sting his words caused.

"I'm not," she quickly replied, the lie tripping easily off her tongue. She hardly felt like a wife. Especially not the wife of a man who threw her away. A shudder rippled over her at the idea of being married to him. That she belonged to him. It might be a matter of legal record, but she was not his wife. She was not married to that monster.

"Or perhaps your heart is attached—"

"It's not," she countered, that not a lie at all.

"How do you know?"

"Because I would feel it here." She placed a hand over her heart. "I would know."

He snorted. An indulgent smile played on his lips. "You're a romantic."

"We are consenting adults. What's wrong if we—" She considered her words. "—amused ourselves?"

He released a breath, his expression sobering once again. "You don't know what you want."

"I do."

"You don't know what you're saying. You're confused."

She sighed. "Don't patronize me. I did not get pulled from that river yesterday. My faculties are fully intact and functioning. I may have lost my memory but not my intelligence."

"Then I trust that a good night's rest will restore your good sense."

Her cheeks burned. "So if I wasn't injured . . . if you knew my name to be *Miss* Anna Smith, then you would have no qualms?" Whether he desired her shouldn't matter so much. But it did. It would mean that he wanted her. That she didn't repulse him. And after Bloodsworth that mattered more than ever. To be wanted, desired.

He opened his mouth, but words seemed to elude him.

With a grunt, she released his hand and started to pull herself back on the bed away from him, disgusted with him. With *herself.* What about her failed to entice a man? "If you could, please send Mrs. Kirkpatrick along. She can help—"

With a growl, he grasped her shoulder, stopping her from further retreat. His knee came down on the bed beside her. The mattress dipped, and she slid a bit closer whether she willed to or not.

He stabbed a finger at himself, directly in the center of his chest. "Don't look at me as though I'm something beneath your shoe because I insist on doing the right thing and not using you as you're begging me to." His gaze raked her, scathing and thorough as though she were still naked and not covered with the blanket he thrust upon her.

"I'm not asking to be used!"

"Oh, come now. You're not asking for anything honorable from me." He thrust his face closer, his body radiating anger.

She pushed at his chest with the base of one palm, her other hand clinging to the blanket at her throat. "I never heard of a man taking such offense over a little flirting. Go. Away." She bit off each word, her face flushing hotly with shame.

"Oh. You are accustomed to flirting in this manner, then? Has that memory returned to you?"

His eyes glimmered with accusation, and she knew then, without a doubt, that he doubted her story. He doubted her, and yet he allowed her to remain with him. Was he toying with her?

"You're hateful," she fairly growled. "I cannot even fathom why I entertained the notion of you . . . of me . . . oh!"

"Nor I."

She inhaled a deep breath through her nose

Indeed. What had she been thinking? She certainly shouldn't crave his touch. Or kiss. Or anything else. That had been a colossal miscalculation on her part. He clearly preferred not to sully himself.

Suddenly, irrationally, she wanted to scratch at his face looming so closely over her, all stark, handsome lines and tempting shadows. She shoved at his chest yet again. "Remove yourself."

His jaw hardened and he closed his hand over hers. She could feel the thud of his heart against her palm.

"You are hardly in a position to issue commands."

And the truth of that statement only angered her further. To be vulnerable, weak . . . it was everything she had vowed to never be again. And yet here she was again. She curled her fingers into a tight fist and dug her nails into her tender flesh.

Their gazes held, locked. The air surrounding them crackled with tension. She couldn't help thinking that he resembled some kind of dark angel risen to tempt her to sin. Considering she had done her damnedest to tempt him, and to no avail, she could have laughed at the comparison.

"Get off me," she repeated, lifting her head off the bed, bringing their faces closer. She didn't know how she dared to challenge him. Naked, leg broken, she was hardly in a position to make demands.

"Oh, now my nearness offends you?" His deep voice mocked. This close, his eyes gleamed with a light in the centers, almost like the moon off inky waters. "What a capricious nature you have."

"You're impossible," she whispered.

"No more than you. Moments ago you threw yourself at me. What's next? A marriage proposal?"

She laughed. True, genuine laughter. "Is that what you think? Marriage? To you?" She gulped a breath, stifling her laughter. "That would be akin to not being married at all. You're never around and when you are you hardly speak. You certainly won't touch—"

The rest of her words were cut off by his mouth. They slammed over hers roughly. She cried out, but the sound was lost, consumed in those ravaging lips. Their teeth clanged briefly in a fierce collision. It was nothing like the sweet, gentle kisses she had fantasized about with great anticipation those many weeks before her wedding.

Nor was it anything like the quick, chaste kiss Bloodsworth gave her after the completion of their vows. It was savage and relentless, punishing. She whimpered and pushed at his chest, and that must have affected him because suddenly his lips gentled on hers.

He nibbled on her bottom lip sweetly, almost apologetically. When he stroked the bruised flesh with one swipe of his tongue, everything inside her shook alert, awake and alive and hungry.

His mouth lifted off hers slowly. Feeling him slipping away and loathing the loss of his warmth, she wrapped her arms around his neck and pulled him back down over her, mashing his lips to hers.

This time she kissed him, nibbled and sucked

at his bottom lip in the same manner he just did with her. When she set her tongue to him, licking, he groaned against her. His hands fisted in the blanket covering her, tugging it lower in the process. Cool air wafted over her bare shoulder.

He was careful with his weight, straddling her, his knees on either side of her hips. Meanwhile she let her hands roam, reveling in the freedom to touch him. Her fingers drifted from his shoulders to his neck, his jaw, his face, and then back around to tangle in his hair.

"Anna," he breathed into her mouth the moment before his tongue touched hers. A chill chased over her at the sensation. Goose bumps broke out over her skin as his tongue began a dance with her own, licking, tasting, stroking. Her belly tightened, grew heavy and aching.

The hand clutching a tight fistful of the blanket covering her loosened and smoothed out over her breast, cupping the mound through the fabric that she wished wasn't there. She arched into that hand, crying out as those splayed fingers pressed and caressed her back.

"Miss Anna, do you need any help yet?"

Owen launched himself off her and the bed, leaving her gasping, her hands bare, empty and bereft. He took several steps until he was a good distance from her.

Annalise lifted her head to glare at the housekeeper.

Mrs. Kirkpatrick grasped the edge of the door, looking back and forth between the two of them in horror. "Forgive me, my lord, I did not realize you were here." Her gaze lingered on Annalise. Self-conscious beneath the woman's shocked gaze, she pulled the blanket back to her chin.

"I was just leaving." Without another glance at her, Owen strode from the room, passing Mrs. Kirkpatrick on his way out.

"Well, then. Let's get you dressed," the housekeeper said as she advanced. But Annalise paid little heed as Mrs. Kirkpatrick buzzed about the room, collecting her bedclothes.

She brushed her lips, still tender and warm from his mouth. He'd proven he wasn't immune to her. He wanted her. And in a week she would be on her feet again. Then he couldn't hide behind his excuses of honor. She wouldn't be bedridden. One more week and he couldn't hide from her anymore.

It would be the longest week of her life.

Owen fled to his chamber as if the hounds of hell were after him. He realized he could have used his adjoining door, but he'd been too rattled at the time to recall that fact.

Now he paced the length of his bedchamber, staring at the adjoining door, listening to the sounds of female voices on the other side. He had no doubt Mrs. Kirkpatrick would be in there for a while helping Anna dress that tempting little body, covering her curves, the breasts with their dusky dark nipples that begged to be tasted.

Groaning, he dragged both hands through his hair. He was mad. She was an invalid suffering from memory loss. He couldn't take advantage of her. Her willingness, the invitation in her eyes—none of it mattered. Not without knowing who she was. *Not being who he was.* He wasn't that much of a scoundrel.

He might be soulless, depraved, but he liked to think there was still some code of honor within him. Some lines he would not—*did not*—cross.

With a growl of frustration, he stormed from his chamber and out of the house, determined to find something to occupy himself. Something to consume his thoughts and help him forget a maddening female who begged for his touch.

Chapter Eleven

"Are you ready?" Mrs. Kirkpatrick asked.

Annalise looked down at her legs, already in position, dangling over the side of the bed. The eager yearning she had felt over the last weeks to finally be rid of the bed, to finally rise and walk, had swerved into something else. An anxious fear that she loathed even though she understood it. It was the same wretched fear she felt all those years ago when she rose from bed after her accident. Each morning she woke and limped—staggered in the beginning—across the small chamber she shared with her mother toward the basin of water.

Even months after her accident she would linger a few moments in bed every morning as dawn seeped through the curtains of her window, praying that today would be the day when she rose and walked like she had before the accident. Sound of body. No limp. No longer a broken girl.

What if I can't walk at all?

What if the moment her foot touched the ground, she crumpled? A wash of bitter fear coated her mouth.

"Miss Anna?"

She snapped her gaze back to Mrs. Kirkpatrick. The housekeeper watched her expectantly, a hint of impatience lurking in her eyes. A good portion of the woman's day was now devoted to her. She doubtlessly wanted to see her up and about, too.

Nodding, she pressed her hands against the side of the mattress and gently eased off the bed. Mrs. Kirkpatrick gripped her arm for support.

"There you go now," she encouraged as Annalise stood, a faint hint of her brogue creeping out.

For several moments she didn't move, testing her weight on her feet. She offered up a wobbly smile. "Good so far." She hadn't toppled to the ground. The only question that remained was if her leg could bear her weight as she walked.

Mrs. Kirkpatrick nodded. "Ready for a step?"

Sinking her teeth into her bottom lip, she nodded, not convinced she was ready at all, but unable to hide from reality. Now was the moment she learned her fate.

The housekeeper tugged on her arm, nudging her to move forward.

Annalise shook her head and shrugged her arm free. "I'm fine." If she was to do this, she needed to see if she could do it on her own.

She didn't breathe as she lifted her right foot and set it down. Now came the true test. She lifted her left leg quickly in a step. And didn't fall.

A small breathy laugh escaped her. She'd done it without collapsing. She smiled widely and then caught herself. She needed to attempt more than a single step to know for certain that she could still walk. Then she could celebrate.

"There you go. On with you."

Sucking in a lungful of air, Annalise pressed forward. One step and then another. She staggered a bit, a little unsteady, cautious, fearful of falling. Mrs. Kirkpatrick hovered close.

Gradually, her steps evened out as she walked. Her leg felt weak, but that was natural after being abed for so many weeks. She frowned as she approached the door to the room.

"Is something amiss?" Mrs. Kirkpatrick asked, eyeing her up and down curiously as she hovered close. "Are you in pain?"

At the door, Annalise stopped and turned, hesitating for a moment before continuing. "No." She walked a little more, feeling her brow furrow in bewilderment at her even, if somewhat tentative, gait. "I'm not in pain."

"Well. That's good news." The housekeeper studied her face before glancing back down to her legs. "Then what is it?"

"I'm not limping."

"Should you be limping?"

I used to, she almost said, but caught herself. She didn't want to refer too much to her past as long as she was feigning memory loss.

"I merely thought . . . I feared there could be a limp." She increased her pace, hope unfurling inside her. She didn't want to think it could be true, but the evidence was glaringly clear with her every step.

"Well, apparently those Gypsy folk knew what they were doing when it came to setting that leg. Appears you can walk on it just fine now."

She could walk. Without a limp.

Her heart thundered madly in her chest. She approached the bed, marveling at her smooth albeit slow steps. The hope in her grew, blossoming into full-scale joy.

The first time she broke her leg, Mrs. Danvers had forced her from bed a week after her fall, insisting she would not harbor any lazy layabouts beneath her roof. By then Annalise was helping her mother in the nursery and with other tasks about the house. She was not allowed to be idle—even in order to heal properly.

Apparently this time around, being off her feet had allowed her leg to heal properly. If Mirela was in front of her now, she would have hugged her to within an inch of her life. And she knew she owed her good fortune to Owen, too. If he hadn't found her and taken her in and given her the opportunity to recuperate, she would still be crippled. If not dead.

"You shouldn't push yourself too hard," Mrs. Kirkpatrick said, "but you should walk daily. Lord McDowell said you need to increase your stamina each day."

"You spoke with Lord McDowell?" She looked sharply at the housekeeper.

The woman nodded. "Aye. Yesterday. He's the one that told me to get you on your feet today, that it was time for you to start walking."

So he had not totally forgotten her. After last week's embarrassing episode in her bedchamber, she had no sight of him. She hadn't even heard any sounds coming from the room next door. She had started to wonder if he still intended to keep his promise to her.

She glanced toward the door that separated their rooms. "Is he here now?"

Mrs. Kirkpatrick's lips thinned with disapproval, and Annalise wondered if she thought her interest unseemly. "No."

Absurd, but disappointment lanced through her. She had hoped he was near, that he would surface to witness her progress. She was no longer the invalid. She could look him in the eyes now instead of from a chair or bed.

She crossed the room again, walking cautiously. Her limp might be gone but she still wasn't quite in skipping condition.

"Don't overtax yourself," Mrs. Kirkpatrick reminded her, standing back now, hovering less.

Her lips curved. "A moment ago you were shoving me off the bed."

"If you overtax yourself, then you won't be able to get up from bed at all tomorrow. You'll be too exhausted."

"Will his lordship return tonight?"

Mrs. Kirkpatrick's lips went thin again, and this time Annalise did not think it was just because she disapproved of her improper relationship with the earl. It was something else, something more. "I don't expect him tonight."

She stood in place for a moment, noticing that the housekeeper didn't meet her gaze, instead bent her head and concentrated on smoothing the coverlet of her bed with her hands.

And then Annalise understood. Owen hadn't been staying here. He was spending the nights somewhere else. Her mind shied away from just where he could be. Another residence? Another woman?

A hot surge of jealousy spread through her chest.

Squaring her shoulders, she looked down at her feet and continued her stroll around the bedchamber, shoving aside feelings of hurt. It was none of her business where he spent his time. Or with whom.

"You don't have to remain, Mrs. Kirkpatrick. I intend to walk a few more paces around the room at least."

"I don't know—"

"It's as his lordship said. I need to increase my stamina."

With a shrug, the housekeeper moved for the door. "Ring the bell if you need anything."

Annalise focused on her steps again. She needed to be strong. Stronger than ever before. When she next saw Owen, he would not confuse her for the invalid he fished from the river. Nor would he mistake her as the woman who had so foolishly offered herself to him. She would not commit that mortifying error again.

He'd see her as a strong, healthy woman, ready for whatever instruction he could give her.

She'd make certain he saw her for who she really was. Or at least who she was determined to become.

Chapter Twelve

The house was silent as a tomb when Owen returned that night. A lamp glowed from a small marble table in the foyer. A groom emerged from the small room off the foyer, rubbing groggily at his eyes.

"Good eve, my lord. Can I attend you and help you retire for the night?"

"Unnecessary, Edmond. Take yourself to bed."

The groom bobbed his thanks. "Very good, my lord." He started to move away, stopping at the sound of Owen's voice.

"How have things fared around here lately?" He'd stopped in a few days ago for some fresh clothes and had not returned since.

The groom blinked at his inquiry as if trying to wake and decipher its meaning. "Er, everything is well, my lord?" It was more question than statement. Clearly he did not know how to reply.

"All has been well? *Everyone* has been well?"

"We are all quite well, my lord, thank you for inquiring," the man answered obtusely, smiling and bobbing his head agreeably.

Owen stared at him a moment longer. With a gust of breath, he finally asked, "And our guest, Miss Anna. Is she well?"

Understanding lit the man's eyes. "Ah, yes. She is quite well. Walking now. Today she managed the stairs for the first time. That was a bit of excitement. Most thrilling for all of us, my lord. There was a bit of cheering. We were all quite caught up in the excitement. She mentioned taking a walk out of doors tomorrow."

"Did she?" He nodded, absorbing this last bit of information. "Very well, then. Good night."

The groom nodded his head. "Good night, my lord."

Owen ascended the stairs, his footsteps deadened by the runner. He required fresh clothes again. A bath, too. He'd spent another night at Sodom, a gaming hell that belonged to his old school friend, Ian. There had been a fair amount of brandy flowing throughout several hands of cards. He could not rightly recall the details. Lately he had spent a great deal of time there, losing himself in drink and cards. He might have even spent a night or two in the bed of a woman whose name he did not know.

The female had been more than happy to offer him use of her bed. She even made the generous offer to share it with him. An offer he had refused for reasons he could not precisely define. As fetching as the curvaceous blonde had been, he wasn't interested in making her his bedmate. He told himself it was because he'd simply craved sleep . . . a place somewhere within the walls of Sodom to rest his head, which felt as though it were stuffed full of cotton.

A wretched situation. He'd let her run him from his own home—the very place he'd long to return to. Inside his chamber, his gaze drifted to the adjoining room. No light glowed from beneath the door and he could only surmise she was asleep. Of course. In all likelihood she was exhausted from a day of walking stairs. He frowned, hoping she wasn't overdoing it. He'd left Mrs. Kirkpatrick with instructions that Anna should resume activities and start building up her strength, but he didn't want her to injure herself. That would only prolong her stay here, beneath his roof.

He closed his eyes against that notion, and that was a mistake because the image that rose, unbidden, in his mind was of Anna. Naked in a tub. Anna stretched out wet and inviting on the bed, the towel clinging to her body, hiding nothing. Only emphasizing the flare of her hips, the generous swell of her breasts, the flat expanse of belly that begged for his touch. His fingers curled inward at his sides in reflex. As if it was all he could do to stop himself from striding into her room and laying his hands on her satin skin.

He turned to his bed. Sitting down, he tugged off his boots. Next he stripped off his jacket, followed by his vest and irreparably rumpled cravat. Realizing it was too late to call for a bath, he strode to the basin and splashed water over his face and bare chest, washing himself, heedless of the mess he was making.

He was bent at the waist, his head practically submerged in the bowl, when he heard the creak of a floorboard. He seized the towel from the side of the stand and dragged it over his face and head. Rubbing it over his chest, he lifted his face and listened.

It came again. Steps in the corridor. It was a little late for a servant to be wandering the halls. Curious, he strolled to his door and opened it.

The flickering firelight from his bedchamber spilled a path out onto the shadowy hall, directly onto the person inches from the threshold of his room.

"Anna?" He eyed her up and down, standing only one arm's length from him.

She froze in place, blinking those large brown eyes at him. The velvet brown glowed, the outer edge a ring of black. "My lord," she breathed.

Gazing at her, he registered that he had never seen her upright before. Her head only came to his chin. The way she stood so utterly still reminded him of a rabbit caught in the eyes of a predator. His gaze crawled over her, devouring the long rope of brown hair draped over her shoulder, the tendrils unraveling from its plait like so many threads.

She wore a modest nightgown, the neckline laced with ribbons almost up to her throat. Her bare feet peeped out beneath the hem, the small, round toes curling into the floor as if shying from his scrutiny.

"You are home," she murmured, indicating that she had been fully aware of his absence. *Home.* Is that how she viewed this place? As her home now? He wasn't sure how he felt about that. It probably wasn't a good development.

He motioned to her person. "You are standing. Walking." Inane, he supposed. He could see as much—even if he hadn't already been informed, he knew.

"Yes."

"You look well."

"Thank you." She paused, moistening her lips, and his gaze followed the glistening trail left by her tongue. "I am." She walked in a small circle as though to demonstrate. "And no limp."

She stopped to gaze up at him with a face glowing with delight. *And no limp.* The words had been uttered as though she expected a limp—as though *he* should have expected as much.

"Should you have a limp?"

Her mouth opened but no words fell. She had that look on her face again. The one that came like a cold wind, freezing her features. He recognized it, knew it signified something. Fear? Regret? He wasn't certain.

"I simply thought that I might—" Her voice broke off. She tried again, "I've heard of people left with a limp after a broken leg."

"Have you? I am happy to see you on your feet then." *Relieved,* he silently added. The quicker she was well and moving about on her own again, the sooner he would be rid of her. An uncharitable thought, he knew, and one that caused him to feel myriad emotions aside from relief. Not all of which he could identify. Nor did he wish to even try.

When he'd left his brother and Paget, he had sought to simplify his life, and this was a far cry from that. From the moment he found her along that riverbank, his life had been in upheaval.

He wanted to find a place where it was just him and the blast of his ugly thoughts and waking nightmares. He was unfit for the company of others. That's why he had to leave Jamie and Paget. Not because he was angry or jealous. He could not taint their happiness. He was a corrupted soul. He couldn't be around them. He couldn't be around anyone.

And yet here she was. He had never asked for her presence in his life. He wanted only solitude, to be left alone with his wounds, and yet somehow he stood here. In the dead of the night face-to-face with a woman who looked at him with eyes bright and full of expectation.

As if she sensed his anxiousness to be rid of her, she replied. "I am certain you are happy. My presence here is quite the burden. I understand that." She tilted her head at a defiant angle, almost as though she dared him to dispute this.

His mouth curved and he glanced away, peering into the dark depths of the corridor, trying to banish his grin. It couldn't be helped. She amused him . . . *affected* him.

He faced her again, his expression sober. "What are you doing from bed so late?

"I'm doing as you instructed."

He arched an eyebrow. He had not been around lately to instruct her on *any* matters. A fact he was achingly aware of as he gazed at her, his every nerve, every sense, heightened and alive and aching at the sight of her. Even garbed in a virginal nightgown and cloaked in shadow, he vividly recalled what she looked like with it off. He swallowed against the sudden tightness in his throat.

"Mrs. Kirkpatrick conveyed your wishes that I should add to my distance each day in order to increase my strength."

"Ah." He crossed his arms and nodded sagely. "I said that, yes." And then he'd gone about his way, leaving her to Mrs. Kirkpatrick's care, trying to fill his days and nights and block out the past, block out *her.*

"And I've done that. *Am* doing that." She waved her arms out.

Astonished, he dropped his arms at his sides. "Is that what you're doing? Right now?"

"I want to become stronger so that you can start helping me."

He ignored that reminder and stepped out into the corridor, looking left and right. "Foolish woman," he muttered.

"Pardon me?"

Even in the gloom, he detected the flood of

color in her cheeks. It didn't give him pause. "You should also be getting plenty of rest. Not walking the halls at night. What if you lose your balance? What if your leg gives out?" He took a step closer, looming over her.

She backed up and wobbled a bit—proving his point. She wasn't as steady on her feet as she thought. Or as she would like him to think. He instinctively reached out and grasped her elbow to help balance her. A mistake. Immediately, heat flared between them, centering on where his hand connected with her.

"I'm fine," she bit out.

"Is this what you've been doing at night? Walking alone? I'm certain Mrs. Kirkpatrick is unaware—"

"Of no doubt. She would have reported back to you if she knew." The accusation rang clear in her voice. He wasn't around. Not as she had expected him to be.

Determined not to rise to the bait, he growled, "If you're so determined to regain your strength—"

"I'm not attempting to merely regain my strength," she hissed, the color still high in her cheeks. It only made her look more fetching. More like the innocent young girl he had no business associating with. Despite the other night when she had practically offered herself to him, he knew her to be innocent. It dripped from her every pore. It was in her speech, her manner, the way her face reddened around him.

"I want to be stronger than ever. Better. I want to protect myself, and you promised to help me do that." She waved a hand wildly. Her breath fell harshly on the air. "Instead you're off cavorting and forgetting my existence."

He felt her words more than he heard them. They gouged deeply. He inhaled a large gulp of breath. She glared at him, the gleaming brown glinting angrily. He understood about survival. About staying alive, staying one step ahead of forces that threatened to pull you under. Even though she claimed no memory of events, she remembered something. Enough. Enough to feel unsafe, vulnerable and desperate. He understood her fear. Her need. That was why he had agreed to help her in the first place. He had forgotten that and pushed it aside for his own selfish reasons.

"I have not forgotten your existence." Hardly.

Her gaze scoured his face, searching for more from him. She just did not realize. He had nothing more to give. Not to anyone. He couldn't be anyone's hero or salvation. He couldn't even be there for himself.

He motioned to her door again. "You need to go back to your bedchamber."

Her breathing evened, the rise and fall of her chest slowing. The anger in her eyes, however, did not lessen.

Her face captivated him. The rounded features, the thrust of her chin. Her mouth was shaped like a heart—the top lip dipping deeply in the middle, the bottom full and kissable. And her eyes. Even in the dark the lushness of her lashes beckoned him. He yearned to just stroke a finger against those lashes, test their softness. Moments passed and still she did move from her position in the corridor.

He dropped his hand from her arm and waved in the direction of her door again. "Go to bed. Before you hurt yourself. Before . . ."

Before he lost his will and touched her again. Everything about her looked so soft and inviting. Her freshness, her innocence, lured him. He couldn't surrender to it—to her.

He couldn't do that to this woman in his care. He couldn't corrupt her with *him*.

As the moments crawled by, she returned his scrutiny. Her gaze roamed his face before stopping to fix on his mouth, and his gut tightened.

Still watching his mouth, she replied, "I'll retire in good time."

His hands curled into fists at his sides. *Stubborn chit*. She was determined to thwart him.

She blinked those wide eyes of hers. "I think I'll take another pass down the—"

Before she could finish her sentence, he swept her up in his arms. She released a little squeak.

He clenched his jaw and strode to her door. She felt like a familiar bundle against his chest. It took everything in him not to pull her closer and nuzzle the sweet-smelling hair.

"Unhand me! I can walk!"

"You can resume walking tomorrow. After a night's rest." She crossed her arms as he carried her into the bedchamber.

"You don't need to carry me anymore," she pouted.

"When you fail to listen and act with good sense, then I apparently do."

"You need not act so concerned for my welfare. I know you want to be rid of me."

He opened his mouth to deny the charge, but knew he could not. He did want her gone. For him. For herself. For both of them. She just didn't understand his reasons.

He stopped before her bed. Instead of lowering her, he continued to hold her, staring down until she lifted her gaze to his face.

"I will keep my word to you," he said.

Her expression lightened, her eyes softening. He hardened his heart against the sight. He was no boy to be swayed by a girl's tender looks. He might have been that boy once. And the girl to twist him around her finger might have been Paget. His gaze roamed Anna, tracing her eyebrows, her nose, her lips. No two females looked more unalike, but he could not recall ever feeling quite so enthralled. Paget, with her ice-blond hair, had simply been Paget. His best friend. There had been no mystery, no fascination for him. Not as he felt now for this woman.

"You'll help me?" she whispered.

"I said as much."

"When can we begin? Tomorrow?"

Discomfort knotted inside him at her sweetly hopeful expression. He was going to regret this. He already did.

"Very well. Tomorrow."

She uncrossed her arms and placed her palm flat on his chest. "Thank you. You can never know what it means to me."

An image of her broken body on the bank of the river flashed in his mind. "I think I do."

He set her down on the bed, desperate to separate himself from her warm, giving body, from the sensation of her hand on his chest. Seeing her on the mattress, however, did not improve matters.

She was dressed more than the previous occasion he stood over her, and no invitation gleamed in her eyes as she hurriedly covered her legs with her gown to make certain no part of her was exposed. And yet he wondered, if she offered herself to him right now, would he refuse? He could not imagine he possessed enough strength to resist her a second time.

Her head cocked as she studied him. "I believe you do understand." And he knew she was recalling how easily he had dispatched the two scoundrels outside the village fair.

He moistened his lips. "I do this for you, and then you go." He hesitated, expecting her to ask him where she should go. With no memory, no family or friends, that must be a worry. And yet her expression remained calm at the prospect of losing his support. Hoping to reassure her, he continued, "I shall provide you with funds so that you can secure a situation for yourself somewhere."

Before she could reply to his generosity—if she even wished to—he turned on his heel and went back into his room, as if a door was the only thing he needed between them to stop her from infiltrating his thoughts.

Annalise stared after the earl, his voice reverberating in her mind. *I do this for you, and then you go.* The words didn't wound her. Nor did they even strike fear in her. The knowledge had always been there that this, whatever it was between them, would eventually come to an end.

Before Jack Hadley found her and claimed her as his daughter, she had been alone. Solitude was nothing new to her. It did not frighten her.

And she was stronger now. Smarter. No longer a girl who believed in fairy tales. She knew she couldn't stay here forever. At least she would be able to depart here with some knowledge and skills to protect herself. And he was beyond generous to offer her funds. She would be fine. And perhaps she would forget Owen, too. Put his memory behind her.

As eager as he seemed to put her behind him.

Chapter Thirteen

Annalise could not say precisely what woke her. She sat up in bed, her body alert and tense. The fire burned low, its light not reaching far into her vast chamber. Then she heard it. A moan from the room beside hers. Rising, she hastened to the adjoining door. She waited on her side, jerking when a rough shout clawed the air. As though someone were hurt. *Owen.*

Concerned, she turned the latch. Pressing the flat of her palm to the door, she swung it open soundlessly.

Hovering in the threshold, she peered into the gloom of his bedchamber. His fire was out. She heard it again. A sharp, guttural cry.

"Hello?" Her voice sounded small and tremulous even to her ears. She cleared her throat. "Are you hurt?"

He didn't answer her. Perhaps he couldn't. She stepped cautiously into the chamber. A ribbon of moonlight trickled into the room from the thin part in the curtains. It was enough for her to make out the shape of the enormous bed. He thrashed around, fighting the covers—and from the sound of it countless other invisible demons.

She stopped beside the bed. He muttered gibberish she couldn't decipher. Deciding he was in the grip of some terrible dream, she turned to go, but he whimpered. It was a small sound. It reminded her of a child, and she turned back around.

"Owen?" She leaned in, her fingers lightly grazing the bed as she assessed his writhing shadow. "Owen, are you—"

He jerked upright, and she staggered back a step, her hand flying to her throat. Her words were cut off, twisting into a sharp cry as he lunged for her.

A hard hand closed around her arm, pulling her down. A scream ripped from her mouth.

She fell against smooth, muscled flesh. Into bruising hands. She fought, punching and slapping as he rolled on top of her. It was all too terribly familiar. She grabbed a fistful of his hair and yanked, yelling into his ear, "Let me go!"

He stilled, his hands gentling on her but not dropping away, still holding her. "Anna?"

She gasped, swallowing back a sob of relief to hear the even calm of his voice. "Please." She gulped. "Get. Off. Me."

"Easy," he soothed, smoothing back the tangle of hair from her face. "What are you doing in here?"

"I heard you cry out—"

"So you thought you would just waltz in here—"

"I was worried about you!"

"Well, you nearly got yourself killed for your trouble."

"I realize that now. A mistake I won't repeat," she bit out, shoving her fists at his bare chest.

"Don't ever sneak into my bedchamber again while I'm sleeping."

She inched her face close, feeling the fan of his breath on her cheek. "Understood. Now let me go."

He rolled off her in one easy move. She rose to her feet and raced for her room, slamming the adjoining door shut behind her. But solitude wasn't to be. He followed, flinging her door open as he slid the last of himself into his breeches, making it clear he had been naked in that bed.

Heat scored her face.

"Anna—"

"We needn't discuss this." She averted her eyes from his gaze and the sight of his enticingly bare chest.

"But I do. I need to explain."

She bit back a response, looking anywhere but at him.

"You're here, under my roof and in my care. I want you to feel safe." A pause followed. "Anna."

She looked up at the sound of her name.

He gazed at her intensely. "I need you to feel safe."

She nodded clumsily, as though she understood that. Understood him. Of course, she didn't. She couldn't imagine why that would weigh so importantly on him.

"Sometimes I have dreams." He dragged a hand though his hair, cringing. "Nightmares, really. Of the war."

She opened her mouth, searching for something to say, to commiserate, but then she wasn't supposed to remember anything of her past.

"When the memories fade, perhaps the nightmares will, too," she offered.

He angled his head, studying her. "You think so?" He sighed and dropped his head back, staring up at the ceiling. He gave a short, broken laugh. "That would be nice. Peaceful dreams. Or better yet, no dreams at all. Just deep, dreamless sleep."

She swallowed against the sudden lump in her throat at seeing him like this. So very human. Vulnerable. "I hope you find that."

He faced her, his eyes piercing. "Do you have that, Anna?"

She shook her head, at a loss for words.

"Of course not," he added. "I need only look into your eyes and see the shadows there to know you do not." His look turned rueful then, his eyes turbulent as a night sea. Her chest tightened. "I'm sorry for disturbing you. Good night, Anna."

He returned to his chamber. For several long moments she stood in the center of her room, gazing at the shut door, her heart racing like a rabbit in her chest.

Owen had agreed to begin helping her today. He reminded himself that he had done far more distasteful things in his life. Things his mind shied away from in his waking hours but could not escape during those brief moments of sleep he managed to steal, proving there would never be an escape. He would never be free. Last night had proved that easily enough.

And yet as he lifted his head from his desk where he had been studying his long-neglected accounts to stare out the window at the day's deepening shadows, he felt only grim reluctance.

He'd heard Anna moving about the house throughout the day, her steady tread on the stairs. He even caught sight of her walking the gardens. She was tackling her recovery with great determination. As far as he could tell, she had not been idle all day.

Rising, he rounded his desk and went to find her. They could manage a small lesson before the dinner hour. A few tips that would show her how to keep vigilant in her surroundings. Some simple evasive maneuvers. Later he'd make certain she could handle a weapon. He'd acquire a small pocket pistol. Something she could take with her when she left here.

Crossing the threshold of his study, his distaste intensified, coating his mouth in a bitter film. He suspected it might be a result of the thought of Anna leaving, disappearing into the unknown. Further evidence that he needed to be free of her . . . before she complicated his life any more. *Before he let himself kiss her again.*

He set one foot on the bottom step just as Mrs. Kirkpatrick hailed him. "My lord, you have a visitor in the downstairs parlor."

He turned and frowned, wondering who would be calling on him. Other than Ian, he had not reacquainted himself with any of his old friends.

At his puzzled expression, his housekeeper hastened to add, "It's your brother, my lord."

Jamie? His stomach dipped. He should have known that Jamie would make an appearance. Owen had not even said farewell to him when he left, simply slipping away before the household awoke, unable to stand another moment of his and Paget's tempered happiness. Tempered only because they continually looked his way with guilt and wariness . . . as if they should somehow not have found happiness with each other. He could not stomach it. They should feel free to love each other without his shadow inhibiting them.

When he and Anna had arrived in Town, a letter was waiting from Paget. After her gentle admonishments for his sudden departure and pleas for him to return for another visit, she had filled the parchment with cheerful, meaningless news. He had merely glanced over the drivel, feeling empty inside at her report of village happenings.

All inane, empty words, but beneath every written word lurked the guilt and fear that he was lost to them. And he was. Only not for the reason Paget thought.

With heavy steps and a sinking sensation settling low in his gut, he pushed open one of the double doors Mrs. Kirkpatrick had left cracked.

His half brother turned from the window that faced the street. A slow smile spread across his features. There was little resemblance between the two of them. Owen favored his mother, while Jamie took after their father with his darker coloring. In fact, he felt as though he were staring at a younger version of his father now. Tall and handsome with a certain brightness in his eyes that had not been there when they served together in India. Owen had never seen his brother ever look so happy. Even before the war. Paget was responsible for that.

Owen was merely glad his brother had left India and returned home before he'd ruined himself. Like him.

"Jamie," he greeted.

"Thought I would find you here." Jamie approached as though to embrace him, but he must have read something in Owen's demeanor because he stopped at the last moment.

Owen motioned to the tray of brandy. "Drink?" He supposed he could have invited Jamie into his study. The room was more appealing with its rich woods and leather than this parlor, which still bore the handiwork of his maternal grandmother.

He had not seen to redecorating it yet. The wall was papered with tiny golden rosettes, and the curtains were a pale rose damask. He remembered hiding behind them when visiting here as a child, trying not to give away his presence with a giggle as the housemaids hunted for him. Too bad he could not hide behind them now instead of enduring his brother's pitying stare.

Quitting this room for the study also meant venturing upstairs. That posed the risk of running into Anna. And how would he explain her to his brother? Not that he couldn't do it. The explanation of her presence was perfectly reasonable. He had found her. Saved her. She was his responsibility. It was a clear enough matter to him, but perhaps it wouldn't be clear enough to Jamie. He might think there was more to it than that.

Owen nodded as he poured first a glass for Jamie and then himself. "What brings you to Town?"

"Some business." Jamie took a long swallow. His gaze flickered away for a moment, and Owen knew that wasn't the entire truth. "And I wanted to see you. Set my mind to ease that you are well." Owen suspected that was closer to the truth. "You left so suddenly, Owen—"

"As you can see, I am well. No need to fret." He

waved his hands out at his sides as if his brother could somehow see evidence of that. "You can assure Paget that I am well."

His brother nodded, not even bothering to deny that his wife was worried about Owen. "I thought we could have dinner together this evening. Just the two of us."

Without deliberation, Owen's gaze slid to the parlor doors as though Anna stood there.

At his silence, Jamie prodded, "Owen?"

He faced his brother again, blinking as if that would chase thoughts of Anna away.

"Maybe we could do this another night?"

"I'm leaving tomorrow, Owen. I don't like to be gone long from Paget, especially in her condition."

Owen nodded. His sister-in-law was with child. He was actually surprised Jamie had slipped away for even a couple days so close to the end of her confinement.

Jamie angled his head, a hint of aggravation gleaming in his eyes as he studied Owen closely. "Do you have other plans? You can't spare a few hours for your brother? We've hardly had any time together since you returned home." His jaw tightened, and Owen knew Jamie was thinking about when he'd abandoned him. When he had left Owen in India following their eldest brother's death. While Jamie returned to take up the reins as the Earl of Winningham, Owen continued alone, fighting for his life and destroying others.

He glanced to the doors again. Anna was expecting him. Knowing her, she'd come looking for him and walk right in on him and Jamie. He winced, already imagining his brother's questions.

"We've talked so little since you returned," Jamie said. "Paget and I were hoping you'd be home for the baby's birth. The christening. It would mean a great deal to us."

Owen shook his head, not answering.

"You don't have to decide now," Jamie hurriedly said. "Think about it. We're family. You should be there."

Owen looked back at his brother, schooling his features to reveal nothing. "I don't have any plans this evening," he finally answered. "We can dine at our old club." Away from here. From her.

Jamie nodded, his features easing with pleasure. "That sounds fine."

Owen led him from the parlor, half expecting to see Anna walking her paces on the stairs. At the door, he crossed paths with Mrs. Kirkpatrick.

"I'll be dining out for the evening, Mrs. Kirkpatrick."

She glanced to the stairs, and he knew she was thinking of Anna, the girl he was once again leaving to her own devices. He lifted an eyebrow, quelling anything the housekeeper might say. She closed her mouth with a snap. Clasping her hands in front of her, she nodded circumspectly.

Nodding in turn, he forced his thoughts away from the notion of a disappointed Anna waiting on him.

He had never wanted a person in his life whom he could disappoint. He wasn't capable of being there for anyone, and it was best that she understood that. The last thing he needed was for Anna to form any attachment to him.

Before he passed through the front door, he couldn't stop himself from taking another look behind him at the stairs. Simply to reassure himself that she was not there.

He did not come for her as promised.

There was no lesson. No shared dinner as she had secretly hoped when she realized he was in residence all day. Nothing. Then he left. And she was alone again for the evening.

She inhaled thinly through her nose. Not such a change. It should not distress her. Much of her life had been lived alone, especially after her mother passed away. She should be used to it by now. The year she spent with Jack had been a whirlwind of teas and parties and fêtes, but she had quickly learned one could still feel alone in a crowded room. She'd made hundreds of acquaintances but no true friends.

Her sisters were all lovely, but two of them were married and lived far from London, one in Maldania and the other in Scotland. They could not be counted upon to keep her company. Marguerite, who lived in Town, had recently given birth. Understandably, Marguerite had been too distracted to really be there for her. And that left only Jack.

Well, becoming a father overnight did not really make one a father. At least not the type she had dreamed of in her girlhood.

She had dreamed of someone kind and strong. A father who would sweep both her and her mother into his arms and claim that he had been searching for them for years. Of course, that never happened. It was foolish to dream, believing in fairy tales led her like a lamb to the slaughter. She had believed in Bloodsworth, believed their marriage would be something genuine. She had been wrong. So wretchedly wrong that it nearly cost her life. She'd never be that wrong again.

Annalise gazed about the flickering shadows of her bedchamber, inhaling the thick silence. Yes. She knew about loneliness.

Still, there was something in *this* silence, in this

emptiness. Her gaze flicked to the adjoining door. This was all the more acute. It drove deep the realization that she had been looking forward to their lesson, to their dinner—to *him*. Perhaps she had hoped for another kiss. Another taste of him.

Idiot. She had begun to let herself believe in the fantasy of him. Had she learned nothing?

Her throat felt suddenly tight, the skin itchy. She pressed a hand to her neck as if she could ease the sensation. She was repeating past mistakes and expecting things from Owen she had no right to expect. She felt connected to him in a way she had not even felt for Bloodsworth.

A soft knock sounded at the door.

Mrs. Kirkpatrick entered the room at her command. "Dinner is ready, Miss Anna."

Ever since she regained her mobility, Annalise had started taking her meals in the dining room.

"Will his lordship be dining at home this evening as well?" She could not stop herself from asking, *hoping*.

A frown creased the housekeeper's ruddy features. "No, Miss Anna. He stepped out for the evening."

He was not coming. Annalise turned her attention to the open balcony doors. She stepped out into the early evening air and stared down at the gardens. "Thank you, but I'm not hungry tonight."

She imagined food would taste like dust in her mouth. Because although she told herself she should not have expected anything from Owen, she had.

She did.

"His lordship's brother surprised him with a visit and they went out for the evening."

The news only mollified her somewhat. Perhaps it was too much to expect he include her, but he could have told her himself.

The housekeeper continued, "You need to eat. Allow me to bring you a tray—"

Like she was once again an invalid who required a nursemaid? No. She shook her head, her hands coming up to chafe her arms against the chill. "No, thank you."

"You need your strength."

"I'm fine." And that was true. She felt stronger, healthier than ever. She was ready for however much Owen could teach her. Only it appeared he would teach her nothing save not to trust a man again. And if there was nothing left for him to show her, there was no reason for her to linger here any longer.

The housekeeper's tread stopped behind her. "I am sure he will make himself available tomorrow."

She swallowed back a snort. She must appear

the pathetic girl indeed for the housekeeper to feel the need to console her. Heaven knew what Mrs. Kirkpatrick thought of her employer's strange relationship with the broken girl he brought home like a stray pup. It was unusual, she would be the first to admit that. She imagined she looked lovesick, pining after the earl. The notion filled her with disgust.

She turned and faced Mrs. Kirkpatrick. "You are very kind, but I am sure I do not care one way or another. I shan't be staying much longer."

The housekeeper's keen eyes evaluated her for several moments before she nodded slowly. "Very well. Of course, miss. Simply ring if you should change your mind. I'm certain Lord McDowell would not wish you to go hungry beneath his roof."

The housekeeper turned and departed. Annalise stared at the still bedchamber. The silence seemed to echo and vibrate all around her.

Her hands returned to her arms and she chafed them once again. She doubted his lordship cared one way or another if she went hungry. Certainly the matter of his word meant nothing to him. She would cease expecting it to. It was simply too difficult for him to honor his pledge to her, and she didn't know why she continued to let him dupe her.

Life had not shown her a string of honorable men. She'd been on her own before Jack found her. She could be on her own again. Stronger than before now, wiser, *whole.* She would persevere even without Owen's help.

She was done waiting, and she'd tell Owen that the first chance she had. And then she would leave.

Chapter Fourteen

Owen's eyes flew wide. He held himself still, assessing, listening to the bedchamber around him. Early morning birds chirped outside his window and the pale gray light of dawn crept in beneath the drapes.

He knew he was in London, in his town house and a world away from the heat and death of the war, but old habits were hard to quit. For once he'd slept solidly. Last night he'd endured a tense meal with Jamie. His brother was full of helpful suggestions. It appeared Paget and he had decided he needed to meet a nice young lady. One of the many debutantes coming out this Season would be just what he needed to bring him back to himself.

The evening couldn't have ended quickly enough.

Then he heard it again. The slight creak of a floorboard. He wasn't alone in his bedchamber. Firelight from the hearth danced on the wall he faced.

He didn't breathe, didn't move, simply waited, listening as the steps drew closer behind him. When he sensed a body close to the bed, he turned and lunged.

His arms pulled the struggling figure down on the bed. A feminine cry filled his ears.

Anna.

"What are you doing in here?" he growled, coming over her. "I thought I advised you against sneaking into my bedchamber."

"Unhand me!" She squirmed beneath him.

He loosened his arms around her without letting go. "Am I hurting you?"

"No." She blew at a strand of hair dangling in her face. He watched it drift back to land on her smooth cheek.

"Good. Then answer me. What are you doing here? You know very well what I could have done to you."

Her glance scanned him. "You don't have a weapon."

He slid his hands to her throat, let his fingers lightly surround the smooth skin of her neck. "These are weapons enough."

"Stop." A shudder racked her, and he instantly removed his hands. He couldn't bring himself to frighten her.

"Why are you here? I was not having a bad dream," he whispered. "Come to play at seduction again?" The question slipped free, an unbidden taunt, an unspoken desire.

Bright color fired her cheeks. "No!" She squirmed beneath him, and he tightened his jaw against the sweet sensation.

She continued heatedly, "I did not know how else to have a word with you but to seek you out myself. You prove ever elusive, my lord."

Her words hit their mark. A hot flash of guilt washed through him. "About yesterday—"

"No need to explain—"

"I want to explain. I—"

"Forgive me, my lord, but it's not necessary." She angled her head on the bed beneath her.

He stared down at her for a full minute. She cared. The fire in her cheeks was not solely from embarrassment. He knew that at once.

"My brother—"

"Your brother surprised you with a visit. Mrs. Kirkpatrick told me." She released a heavy breath. "But you owe me no explanation. You owe me nothing at all." She blinked those amazing eyes of hers. "You've done more than enough for me. You've seen to my care. I'm fit and hale once again. Thank you for that." She uttered these words so properly, so very primly, that he felt some primitive urge to shake her well up inside him. "It's time for me to go. It was unfair of me to exact a promise from you for more than you've already done for me."

"Unfair?" Her words sank into his stomach like heavy stones. "'Fair' doesn't come into play here, Anna. Something terrible happened to you and that wasn't fair, was it?"

War . . . the deeds he'd committed in India . . . none of that had been fair. What made her think fairness was to be expected in this life? It wasn't fair that he couldn't forget their kiss. Her taste. It wasn't fair that he was in anguish to experience it again.

He pulled back farther and his gaze roamed her. She had dressed for the day in a modest gown of robin's egg blue. Even so, the fabric was snug across her breasts. Wherever his housekeeper had unearthed the gown, it was meant for a female far less endowed.

She looked away, again confirming that she remembered far more of the events that led him to find her on that riverbank. For whatever reason, she didn't trust him enough to confide in him. "I would not know about that."

He sighed. "I promised to instruct you—"

"It's clear I'm unwanted here." Her long lashes blinked slowly over her eyes, as if she was fighting some unwanted emotion. "Let's just be done with this . . . and each other."

Her words rattled about his head. She was giving him a way out. He could simply say yes and let her go.

"That's what you want?" He paused to swallow. "To go?"

She nodded jerkily, sending her brown hair tossing around her shoulders. The top half of it was pulled back with a pair of combs, leaving the rest to fall all around her shoulders. She looked young and fresh. He wished she had taken the time to arrange her hair. The temptation to touch that unruly mane, to run his fingers through the rich mass, was far too tempting. It took her a while to reply. "I think we can both agree that I've outstayed my welcome."

He inhaled a sharp breath. Again he needn't say anything. He only had to rise and let her go. Give her the money he promised to help her get settled somewhere and turn his back on her.

He glanced down at himself, recalling his lack of clothing. Lifting his gaze, he caught her observing him in turn. Her eyes skimmed over his bare shoulders and chest. When she lifted her gaze to his face, the color deepened in her cheeks.

Again he recalled her in her bath . . . after her bath. Of course she could not have forgotten that either. Did she regret her behavior that night? Did it torment her as much as it tormented him?

"If you'll give me a moment, I'll dress myself and meet you in the gardens. We should be able to begin your lesson there."

Her gaze snapped back to his face. "What?"

"I made a promise to you. I apologize for putting it off . . . for failing you last night. You shan't leave here until I've made good on my word to help you."

He told himself it was the honorable thing to do. That was the only reason he refused to let her go. He wanted to cling to what small scrap of honor he still possessed.

She studied him for a long moment, her expression bewildered, her fine eyebrows knitted close. Doubtless, she wondered why he should care to keep her here any longer when she was so agreeable to leaving.

He was equally bewildered.

"Have you eaten yet? We should not begin until you're properly fed. You'll need your energy."

After a long moment she nodded, but uncertainty still lurked in her wide eyes.

He slid his hands along her arms, trying not to enjoy the feel of her in his hands too much. He firmly set her from him.

Flipping back the counterpane, he rose in one smooth motion. If possible, her eyes grew even larger. Her gaze scanned his length before jerking elsewhere, darting wildly around his room. "Y-You are unclothed!"

He smiled, enjoying her discomfort as he strolled naked toward his wardrobe. After the torment of finding her in her bath in a similar state, he thought it sweet justice. "Speaking of clothes, we really need to find you some garments that are tailored to you."

She glanced down, brushing a hand over her bodice as she got to her feet.

"Not," he added, "that I don't appreciate the cut of your bodice. You have lovely breasts, Anna. I'm just not certain you want to flaunt them so much."

"Oh!" Her fist came down to strike her skirts. "I shall see you downstairs," she called, whirling around.

Chuckling, he watched her flee, impressed with how deft and quickly her feet moved beneath her skirts. She had made a miraculous recovery.

The door clicked shut behind her as he dressed himself.

It was only moments later that he realized he was still smiling.

Chapter Fifteen

She was waiting for him when he arrived in the dining room not half an hour later. The curtains were drawn and some rare morning sunshine spilled into the narrow room. He blinked as if his eyes were sensitive to light. She tried to school her features and not devour him with her gaze. The image of him naked, however, was burned into her eyes. She'd seen him without his shirt on, but he looked even better fully naked. Every inch of him exuded power and strength.

She straightened her spine, focusing on presenting a composed air in her chair. The only outward sign of her nervousness was her right hand. It twitched madly in her lap, safely out of sight, so she allowed herself the weakness.

He offered her a slight smile and inclined his

golden dark head in a bare nod before turning to the sideboard a maid had laid out only moments before, the bounty of which made her feel rather guilty. The amount of food available could feed an entire household and not simply the two of them. She had seen such largesse in Town the last year but still had not grown accustomed to the sight of it all.

She took advantage of the moment to study his back, which even beneath his jacket was obviously strong, his shoulder blades shifting beneath the fabric. Unlike other *ton* gentlemen, his garments weren't padded in the shoulders. He was lean and muscled. Her gaze caught on his broad wrist as he spooned eggs onto his plate. Her throat thickened and she fought to swallow.

Tearing her gaze from him, she lowered her spoon into her poached egg and continued to watch from beneath lowered lids as he sat down across from her, his plate piled high with eggs and kippers and various breads. Perhaps such largesse was appropriate, after all.

"Is that all you intend to eat?" He nodded toward her plate just as she took a bite of toast.

She chewed before answering. "Ever since I broke my leg I feel as though I have been pelted with food."

"For a week you were out of your head with

fever and did not eat at all. It was everything we could do to get water down you."

Her spoon stilled and she looked up at him across the table, trying to picture him tending her alongside Mirela, although she knew he had been there. Mirela told her as much. Still . . . since she opened her eyes he had been maddeningly elusive.

"Even after you woke, your appetite was hardly recovered," he said. "You should be eating now."

"I'm well. Hardly wasting away. Fortunately, I could afford to lose a stone or two before."

The sound of his knife on his plate stilled, the silence filling the space between them. She looked up, bewildered at what she had said.

His eyes pinned her, the dark blue penetrating.

She moistened her lips uncertainly.

"When are you going to admit you remember more about your past than you're telling me?" Even his lips looked hard, pressed into a grim line.

Her pulse hammered at her neck. She suspected he had always thought as much—that she knew more, that she was lying—though he never demanded the truth from her. Until now.

"What are you saying?" she hedged, reaching for her tea, groping for time to recover, to decide what she needed to say other than the truth. Because she could not touch the truth. Not with him. Dread gnawed at her at the mere idea of telling him she was another man's wife.

She believed him to be an honorable man, and honorable men did what they thought was right and just. They followed the law. Just as he had followed orders he might not have believed in or wanted to obey.

Returning a wife to her husband, a fellow peer of the realm, would surely seem the right thing to do. Or he could turn her over to the local constabulary, thinking they would do the right and just thing. She could not fault him if he chose such a course. But she had no doubt that Bloodsworth's name and power would persuade the authorities to release her back into his care.

She couldn't count on Jack to help her, either. His motivation had been clear from the start. She was to marry well. She had done that. She had given him a duke for a son-in-law.

An image of Bloodsworth rose up in her mind, and she couldn't breathe. She could not go back to him. She could not risk anyone discovering her identity. Not even the man who had saved her life.

"You know my meaning, Anna. I'd like the truth."

For some reason, she wanted to snap out that her name wasn't Anna. She was Annalise. *Anna-*

lise. Just once she would like to hear the sound of her real name on his lips.

Instead, she merely said, "I am sure I do not."

"You're lying."

Her face warmed. She set her tea cup down with a soft click, one finger lightly tracing the delicate rim.

He pressed on, his deep voice cutting, "Why are you lying? I can help you if you tell me the truth."

An ache pulled at her chest. It would be so easy to tell him, to confess everything. She wanted him to help her, to take care of everything, to save her and make her life easy. Only he couldn't do that. No one could.

"What are you afraid of?"

Her gaze snapped back to his face. "I'm *not* afraid."

It was as though he had said the magic word. It brought an almost a visceral reaction. *No more being afraid. No more fear ever again.* She had made that promise to herself and she would keep it.

A slow, wicked smile curved his mouth. "You're lying again."

She angled her head. Her hand in her lap clenched into a fist. "Stop saying that." *This time I'm not lying. I'm not afraid. I'm not.*

"It's not just for sport that you want me to teach

you how to protect yourself. You know what happened to you . . . you know *who* hurt you."

She swallowed past the ever-thickening lump in her throat. In her mind, she could only see Bloodsworth, hear his voice. *Nasty bit of rubbish.*

"You're wrong. I can't remember."

"Liar." His lips formed around the word slowly, like he was savoring it. The word was just a breath, a whisper that enraged her, as he knew it would. Because, of course, there was a loathsome kernel of truth to it.

And if she were being completely honest with herself, she knew he wasn't entirely the target of her ire. It was Bloodsworth. His image in her mind. His voice in her head. The nightmare of what he did to her. It was forever there, nipping at her every action, every thought. It would be the memory by which everything else in her world centered. And she hated him for that.

With a choked sob, she lurched up from her chair and flung her napkin across the table at Owen. The fabric fell short, landing in his plate of food.

She was halfway to the dining room doors before he caught up with her, seizing her arm and whirling her around to face him.

"What are you running from?" His face was so close to hers, those eyes of his probing, searching.

She sucked in a breath, feeling stripped, bared and vulnerable. She felt the wild, desperate urge to look away, escape. No one had ever looked at her—*into* her—as he was at that moment. "N-Nothing."

She could see the darker rim of blue circling his eyes. He shook his head once, the movement hard, decisive. "No. You're afraid right now."

"I'm not—"

"I can see it in your face. Those beautiful eyes . . . they're full of fear."

Perhaps. But not in the way he thought. His eyes on her, the sensation of his body against hers, the hardness . . . it brought back the wanting, the deep pull at her core she had felt only with him. *God.* He made her vulnerable, weak from wanting him.

Her desperation to break contact, to end this dangerous conversation, spiked a chord deep inside her.

"You have a habit of manhandling me, my lord." She feigned a wince and glanced down to his fingers wrapped around her arm. "You're hurting me now," she lied.

He frowned, and his grip on her arm softened. She took advantage and pulled her arm free, moving quickly from the invading breadth of his chest.

But not quickly enough.

She was both thankful and regretful for the lack of servants present when he caught her up in his arms and pressed her against one of the dining room's double doors. Her feet dangled, her toes barely grazing the carpet as his body aligned flush with hers.

Her breath escaped her lips in a small swoosh, and she tried not to look down, to observe the way she *felt* her breasts swelling in her gown, pushed tightly against his broad chest. Her cheeks burned as she felt the tips harden and pebble within her corset.

"That was clever," he remarked. "But how will you get out of this?" One of his eyebrows winged high. "Any ideas?"

She studied him carefully, trying to focus as languid warmth slid through her veins. "Is this the start of our lesson, then?"

He shrugged one shoulder as if to say, *Why not*? "You're overpowered. Trapped. What now?"

She bit her lip, considering, and then shoved at his chest with both palms. Nothing. He was one giant wall. Impossible to budge.

"You're going to have to do better than that." His smile was almost smug. "You're not capable of overpowering most men, so you're going to have to be smarter. You're intelligent. Use that mind of yours."

He thought her intelligent? She tried to not let the compliment distract her.

His face was so close she could slap him, and maybe that's what she should do. If she were desperate to escape someone hurting her, she would do anything. That seemed logical, even as a part of her rebelled against hitting him.

It was almost as though he read her thoughts. His jaw locked, a muscle feathering the flesh of his cheek as if he were bracing himself for her to strike him in the face.

She stilled her hand. No. He expected it. It would get her nowhere.

In this scenario, trapped as she was, she needed a weapon. She glanced around, hoping she could find something to grab and use. Nothing was within reach. That men were stronger struck her as terribly unfair. That she would forever be at their mercy ate at her like a hungry poison.

Her gaze locked on him again. "Aren't you supposed to be teaching me what to do in a predicament like this?"

"I am."

"Use my head," she snapped. "That's your advice?"

He angled his head, a hint of a smile on his lips.

Frustration welled up inside her as she gazed at that smile, at that mouth. Far too beautiful for any man. Warm and soft looking in contrast to the rest of him, which felt so hard and unrelenting. It looked inviting. Her body hummed with awareness.

Familiar heat crept up her cheeks. She couldn't believe she was contemplating his mouth when she was supposed to be devising a way to break free of him.

But perhaps that was it.

Perhaps she had her weapon. It was *her.*

Chapter Sixteen

With the blood roaring in her ears, Annalise leaned forward and brushed her lips across his, hoping to catch him off guard. She felt his sharp intake of breath the moment she pulled back to read his gaze.

His eyes gleamed down at her and she knew she had succeeded in surprising him. "What was—"

She moved in again, letting her lips linger longer over his, cutting off his question.

With her mouth on his, it was a difficult task to focus on the rest of his body, to assess whether he was relaxing, loosening his hold on her as they kissed. Well, as *she* kissed him. He stilled. She supposed she had shocked him motionless.

Eager to illicit a response, she brought both

hands up between them to cup his face, reveling in the bristly scrape of his cheeks against her palms. She kissed him deeper, hoping she was doing it properly. She was hardly experienced in this area.

She broke the kiss with several quick, desperate pecks to his top lip, bottom lip. Then again with a longer kiss, drinking from his mouth.

Suddenly he moved. His grip on her loosened. He enveloped her. His arms came around her, lifting her more fully against him.

She had not thought it possible to be any closer, but all at once they were. Almost as though they were one body instead of two. Her heart pounded against her rib cage in direct rhythm with his own galloping heart, which she felt through the layers of their clothing.

It was a far cry from what she hoped might happen—his arms and body relaxing enough for her to escape. On the contrary. Everything about him hardened, became more alert, more fierce. He held her like he would never let her go. And good heavens his lips . . . They did wicked things to her, kissing deeply, thoroughly.

When she moaned, he tasted her mouth, his tongue stroking the wetness inside. Her fingers tightened on his face, clinging to him. He swallowed her moan and continued his sensual assault.

Dully, the realization pushed through her sensations that she had not stopped to consider the distraction this would prove to *her.*

She had wanted him to drop his guard so she might slip free. She valiantly tried to remind herself of this as his hand moved over her back. His fingers splayed wide, each finger leaving a burning imprint.

"Anna . . ." He sighed her name against her mouth.

She slid her fingers through his hair, reveling in the freedom to do so, to feel and savor the strands, thick and soft and filling her palms.

Likewise, one of his hands slid up her back and dove into her hair. A few pins hit the floor, clattering against the wood. She felt the coiled mass of her hair loosen, but it didn't fall, even as his fingertips slid against her scalp. She shivered at the delicious friction.

More pins fell and the rest of her hair tumbled down. She cried out softly, and he stepped back hastily with a sharp breath and muttered, "Sorry."

His gaze locked on her face and she felt brazen, wanton, with her hair spilling loose all around her. Pressed up against the drawing room wall. Her lips tender from kissing.

He made a sound, a warm huff of breath against her cheek that bordered on a groan. "What am I saying? I'm not sorry at all." He reached out with one hand, touching her thick mass of hair almost reverently, gathering it in a fistful.

He curled it around his hand, wrapping it ever so gently until it covered his knuckles. He brought his hand to his nose, the movement tugging her closer. Gaze still locked on her, Owen inhaled. "You have beautiful hair. You smell like bergamot and . . ." He angled his head to the side. " . . . lemons?"

She didn't know what to say. She felt hopelessly out of her depth, as though she were adrift at sea with nothing to grab hold of to stay afloat. Not entirely unlike being tossed in churning waters. Except without the terror.

Had she thought to seduce him at one point? Absurd. He was the seducer.

She was transfixed, marveling at his words, at him.

She moistened her lips. "Th-Thank you."

He brought her hair back to his face, his eyes drifting shut as he very deliberately brushed her hair to his lips. Her breath caught. This was quite possibly as enticing as his kiss had been, and she couldn't help imagining the myriad other things he could do with that mouth. To her.

It dawned on her then that his eyes were closed. He wasn't looking at her. He wasn't even holding her anymore—at least not like before. No longer as a captive. The gentle hold on her hair hardly qualified as a firm grip. She could get away.

As soon as that realization sank in, she tensed. And then she knew she had to act before *he* realized she recognized that her opportunity had arrived. Without a sound, she launched herself past him and dove through the other door. Not until she reached the foyer did she risk glancing behind her.

He emerged from the dining room at a slow pace, blinking and looking as though he had just woken from a deep and languorous sleep. She silently applauded herself for escaping while still holding herself rigid, wary that he might pounce on her again. She wasn't ready to be his prisoner. Not yet. Not so soon after his kiss.

He stepped in her direction and she stepped back.

"Anna?"

She took pride in the befuddled look on his face. "I believe I successfully escaped you, my lord. Thank you for the advice."

"Advice?"

She tapped the side of her head for emphasis and echoed his earlier words. "Use my mind."

He stared, his befuddled look disappearing. A cool, impassive expression slid into place, and with its arrival she felt her own satisfied smile start to slip.

"I did not give you nearly enough credit, Anna. You are far cleverer than even I knew."

She swallowed, feeling somehow guilty. Which was ridiculous. He had challenged her to get away. That is what she had done. So she had used her wiles to achieve that. Wasn't that resourcefulness?

He nodded. "You are a true survivor. Now I know you shall use whatever tactics available to you."

Instead of complimented, she felt somehow insulted. Small and meager.

He appraised her in a thoroughly scathing manner, and that only made her angry. She had escaped him. *She* outmaneuvered *him*—as he had asked her to do—and now he was trying to make her feel bad about it.

"I'm sure I've done nothing worse than you in the name of survival."

His nostrils flared and long moments passed before he answered her. "Indeed. You hold not a candle to me. You cannot imagine my actions. Were I you, I would not aspire to such lowly depths."

He advanced on her then, and she quickly

glanced around, unsure whether they were still practicing and he meant to attack her, pin her to the wall again. She did not relish being held captive. Especially not with him looking at her with his eyes relentless and deep as a midnight sea.

Should she flee? Or grab the nearby vase to wield as a weapon? She held her ground, her heart pounding savagely in her too-tight chest as he came closer.

Before reaching her, he turned and ascended the stairs. "I shall join you in the gardens momentarily."

He still intended to instruct her in the gardens? Her cheeks burned at the notion. Especially considering what had just occurred not five minutes ago.

His voice stroked over her, velvet-deep, leaving a trail of gooseflesh as he called down to her, "We shall continue with our instruction then."

The thud of his steps faded on the stairs, drifting away on the floor above. She slowly made her way to the parlor, passing the furniture that seemed too dainty and feminine to belong to Owen. The man who had pressed her against the dining room wall did not seem like a man capable of softness of any kind.

She pushed open the French door and emerged into a gray morning, enjoying the evenness of her stride, the smooth roll of her gait. It was still strange and new, this walking without a limp. It seemed as though the ache deep in the bone of her thigh had always been there. As natural to her as breathing. And now it was gone.

She strolled the circuitous garden path, cutting swiftly through the moist press of air, determined to continue to build her strength. For all she knew, Owen would disappoint and not show up again.

A popping twig snapped her to attention. She glanced around but saw nothing in the garden's hedges and trees. She continued, not decreasing her pace. She walked for several minutes more before Owen suddenly appeared, stepping out into her path from behind a tall hedge of heather.

She yelped and jumped back a step, her hand flying to her throat. "You gave me a fright!"

"I thought I might."

"Then why on earth did you jump out at me like that?"

"To verify how observant you are."

She crossed her arms. "Not very, I suppose."

"I've been here watching you, moving about the trees and shrubs for the last five minutes."

"I thought I heard something," she muttered.

He stepped closer and started circling her. "I saw that you did. So why did you not do something? Call out? Get away? Go back inside?" His breath fanned the many loose hairs at her ear. "Nothing will get you hurt, killed faster, than ignoring your instincts. That tiny little voice in the back of your head? Listen to it." His voice washed through her. The hairs near her ear fluttered and she swatted them in aggravation.

Owen ceased to circle her. Standing in front of her, he looked her squarely in the face. "You have to be aware at all times."

She dragged her gaze from his mouth to his eyes, and couldn't help marveling that she had never been more aware of another person, a man, as she was of him. How could she have not known he was within five feet? The way her body hummed and her skin tingled, she should be able to detect him from across the city.

He pointed at his eyes. "Watch. Keep your eyes sharp. Head up."

She nodded, her lips compressing as she focused on what he was saying, absorbing his advice. In the back of her mind Bloodsworth rose up like a childhood specter.

He continued. "Listen." He motioned to his chest. "With everything, all of you, your very skin. Do you hear any sounds?" He lifted his hand to her chest, and she sucked in a sharp breath at the contact, the warmth, the solidness of his hand, the imprint of each strong finger burning into her. "Is there something that doesn't belong? Do you hear nothing at all? Sometimes absolute silence tells you when danger is afoot, too."

She inhaled another deep breath and struggled to focus on his words. On the air. In her surroundings. Beyond difficult when there was him. Everywhere. Swirling around her. Consuming her, filling her senses to the exclusion of all else.

She blinked, struggling to focus as he continued, "If you're watchful, aware, the odds are much less that someone will target you. They will move on and look for easier prey."

She wondered how he would respond if the villain they were discussing happened to be someone you were close to. Like a husband. Her stomach curled sickly at the thought and she shoved it away, refusing to give Bloodsworth such power over her.

"Close your eyes," he commanded.

"What?"

He angled his head, repeating slowly, "Close. Your. Eyes."

Nodding as though that were the most natural request, she closed her eyes, jamming them tightly shut.

He chuckled lightly. "At ease."

She nodded again and let some of the tension ease away.

"Better."

With her eyes closed, the sound of his voice was like a physical touch, and the hand that he pressed flat to her chest was a torment. She could feel his pulse, the very beat of his heart in rhythm with her own. Her breasts tightened against her bodice, tingling. Mortified, she prayed he did not notice.

A ragged breath left her when he dropped his hand. "I'm going to move away now. I want you to listen with your eyes shut. Raise your hand and point to the direction where you think I am. If you mark me, I'll tell you."

She nodded. Darkness swirled behind her eyelids. She strained to hear him. A whisper of fabric. The fall of a footstep. Nothing.

She lifted her arm uncertainly and pointed to her right. Nothing. Frowning, she lowered her arm. Another moment passed and she stretched out her arm straight in front of her. Again, silence. Apparently the instinct he wanted her to cultivate did not exist within her.

"Your instincts are better than that." His disembodied voice whispered directly to her left, so close she was she certain she could touch him. She reached for him only to grope air. He had already moved. The man was like wind, moving without a sound.

Suddenly a fingertip stroked the bridge of her nose.

She made a growl of frustration, swiping at the hand, but it was already gone. She opened her eyes to find him directly in front of her. So close she could mark the darker ring of blue around his irises. The air trapped in her lungs to find him so close, his mouth once again there, hers for the taking.

She bit her bottom lip. His gaze dipped to her mouth, and heat swept up her neck to swallow her entire face. She held herself erect, stopping herself from leaning the half inch forward and pressing her mouth to his. The taste of him was still there from earlier, and she yearned for another sampling.

Moments passed, and he angled his face, convincing her that he intended to kiss her. That he was just seconds away from closing that scrap of space and claiming her lips with his.

Suddenly he pulled back. "Close your eyes," he chastised.

Nodding hastily, she shut her eyes with an indignant huff, but the heat still swarmed her face. She could not get the image of him hovering before her—his lips so close, ready to kiss hers—out of her mind. Her entire body strained, listening for a sound. Nothing. But that did not mean he wasn't before her, ready to kiss her again. Her pulse quickened with excitement.

Disappointed that he had been near enough to touch her and she had not sensed him—and convinced she would not fail in that regard again—she whirled around, wildly swinging her arm, hoping to make contact.

"Now you're letting frustration guide you. The moment you lose control, some villain has control over you. Stop. Concentrate."

It was hard to think of villains with his deep voice curling around her. She knew he was still there. She felt him, sensed him. She took one sliding step forward, convinced she was moving toward him.

Her lips tingled, throbbed, recalling the pressure of his lips there, *still* feeling the intensity of his earlier gaze. Perhaps he was on the verge of finishing where they left off. The way he had been looking at her mouth, she suspected he'd wanted to.

"Owen," she whispered, turning her face upward in offering.

She stood like that for several moments, face tilted, body leaning, straining forward until a stillness came over the air. Suddenly she felt chilled. As though all the warmth had suddenly been sucked out of the garden.

"Owen?"

Silence answered her. A bird chirped from a nearby tree. In the distance a horse whinnied. Gradually, she opened her eyes, as though emerging from a sweet dream that she didn't want to leave. Because her gut warned her of what she already feared. What she already knew.

She scanned the empty garden, moving around a hedge, surveying everything all at once.

He was gone.

Owen's initial impulse was to storm from the house, but he'd run away enough times since meeting Anna. He wouldn't flee her anymore. He'd agree to help her and he would see this through. At any rate, running only prolonged her stay in his life, her invasion into his world.

He ran his tongue over his lip. He could still taste her there. Pressing his mouth into a hard line, he walked rigidly into his bedchamber. Safe inside, door shut, he dragged both hands through his hair and allowed some of his composure to slip.

He caught a glimpse of himself in the cheval mirror. His reflection gave him pause. He looked wrecked. What was she doing to him? She had kissed him as boldly as the most experienced female, only she wasn't. Nor had the kiss been. In the beginning.

At first her lips were tentative on his. Firm but unsure. Moving slightly. But not for long. He had seen to that.

With a groan, he dragged his hands through his hair yet again. He had almost kissed her in the garden. Working so closely with her would be a torment, but he would do it. He had to. Then he could be free.

His brother's voice echoed through his mind. *I want you to find what I have found with Paget.*

It simply was not possible. And certainly not with Anna. She was running from her own demons. That much was clear to him. Something haunted her. He could see it in her eyes. She was as broken as he was.

Chapter Seventeen

"My lord, this just arrived for you."

Owen looked up from his breakfast. A groom held out a silver tray with a single missive in the center. He swallowed his bite of toast and plucked it from the tray, shooting a look to where Anna sat, sipping her chocolate. Morning sunlight struck her brown hair, reminding him of a chestnut bay he owned as a boy, the shining coat he had brushed so lovingly.

Her gaze met his before sliding away. A pretty pink filled her cheeks, and he knew she was remembering yesterday. The kiss that had started as a means for her to distract him had turned into something else. Something more. He'd thought of little else since, wondering how he could continue in this manner with her and not kiss her again. Touch her. Taste her.

He'd made a mistake not taking up the invitation from the blonde at Sodom. Perhaps if he had done more than share her bed and actually sated himself between her thighs he would not feel so close to succumbing to this woman. *Perhaps it was simply Anna.*

He shook off the distracting thought and forced his attention to the missive, opening it and scanning the words. He sucked in a breath, a heaviness building in his chest as the parchment dropped to the table with a whisper.

"What is it? Is everything all right?" Anna's soft voice brushed the air.

Blinking, he tore his gaze from the discarded letter and faced her. It took him a moment to respond, his brother's words within that letter pulling him in different directions all at once. He had determined to never return home. But this made him reconsider. As Jamie knew it would.

"Splendid. My brother's wife safely delivered a son." The corners of his lips lifted in a smile that felt false and all wrong on his face. Jamie and Paget had a son together. It seemed a strange thing to confront. Even odder than returning home to find them married. This. A child. Perhaps for the first time he understood how fully removed they were from him. That he would never have them back—that things would never be as they once were. In India, Jamie and Paget had been a world away. But now they suddenly felt like it.

"That's wonderful news."

He nodded and took a scalding sip of coffee, suffering the burn down his throat almost with pleasure.

She stared at him, her brown eyes sharp and measuring. "You don't behave as though it's wonderful."

"They want me to come home."

She studied him for a moment. "Of course they do. You should go. They're your family."

His fingers played with the spoon beside his plate. "It's not easy. Being around them." During his last visit he had felt like an outsider looking in, doubtlessly making them as uncomfortable as he was.

She nodded as though she understood. She didn't. She couldn't. Her gaze resumed its study of her cup of chocolate, a finger lightly tracing the rim. "This is your nephew. Your first, I presume?" At his single nod, she continued, "You should go."

His jaw locked. Resentment stirred inside him. Mostly because she was right. He should go. But that did not change the fact that he did not wish to return home and suffer the happy company of his brother and Paget. Would there be that air of guilt swirling around them simply because he was there? The birth of their son was likely the happiest moment of their lives. He did not want to cast his shadow over it.

He rose, dropping his napkin on the table. "I have no place there anymore." His voice rang with clear finality—almost as though he expected an argument from her.

She tilted her head back to look up at him as he hovered over the table. "Then stay here." She uttered the words so simply. As though she harbored no judgment.

He nodded briskly. "Indeed. I'll meet you in the foyer in an hour. Do you ride?"

She nodded, tucking a stray strand of hair behind her ear. "Passably."

"Then we shall improve on that. No individual can be truly independent with mere passable skills in the saddle."

Her eyebrows arched over those expressive eyes of hers. "I should become a more than passable rider, then." A smile brushed her mouth.

His gaze skimmed her ill-fitting blue morning gown. "See Mrs. Kirkpatrick about a riding habit."

"I will. Thank you."

With a slight bow, he departed the dining room, his strides stiff. He could feel her gaze on his back. Even though there had been no hint of judgment in her gaze at his refusal to return to Winninghamshire, he felt her disappointment just the same. For some reason, it mattered to him. It rankled. For some insane reason, her good opinion signified.

He wasn't even to the doors of his study yet when a sharp expletive burst from his lips. He stopped and stared unseeingly ahead of him. The truth stared back.

There would be no ride this morning. How could he ride at his leisure knowing he had a nephew? A new life with whom he was inexorably connected. Jamie and Paget had a son. And despite the distance he felt yawning between them, both literally and metaphorically, they wanted him there.

And she thought he should be there, too.

Like it or not, that mattered to him.

Turning on his heel, he marched back toward the dining room, his movements stiff and mechanical. He arrived at the narrow double doors just as Anna emerged. He pulled up short of colliding into her.

"Oh." Her hand fluttered to her throat. "Did you forget something, my lord?"

"I changed my mind."

Her brow knitted. "You changed your mind?"

"We won't be going for a ride this morning."

Her expression fell. "Oh. I see."

No. She didn't.

She lowered her gaze, avoiding looking at him. She was disappointed. He needn't see her eyes to know this. He felt her disappointment radiating off her in waves. It dawned on him that he hated to disappoint her again even if he was following her advice. And although the reason would be understandable, he had no wish to do so again. How could he even be assured she would be here when he returned? A jolt of discomfort coursed through him at that possibility. Had she not already suggested it was time for her to take her leave?

Before he could consider his next words, he heard himself saying, "Pack your things."

Her head shot up, her brown eyes suddenly bright. "Are we going somewhere?"

"Home. To Winninghamshire."

She blinked, her expression mirroring the shock he felt at his announcement. "You wish to take me home with you?"

He winced. When she uttered it like that, he regretted ever saying such a thing. It made them seem close . . . intimate. Something they were not. Something they could never be.

He nodded brusquely, quelling his doubts. "I can work with you there just as well as here. Perhaps better." He shrugged one shoulder. "I can instruct you in firearms. Such knowledge is useful. And that instruction is better suited for the country."

She looked elated. Like a child awarded a toy. "I shall pack. It won't take long."

He surveyed her ill-fitting gown. Indeed. Her wardrobe was limited—a matter he still needed to correct, but there was no time for that now. According to the letter, if they hurried they might make it to his nephew's christening.

She sped past him, her gait somewhat lopsided in her haste.

"Easy," he called after her. "Injuring yourself all over again will only slow us down."

She shot him a glance over her shoulder, but slowed her steps.

He watched her take the stairs. As she disappeared from sight, he noticed that a smile shaped his mouth.

He had not even realized he'd been smiling.

They did not arrive in time for the christening. He had mentioned to Annalise that he hoped to make it in time for the event, but when they arrived at the manor, the stodgy old butler informed them that Lord and Lady Winningham were in the village for their son's christening and should be home shortly.

There was the slightest flicker of regret in Owen's eyes before he masked it. "Very well, Jarvis. Will you see that our belongings are settled into rooms for the night?"

The butler inclined his head. "Very good, my lord."

Annalise rotated in a small circle in the grand foyer. It was a most impressive house. Not quite as awe-inspiring as Bloodsworth's ducal seat, but this manor house was warm and comfortable. It felt like a home. Not just some grand mausoleum. Children could be reared in this house. Children had. Children like Owen.

She surveyed him beneath her lashes, wondering about that boy. What manner of child had he been? Was he always the aloof, silent sort? Or had he run shouting beneath the vast domed ceiling? She grinned, imagining a harried tutor in pursuit of him.

"Would you and your companion care for refreshments in the drawing room until Lord and Lady Winningham arrive?"

Annalise could detect nothing in his voice as he uttered the word "companion." The rail-thin butler was the very image of decorum, his aged, wrinkled face revealing nothing, but the word jarred her nonetheless as they were led to the drawing room. She felt its weight, the implication.

For the first time, she contemplated her presence here. How would Owen explain her?

She did not have long to contemplate. Voices erupted from beyond the doors. Happy and overlapping, it sounded as though a festive party had returned from the christening.

Owen rose from the chair he had only just occupied as the raucous chatter drew closer. Footsteps sounded outside the drawing room. Annalise folded and refolded her hands in her lap, unsure what to do with them—or herself, for that matter. Should she rise or remain sitting?

The door pushed open before she could decide. A handsome man cleared the threshold, pausing only for a fraction of a moment when he spotted Owen. His gaze swept over him as he continued forward in halting steps.

"You came," he exclaimed, reaching Owen and pulling him into a hug. Clearly he was the brother, although the similarity was minimal. Lord Winningham possessed hair darker than her own. His olive complexion hinted at Mediterranean ancestry, a direct contrast to Owen, who looked like he descended from Vikings. Both possessed like height and build, however.

The brothers' embrace seemed awkward—like they were unknown to each other and not kinsmen at all.

"I departed as soon as I received your letter," Owen said, stepping free. "My apologizes for missing the christening."

Lord Winningham scanned him from head to foot as if he could still not reconcile the sight of him in his drawing room. "Of course, I am simply happy you came to meet your nephew. Paget will be overcome. Best brace yourself."

More people arrived then. Two men: one older and one young; and two young women chattering happily.

Annalise's gaze fell unerringly on the woman with pale blond hair. She was small and lovely. With her fair hair and dark brown eyes, she possessed a haunting beauty. Her eyebrows and lashes were the same shade of brown as her eyes, and it was a striking contrast to her hair. She looked almost otherworldly.

Annalise knew at once that this was Paget. She would have known this even if she did not hold the small, swaddled infant in her arms. Lord Winningham arrived at her side in several long strides, taking the baby from her arms so that she might greet Owen.

There was no hesitation in her. None of the awkwardness that belonged to her husband as she tugged Owen down to her so that she could wrap her arms around his neck. She squeezed her eyes shut in a long blink as she embraced him, either indifferent to or unaware of his reticence.

"You came." She breathed the words over his shoulder as though she were expelling a long-held breath. And Annalise knew. She understood. She was more than the girl who had married his half brother. They shared a past. A history. Perhaps Owen had loved her. Perhaps he still did.

A knot formed in her stomach at the notion, and she had the wild urge to rise and flee from the room. Jaw clenched, she forced herself to sit still, remembering she had suffered far worse than this discomfort in her life.

Unfortunately, at this moment, this reality was the only thing that signified—and nothing quite stung as the sight of Owen in close proximity to a woman he very well might still love. No matter that the lady was married to another and a new mother. If Owen loved her, he loved her. The heart possessed a will of its own.

Owen patted the countess's back. "Of course. How could I miss meeting the future Earl of Winningham?"

She pulled back and beamed up at him. "He is beautiful, is he not? Hopefully, he'll have many years tromping around the countryside first. As we once did." She smoothed a hand over his chest with a familiarity that gave Annalise a pang in her stomach. Which was absurd. The lady was his brother's wife. And even if she were not, she had no reason to feel possessive of Owen. His affections were not hers to keep. They were not hers at all.

"Do you not recall?" the countess continued. "We would leave home at dawn some days and not return until sundown."

"Yes. Unless your father managed to find you first and haul you home."

Chuckles followed this remark. "Oh. I never worried when she was with you," the older gentleman murmured.

"Of course you didn't, Papa. I was with Owen."

Owen's smile grew pained. There was a stillness, a quietness to him that reminded Annalise of when they first met. She realized she had grown accustomed to a certain degree of ease from him. But here, among his own family, he behaved almost as a stranger in their midst.

Paget reclaimed her baby, her voice softening into a croon. "I can only hope little Brand here is just as responsible and trustworthy. The girls in the village shall be lucky indeed to have such a champion in their midst."

"You named him Brand?" Owen asked in a quieter voice, stepping forward to peer down at the tiny bundle of new life.

"There was no finer namesake," Jamie spoke up.

"Your brother is watching down now with pride," the countess's father inserted.

Owen nodded, looking rather humbled as he stared down at his nephew.

"Here. Take him." Lady Winningham thrust him into Owen's arms even as he shook his head in protest, his expression suddenly alarmed.

"There now. Just watch his head," she instructed.

Baby secured in Owen's arms, Paget stood back, her dark eyes shining with pleasure. Her husband draped an arm around her shoulders. Together they watched Owen, obviously so thrilled to have him there. To have him holding their son, albeit awkwardly.

Annalise marveled that Owen claimed to feel like an outsider among his family. Right now that was how she felt. The fact that no one had yet to acknowledged her amid the little reunion did not help. If she could slip from the room unnoticed, she would have. At this point she only hoped to remain ignored, overlooked.

It wasn't to be, of course. "Oh. Forgive me. How very rude." Lady Winningham's gaze swerved from Owen to Annalise and back again. "You brought a guest, Owen."

The question hung in the woman's voice. *Who was she*?

Owen looked up from his nephew. "Yes. This is Anna."

Everyone in the room blinked and looked at each other, uncertain how to react to this less than verbose of introductions. Annalise hesitated, wondering if he would offer more explanation than that. He didn't, returning his attention to the baby, catching one tiny fist with two of his fingers.

Heat crept over her face. "It's a pleasure to meet you all," she murmured, her gaze scanning everyone.

Owen's brother and sister-in-law exchanged glances. The embarrassing heat in her face twisted to anger. Had he no plans to explain her presence? Heavens knew what conclusions they were drawing.

"Paget, we must take our leave," the other young woman said. "What a truly splendid day." She stepped forward to kiss the countess lightly on both cheeks. "John and I are so happy for you." She faced Owen. "Good to see you again, Owen. And farewell to you, my little darling." She stepped forward to stroke baby Brand's cheek.

Paget's father departed the room with them, leaving the four of them alone.

A moment passed before Owen stepped forward

and returned the baby to Paget's arms. She happily accepted her child, saying, "I do hope you will stay longer than last time, Owen." Her gaze flicked to Annalise. "You and your guest . . . Anna."

Annalise offered up a tentative smile.

"We can only stay for a short time, I fear."

Paget frowned. A strained silence fell again. Jamie's jaw clenched, as he looked from his wife to Owen, clearly disliking that Owen had not pleased her with a promise for a longer visit.

Annalise blew out a breath. She was sorely tempted to demand that they all cease with the silent stares and confess whatever it was they were thinking.

"If it would not be any trouble," she said, "I should like to rest in my room for a spell."

"Oh. Of course. How thoughtless of me," Paget said. "You must be tired from your journey. Let me ring for Miss Spence to show you the way."

"I can show her." Owen moved to her side, helping her to her feet.

Paget nodded once, smiling tremulously. "Oh. Very well. Ms. Spence likely put her things in the rose room. You know the way. This is your home, too, after all."

"It was my home," Owen corrected.

Paget visibly swallowed. A faint pink tinged her cheeks, and Annalise felt sorry for her. Jamie's lips thinned, clearly displeased with his brother's terseness.

As if realizing that he had come across harshly, Owen added, "But I'm glad for the invitation and honored you both would want me here."

Paget released an audible breath, her face brightening at his words.

Owen led her from the drawing room then, his fingers light on her elbow. He strode quickly. She practically had to skip to keep pace.

"I need a drink," he muttered beside her. He stopped before a door on the second floor, pushing it open for her, his expression distracted, his gaze not even on her.

She spun to face him, not yet ready to move inside until she aired her grievances. "How could you bring me here?"

His gaze snapped to her face. "What do you mean?"

She waved a hand. "Are you intending to explain my presence? Ever? What must they think?"

"That you are my guest," he replied curtly. "Just as I said."

She snorted. "Goodness knows what conclusions they are drawing of me even now. They must think that I'm—that you and I—" She broke off, too mortified to put it into words. Shaking her head, she hissed, "I should have never come here."

"Well, you're here now." He looked at her coolly, and his apathy only infuriated her further.

"How long must we stay?"

He cocked his head. "Need I remind you that you encouraged me to come here?"

"That was before."

"Before what?"

"Before I realized you're in love with your brother's wife."

The words spilled free. She had no idea they bubbled so close to the surface. She sucked in a shuddering breath, horrified, regretting the awful words and all they revealed of her feelings.

It was like a curtain dropped over his face. Typically stoic, his features were harder than ever, granite. "You are mistaken."

She worked past the lump in her throat, swallowing deep. "Am I?"

He angled his head, a dangerous glint entering his dark blue eyes. "You don't know what you're talking about, Anna."

She rolled back her shoulders, composing herself, knowing this was not a conversation she wanted to have with him. "It's none of my concern."

He was silent for a moment, studying her, the blue of his eyes dark and stormy. "Then why say anything?" He stepped closer.

Because I felt like a fool sitting in that room.

"I don't know," she lied, lifting her chin a notch. "Forget I ever said anything." Indeed, she wished *she* could forget the wretched words had ever escaped her.

She started to close the door on him, but he caught it with one hand and backed her inside the room, closing it and sealing them in.

"What are you doing? They already think me some strumpet you've dropped into their midst." Her cheeks burned as she recalled their uncomfortable expressions when Owen introduced her simply as Anna. As though she wasn't important enough to possess a surname. She shook her head. "Go! The servants are probably whispering already that you're in here with me. What will your family think?" She stepped around him, intent on opening the door and expelling him from her room.

His hand fell on her shoulder, turning her and forcing her back against the shut door. He was close now. The broad wall of him all-encroaching heat.

"Let me be clear. I am not in love with Paget," he murmured, so close his breath fanned her lips.

She shivered. "It's not my—"

"Don't say it's not your concern when it so obviously is," he bit out, his gaze crawling over her face slowly, thoroughly.

Her stomach clenched at that penetrating stare.

She compressed her lips, holding silent. She resisted the urge to fidget, feeling very much like a cornered animal beneath his probing gaze, his words hanging between them. Words it was impossible to deny. Not when he consumed so much of her thoughts. Right or wrong, he filled her head, infected her blood, it seemed. Standing this close, she could not draw enough air to fill her lungs.

His eyes moved from her eyes to her lips and back again. She felt his gaze like a touch, an actual caress. She couldn't fathom her reaction if he actually did touch her . . . kiss her. She might just go up in flames.

"I grew up with Paget. We were children together. We were close, but then life happened." His lips curled in a grimace. "War happened. Brand died. Jamie came home. I stayed in India. They fell in love."

She moistened her lips. "And you're sorry for that?"

He dipped his head, bringing those pale night blue eyes so close she could see the dark ring around the irises. "There isn't one fraction of me that longs to be with her, that longs to . . ." His words faded.

Annalise's body leaned forward of its own accord, as if seeking the rest of those words, craving them like a touch. "Yes? What?"

His eyes roamed her face, searching. She squirmed, struggling to maintain eye contact. A battle when those eyes looked so deeply into her own. A battle she finally lost, her gaze ducking away.

His hand slid along her face, capturing her cheek. With a single, powerful tug he forced her gaze back. "I don't long for this with her, with anyone else."

He didn't leave her to wonder what *this* was. He showed her.

His lips brushed her lips, softly, teasingly at first. She lifted her face closer, like a moth to the light, hungering for more no matter the imminent danger.

Warmth spread through her as he increased the pressure of his mouth, sliding his arm around her and pulling her closer until she was plastered against him.

She melted against him, her body softening and yielding.

Her thoughts reeled. *I don't long for this with anyone else.* Implying he only longed for her, then? Had that been his meaning? It was a heady, marvelous thought and only heightened the desire thrumming through her. It only made her want to crawl inside of him until they were fused together.

He slanted his mouth and kissed her deeper,

his tongue licking at the seam of her lips. She sighed and his tongue delved inside, stroking her tongue.

His hand skimmed her spine, drifting up. She felt his fingers dancing over each vertebrae even through the fabric of her gown, grazing her bones as though savoring and memorizing the feel of them.

She sighed into his mouth, drinking in his kiss, his tongue, as she ran her hand up his neck. She lost her fingers in the thick strands of his hair, reveling in the silky tendrils filling her palms.

He came up slightly for air and breathed her name into her mouth in a hot little gust. It drove her wild. Especially with the echo of his words in her head. He longed for only her.

Need pumped through her blood for him. She brought one hand to his cheek, loving the scratching rasp there. He was everywhere and not nearly close enough. She moaned and pulled his head closer, mashing her lips until they were a tangle of lips, teeth, and tongues.

Suddenly he broke away. Air sawed from his lips as he panted down at her, studying her with eyes far too bright with emotion. Gone was her cold-eyed rescuer. In his place stood a man gripped by desire. For her. It was wholly satisfying. She smoothed her hands over his shoulders, eager, prepared for more than another kiss from him. She wanted what came next. She wanted it all.

Then he suddenly opened the door behind her.

She gaped for a moment, snapping her mouth shut when he stepped out in the corridor and turned back to look at her.

"I shall explain your presence here to my brother and his wife. I apologize if I made you uncomfortable earlier."

Annalise stared, hardly hearing his proper and correct speech. She realized she should feel appeased, but she felt only acute disappointment at the abrupt loss of him from her arms. He had kissed her and the earth moved beneath her feet. Had he not felt that, too?

She forced herself to nod and reply with something similarly polite and correct. "Thank you. That is of much relief."

"I would not have you embarrassed ever again by my thoughtlessness. Or hurt."

She angled her head, wondering if he was referring to more than her earlier mortification with his family. But then he turned and strolled down the corridor with swift steps, leaving her looking after him and wondering at that remark.

Chapter Eighteen

They were ready for Owen as soon as he entered the drawing room.

"Who is she?" Jamie asked baldly, his expression disapproving in a way that reminded Owen of his youth, when his brother had frowned on his wild ways.

"Jamie," Paget murmured, her voice chiding as she rocked the baby in her arms.

He longed to reply that Anna was none of Jamie's concern, but he had promised her that he would set matters to rights. He had brought her here without thinking through how he would explain her presence. Humiliating her was not his wish.

"I found her."

"You found here?" Jamie looked incredulous. "Like a lost penny?"

He winced. "It's not like that. When I left here I found her near the river. She was injured. Unconscious."

Paget smiled with that tenderness that was so like the girl he remembered. "You rescued her."

Jamie processed this for a bit, his eyes failing to go all soft and dreamy in the manner of Paget's. "Has she no family? Is there no one you can return her to?"

"It's complicated. She can't remember," he offered, even though he didn't entirely believe that to be true. He had no intention of filling in all the details for his brother.

Paget looked knowingly to her husband. "Remember when Owen rescued that injured falcon?"

And that was so very Paget—seeing only the best in him.

"Only she's not a pet, Paget." Jamie looked him over. He knew him better than that. "She was at your house when I visited? How is it you never mentioned her to me then?"

Owen shrugged. "It never occurred to me."

Jamie narrowed his gaze on him. "You've taken this woman into your care and you know nothing about her?"

Owen nodded, a slow smile curving his lips. For a moment he felt like that boy he had once been, needling his older brother and getting beneath his skin. "Yes."

"And what do you plan to do with her?"

Paget tsked. "Jamie, I'm sure Owen knows what he's doing. He doesn't answer to us."

"Indeed." Owen nodded once. "Since when am I required to keep you abreast of all my activities?"

Jamie squared his shoulders. "When you bring her into my home, I think I have a right to know."

The smile slipped from his lips. Anger began to simmer inside him. His brother spoke as though Anna were some dangerous criminal with whom he consorted. "I thought you wanted me here. I can go."

He turned to leave, but Paget rushed to his side and pulled on his sleeve with her free hand. "Please, Owen, stay. You *and* your guest. Anyone can see she's harmless." She sent a quelling glance to her husband. "We're so glad you are here. You know Jamie. He's merely being that overbearing older brother. It's an old role to shake."

Jamie nodded stiffly. "Forgive me. We don't want you to leave. I just worry about you." He sighed. "Although I know I have no call. You've been a grown man for some time now."

Paget dropped her hand from Owen's sleeve and went back to rocking little Brand. "I must confess we were planning to introduce you to a few ladies new to the area since you last lived here, but I can see that would be awkward now that you are here with your, er . . . companion."

His lips twisted wryly. "It's not like that, Paget."

"Oh." She blinked and nodded as though she understood, even though she could not possibly understand. How could she when he himself did not? "I thought, well, the way you looked at her." Her cheeks turned pink. "And the way she looked at you."

He resisted the urge to ask her to elaborate on how precisely Anna had looked at him. Instead he shook his head decisively. "No. It is not like that at all between us."

And yet even as he uttered those words, he could only think about that mind-numbing kiss he had just shared with her. The taste of her, the sounds she made in the back of her throat as he touched her, her hands in his hair. It was etched in his memory, lodged forever in his blood.

Brand started to whimper, and Paget made soft, shushing sounds. "Gentlemen, excuse me. Owen, I'll see you at dinner." Her look was pointed as she added, "With Anna, I presume."

He nodded.

She started to move away, but then paused as though recalling something. "Forgive me for saying, Owen, but you really should find her some decent attire. Her gown doesn't even fit properly. I hazard to guess that the rest of her wardrobe is no better."

He smiled. Trust Paget to concern herself with such matters. He inclined his head. "Very well."

Nodding in satisfaction, she left the room. He looked back to find his brother gazing after his wife and son with his heart in his eyes. He couldn't help chuckling.

Jamie's gaze shot back to him. "What?"

"It's still a marvel. You in love with Paget. When we were children I didn't think you could abide her."

Jamie smiled. "Yes, well, want to know a little secret?"

"What's that?"

"I was always a little bit in love with her."

He lifted his eyebrows. "Indeed?"

"Sometimes it just doesn't make any sense." He shook his head, his expression serious. "Logic doesn't apply. Only what's in here." He tapped his chest, directly over his heart.

Owen stared at him a long moment before snorting. "Didn't take you for a romantic."

"I suppose I am now. Paget saw to that. And

someday I hope you're lucky enough for a woman to make a romantic out of you."

Owen searched for a retort, something dismissive, but nothing came to mind. No. The only thing that filled his head was the female one floor above. He doubted there would ever be a woman in existence to make a romantic out of him, but Anna certainly filled him with emotion, a blistering desire that made him feel like a green lad again. His hand curled into a fist as he battled the urge to corner her upstairs and continue where they had left off.

"Well, well, brother," Jamie murmured, peering at him closely with speculation bright in his eyes. "Perhaps that day is sooner arrived than expected."

"I don't know what you mean."

Jamie smiled. "I merely look forward to acquainting myself further with your Miss Anna."

Owen frowned and moved toward the doors, saying over his shoulder, "She is not *my* Miss Anna, Owen."

"Quite so."

He hesitated at the threshold. "She's temporarily in my care. There is nothing more to our relationship."

"And yet you brought her here with you. Why not leave her in Town?"

Why not indeed? "As I said, she's in my care. We're not having an affair."

Jamie nodded, his expression mocking. "Of course."

With a muttered epithet, he quit the room, refusing to let Jamie's knowing smirk get beneath his skin. He was not romantically involved with Anna. A few ill-advised kisses did not constitute an affair.

Not yet.

Dinner was a tiresome affair. Lady Winningham pelted her with questions which she could not answer. Not without revealing more of herself than she wished. She felt Owen's gaze on her during these moments, watchful as a hawk, likely waiting for her to slip up as she fielded any one of the very natural questions regarding her history. By the time she retired to her room and dismissed the maid waiting to help her undress, her head throbbed.

Sinking down before the dressing table, Anna rubbed at her temples and stared at her murky reflection. Dropping her hands, she studied the woman staring back at her, wondering what she was doing here. Was it just Owen's promise to help her or something more?

She sighed and shook her head, acknowledging to herself that she was growing increasingly infatuated with Owen. That early kiss had robbed her of every scrap of reason she possessed, leaving her craving more.

She released the pins one by one from her hair, hoping that might alleviate her aching head. The brown mass tumbled around her shoulders and down her back. Burying her fingers through the strands, she massaged her scalp until feeling rushed back in.

A solid rap on the door had her swiveling around on the stool. "Come in," she called, assuming the maid had returned to pester her further. The girl had been appalled at her insistence that she could ready herself for bed.

Owen entered.

She straightened her spine where she sat.

"Oh. Hello," she murmured, suddenly self-conscious of her loosened hair. She ran a hand over the mass. His gaze followed the journey of her hand.

He closed the door behind him. "No one saw me enter," he assured her, clearly remembering her earlier concerns.

"Oh. Thank you." She swallowed, her nerves stretched tight at his sudden presence in her chamber. He had discarded his jacket and cravat and wore only his shirt. The fine lawn fabric was parted wide at his throat, giving her a glimpse of his upper chest. The golden skin there, the flesh she knew to be dense and compact, smooth to the touch.

Be calm. Don't act nervous simply because he's within ten feet of you.

"We'll leave in the morning."

She nodded. That soon? "Very well. I'll be ready."

"I'll meet you in the foyer after breakfast. Dress warmly. I'll teach you to shoot before we return to Town."

She nodded, her gaze trained on him, drinking in the sight of his face, the deeply set eyes that seemed to see everything, all of her, in the sweep of a glance.

He continued, "It's a useful skill to possess. Especially if you're going to be—" He stopped.

She looked at him, eyebrow arched, waiting.

"Especially when you're on your own," he finished.

She nodded, understanding. And wasn't that her plan? To find a place for herself. To live freely and independently. No Bloodsworth. No Jack, a man who never wanted her around until he decided he wanted a blue-blooded son-in-law. No. She would be better off alone.

"Your fire is low." He stepped deeper into the

bedchamber and moved toward the hearth. She watched as he squatted to add more wood.

Her fingers curled around the edges of her bench, gripping it as though she needed to hold onto something. His shirt pulled taut across his back, the shoulders working as he lifted logs and stirred the wood with a poker.

He stood, dusting his hands together. "That should keep you warm. It's a big house and can get drafty. Don't hesitate to ring for a maid if you should need the fire tended in the night. Do you have enough blankets?"

She stared, unaccustomed to having anyone care for her comfort to such a degree. To any degree. Especially when there was nothing in it for him.

She glanced to the bed with its thick coverlet. An additional blanket sat folded at the bottom. "I'll be fine."

With a slight incline of his head, Owen moved to the door.

She stretched out a hand as though to reach him. "Wait." The word escaped her without deliberation. And it was madness. This overwhelming urge she felt to keep him near her.

He turned, and she closed her eyes in a slow blink and dropped her hand. She shouldn't be toying with him like this. She could never have him. Like it or not, she was a married woman. She wasn't free to be with him.

She swallowed, shoving back down whatever it was she would have said. She moistened her lips. "Thank you. You are very kind, Owen."

Owen gazed at her for a moment, his eyes gleaming in the glow of the firelight. Then he advanced on her with an easy stride, each step making her heart thud faster in her tightening chest.

He stopped before her. She flinched but managed to hold still as he stretched a hand toward her. He paused for the barest moment before gathering a heavy handful of her hair in his fist. It was their only contact but it felt vastly intimate. It reminded her of the last time his hands delved into her hair. Only then, his mouth had been on hers. Did he intend to kiss her again? The thought brought heat flooding to her face. Desire pooling low in her belly.

"Kind, hm? That's not something I hear often." One corner of his mouth lifted. "With good reason."

She resisted leaning forward, closer to him, closer to the hand caressing her hair. "Perhaps you're not letting others see the real you."

"As you do?" His gaze turned rueful. "Perhaps." He shrugged a shoulder. "Or you're just seeing what you want to see."

Her gaze drank him in, the hard planes and valleys of his face, the well-shaped lips, the eyes that looked at her with such intensity, as though he was memorizing everything about her.

She swallowed, wishing she could look away, but was hopelessly drawn to the sight of him. He was achingly beautiful. Like something out of a dream. She supposed that was how she would look back to this time with him. Something beautiful and blurred in her memories. "I don't believe that."

His smile deepened, yet it was mirthless and somewhat indulgent. "Of course you don't. You're the type of girl who only sees the best in everyone."

She frowned, hoping that wasn't true. She couldn't be that trusting. Not again. That had been her mistake with Bloodsworth. She had never seen him for what he was until it was too late. Owen, however, was no Bloodsworth. She wasn't wrong about him.

He let her hair slip free from his fingers. His hand moved to her cheek, tracing its curve down to her chin. Warmth spread through her at the contact.

Her breath hitched, the air seizing in her chest. This time she didn't stop herself from leaning forward, angling her face up for him. Her entire being ached for him. He had to know. If he even felt a fraction of what she felt, he would touch her, take her, claim her.

His hand left her face then. She blinked as he stepped back. His fingers curled, clenching into tight fists at his sides. "Good night, Anna."

She inhaled a shaky breath and ran a hand through her hair, still feeling him there, his fingers wrapping around the tendrils.

"Good night, Owen," she murmured, trying not to appear as though she had desperately wanted him to kiss her again.

The door clicked shut behind him, leaving her alone with nothing but the pop of the fire to fill the silence.

The following morning, Annalise waited in the foyer for Owen. Her bags had already been stowed in the carriage. She had taken breakfast alone in the dining room. She knew Lord and Lady Winningham were keeping late hours, tending to the baby themselves. Most aristocrats would leave such matters to the staff, but she had spent enough time among members of the *ton* to know that Lady Winningham was not like other ladies.

Still, as she ate alone, she had thought that Owen might join her. Perhaps he was limiting his time with her. After he had left her last night, it seemed clear that there would be no more kisses. He would be a gentleman and make no such advances on her again. Or perhaps he simply did not desire her enough to breach impropriety. Lowering as the thought was, it resolved her to stifle this infatuation she felt for him. It would be best. For both of them.

She folded her hands in front of her and tried not to feel awkward standing alone in the vast foyer space, the groom in the corner watching her silently.

"Anna. Good morning." Lady Winningham appeared. "Did you breakfast already?"

She sketched a quick curtsy. "Yes, my lady."

The countess tsked. "I am sorry I wasn't awake yet to join you. Brand kept us up quite late. He still doesn't have his days and nights straight. He is sleeping like a log now. Naturally."

Annalise smiled, suppressing a small stab of jealously that this woman possessed all she had ever dreamed for herself. A family. A loving husband. A healthy child. All things that could never be hers. Just as quickly as the thought entered her head, she banished it, hating that she should even entertain such graceless sentiments. She should simply be grateful to be alive after the tragedy of her wedding night, not envying this woman her happiness.

"Nothing to fret over," Annalise assured her. "We're leaving this morning."

"Yes. Owen said as much. We're very sad to see you go." A mischievous light entered her eyes. "You're waiting for Owen, then? I think I know where he is. Come this way."

The countess strode ahead, not giving Annalise a chance to explain that she would gladly wait for him in the foyer. Clearly, she was expected to follow.

She fell into step behind the lady. They didn't stop until they reached a partially open door. The countess peered within first, her movements careful, as though she wanted to remain unnoticed. A satisfied smile spread across her lips. Nodding, she looked back at Annalise and motioned for her to peer within.

Annalise stepped forward, and her heart constricted at the sight. Owen sat in a rocking chair, the tiny Brand in his arms. Morning sunlight spilled through the parted damask drapes. She had never seen him look so peaceful. The hard features of his face were relaxed as he gazed down at the sleeping babe. He rocked him back and forth, humming something faintly. Gone was the awkwardness of yesterday when the child had been forced into his arms. He looked natural cradling that sleeping baby, and sudden longing pinched her chest.

"He will make a wonderful father someday," Lady Winningham whispered in her ear.

Annalise glanced back at the countess, taken aback at the directness in her dark eyes. She nodded mutely.

Of course he would make a good father. She knew that without even seeing him rocking the babe thusly. He had exhibited gentleness before. Beyond rescuing her, he'd cared for her, helped tend her injuries alongside Mirela. What nobleman would do that for a stranger? She knew firsthand there was tenderness in him even as he'd held himself apart from her so often.

Fast on the heels of this thought came another. *You're more than infatuated with this man. You're falling in love with him.*

She inhaled a ragged breath. Of all the foolish, stupid things to do. She couldn't afford to love this man. She wasn't free to love him. Even if he could care for her in turn, she would be leaving soon to make her own way in the world.

She shifted, desperate to flee from the sight of him holding the child, to erase the image from her mind. The floor creaked beneath her weight and

Owen's head snapped up at the sound. Instantly, the softness fled from his face, a curtain falling over his eyes, quickly masking anything he might have been thinking.

She backed away from the door, bumping into the countess. "Pardon me. I'll wait for him in the foyer."

Turning, she fled down the stairs.

Chapter Nineteen

Owen found her waiting for him in the foyer. He tried to suppress his annoyance, but it was too fresh, simmering beneath the surface.

He had felt exposed when he looked up to find her watching him holding Brand. Humming a Gaelic lullaby he recalled from his youth, rocking Jamie and Paget's child—a child named after his eldest brother, no less—had been a vulnerable moment. And she had witnessed it.

His annoyance wasn't alleviated by the fact that Paget stood just behind Anna, a satisfied sparkle in her eyes that told him she was responsible for bringing Anna to the nursery.

"Come," he snapped. "I've said my farewells."

He strode out the front door, tugging on his

gloves and lifting the collar of his coat against the brisk morning.

"Are we leaving directly?" she asked behind him. "I thought you were teaching me to shoot this morning."

"I am." He opened the carriage door before the groom could reach it and assisted her inside. Once they were settled on the squabs and the carriage was moving, he elaborated. "There is a spot just up ahead. We'll stop there."

Those wide brown eyes stared at him so solemnly, as though he might jump across the seat and bite her. He turned his attention to the window, watching the familiar scenery roll past, hating that she would look at him with such apprehension and yet knowing it was for the best. There could be no comfort or familiarity between them. That could lead to only one thing.

They drove for several more moments before he heard himself saying, "Tell me, Anna. In your limited recollections, do you think it a habit of yours to spy on people?"

She cleared her throat. "Lady Winningham led me to the nursery. I did not mean—I did not know—" She sucked in a breath. "I'm sorry. I should not have pried."

He had suspected Paget motivated the encounter, and to hear Anna say as much made him feel wretched for taking out his frustration on her. She was as much a victim of Paget's machinations as he.

"I suppose we must count ourselves fortunate that I did not startle and drop Brand." He smiled to show that he was teasing.

A grin of relief brightened her features, and he almost regretted his levity. She was far too lovely when she smiled like that. And he was far too weak to resist her. He turned his attention to the window and stared out.

When they stopped minutes later, he helped her down and led her from the road into the trees.

"Where are we going?" she asked.

"I didn't want you to walk too far on your leg. There's a spot ahead where I used to target practice with my brothers and father."

Anna stared at her feet as she walked. "Thank you."

She was always thanking him. Almost as though she didn't know kindness or consideration. *As though she didn't know love.* He drew a deep breath at the notion, marveling that someone like her shouldn't have been loved before. It troubled him far more than he liked. She deserved love.

He slid his hand from her elbow and down her

arm, catching her fingers in his. Her smaller hand felt good, and he longed to strip the glove from his hand so he could feel the sensation of skin on skin.

The grass was taller, whispering against her skirts and the fabric of his trousers as they walked.

"Jamie said there should be targets there."

She glanced up at him. Sunlight ribboned through the tree branches overhead, dappling her features in shadow and light. "Do you have a pistol?"

He patted his jacket where the weight of it rested. "Always."

"You always wear one?" She lifted her legs high as she walked, almost as though she sought to step over the grass that came to her knees.

"Mostly. Not at home. But always when traveling."

"And why is that? Is England not civilized?"

"It's shocking how quickly one can step outside civilization." He thought of their picnic. That scenario could quickly have twisted into something lacking all civility. Something ugly. He'd seen the savagery in the eyes of those men.

"Do you think danger lurks at every turn?" There was no judgment in her voice, just a faint curiosity as she flicked her gaze at him before staring ahead again.

"It can." He stopped as they reached the three trees tangled close together that he and his brothers had used to hold various pieces of glass for target practice over the years. He dropped her hand and moved to the trees to position five of the glasses Jamie had left on the ground.

Returning to her side, he said, "Perhaps more importantly for this discussion is what you think."

She looked up at him, her smooth forehead furrowed. "I know it does. You can never be too prepared."

Staring into those radiant eyes, he knew she was speaking from experience. A history she wasn't ready to share with him. Perhaps she never would. Perhaps she would be gone from his life before he ever had a chance to know the mystery behind the shadows in her eyes.

He reached inside his jacket and removed his revolver. "Then let us better prepare you, shall we?"

He motioned her closer, and then tried to ignore the sweet scent of her as he pointed out the different parts of the weapon, including how to load the balls into the chamber and cock the hammer when ready to fire.

Handing it to her, he instructed her on how to hold it and aim. "Understand?"

"Yes."

Despite her response, she sounded nervous, and the revolver dipped as if too heavy for her hands.

"Why don't we do the first one together?" He stepped behind her. With a tug, he pulled her flush against him, his chest aligned to her back. Even tense as a board, she fit him perfectly. He pressed his cheek alongside hers, sliding his hands over the length of her stretched arms until his hands reached her wrists. His fingers circled the delicate bones there. He felt her pulse through his gloves.

Struggling to focus, he squinted and followed her line of fire. "Are you aiming at the middle bottle?"

"Yes," she breathed, still sounding nervous.

"Good. You're spot on."

"Am I?"

"Yes. Try not to jerk your arms when you squeeze the trigger. Go ahead and pull back the hammer," he encouraged. "Fire when ready."

She cocked the hammer and after a very long moment in which he savored the closeness of their bodies she squeezed the trigger. Her body jerked, but he absorbed the force into himself. She released a small gasp as the ball flew loose and struck the tree. Bits of bark flew at the contact.

"Not bad. You shifted your aim low when you fired. Hold your arms steady and try it again."

She fired again, this time shattering the glass.

She laughed, delighted. He moved around her, staring down at her flushed face.

"I hit it, Owen!"

"Very good. There are three more in the chamber. Want to try it alone this time?"

She nodded enthusiastically.

He stepped back, giving her space.

"Steady arms," he reminded her, watching as she squared off to aim. "Remember not to jerk them when you fire."

She breathed some quiet words of affirmation as her face screwed tight into a look of intense concentration. It was adorable.

A loud pop cracked on the air. She jumped slightly but shattered another bottle.

He whistled. "Impressive. We might have discovered a marksman in you."

She flushed.

"Again?" he asked.

She nodded and fired again, her body falling back a step from the recoil. He didn't have to suggest she fire the fifth shot. She stepped forward, set her chin at a determined angle, locked her arms, and fired the last ball.

She hit the final bottle.

"You're a natural." She still wore that grin on her face. It was infectious. He felt himself smile. "How do you feel?"

She angled her head, studying the shards of glass marring the ground. "Surprised."

"That you're a good shot?"

She nodded.

"Just remember, if you ever have to do this in reality, stay calm. You may only get off one shot. You want to make it count. It might be your only chance. You can't miss."

She faced him and offered him the revolver. He shook his head. Pulling out his pouch, he shook five balls into his palm and held them out to her. "Once more. And why don't you load?"

Nodding, she copied his earlier movements and carefully loaded the chamber.

"We're out of bottles."

"So call your shots."

She hesitated before peering intently at the tangled trio of trees. "Third tree on the right. Bottom half of the trunk."

Then she fired, hitting the third tree in the vicinity she had just predicted.

"Excellent," he praised.

She fired the remaining four shots, if not spot on, then remarkably close.

Afterward, Anna turned to face him, beaming, and his heart squeezed to see her so happy, so triumphant. If nothing else, this had been an excellent exercise for her self-esteem.

"Is this what it's always like?"

"I don't know," he said. "What's it like?"

"Marvelous." She scrunched her nose, evidently seeking a better description. "Empowering."

He frowned. It had been a long time since he'd ever felt exhilarated when firing a revolver or rifle. He fought the tide of dark thoughts. He didn't want to mar the brightness of this moment for her.

"Once, yes. It was like that."

Her smile slipped and she considered him for a moment. "But no longer," she replied, far too perceptive.

Owen collected his revolver from her, busying his hands. "I think that's enough for the day. You have the idea. The revolver is yours to keep. I'll give you the case when we return to Town."

He felt her still beside him and lifted his gaze to her face.

"You're giving it to me?" She blinked.

He nodded. "I'll feel better knowing you have it. When you're gone." Something in him sank as he uttered those words. He told himself it was simply concern for her out there alone in the world. Nothing more than that.

The brightness faded from her eyes. "You've done so much for me. Thank you."

Although she didn't sound grateful.

Together, they walked. This time he did not

hold her hand. He touched her only to assist her into the carriage.

"I said the wrong thing, didn't I?" she asked. "Earlier?"

At her question, he faced her, bewildered. He didn't think this woman could ever say the wrong thing. She spoke with her heart. "What are you talking about?"

"Firing a gun. It's not marvelous for you, is it?"

He tucked a strand of hair behind her ear. "I don't care for what I am," he admitted. "What the war turned me into."

"And what's that?"

He simply stared at her, unwilling to say it. It had been said before.

"Oh. That's right." She nodded slowly. "A killer."

He didn't protest.

She continued, "Isn't that what a soldier is?"

"It's not that simple."

"Has it occurred to you that you're doing a disservice to those who lost their lives? Your fellow comrades?"

He tensed, his ire sparking to life. "What are you saying?"

"They're dead. You are not. Should you not live to honor them? As your brother is doing?"

"You sound like Paget."

"Perhaps she's right."

"Marrying and begetting children will not *fix* me or erase the things I've done."

"And what is it you've done that any other soldier has not?"

"Don't you understand?" He moved across the carriage to sit beside her. "I don't care what other soldiers have done. I only care about my actions."

"And what did you do?"

He turned to the window, studying the tiny motes of dust dancing on the thin stream of light pouring into the shadowy confines of the carriage. "I was a sharpshooter. They gave me assignments. I would sneak into villages, enemy camps, and kill men before they even had a chance to arm themselves. Sometimes they sat at a fire, sipping their coffee, and I ended their lives. One man I executed sat at dinner beneath a tent. There were women at that table with him. Children. And I put a ball straight through his head. When I close my eyes, I still hear their screams."

He was lost in the recollection until the brush of Anna's hand on his face brought him back. She cupped his cheek with a tenderness he did not deserve. He snatched hold of her wrist, squeezing the delicate bones. "Do not comfort me."

"What shall I do then?" she whispered. "Pretend I don't care?"

"I don't want you to care. You shouldn't care."

Her gaze scanned his face. "Too late," she whispered, and firmly pressed her lips to his.

He didn't move for a long moment, didn't respond to the pressure of those lips on his. Her hands slid around his neck, her fingers toying lightly in the strands of his hair.

He could not resist. With a groan, he hauled her against him and kissed her like a man starved.

Anna sighed into his mouth, releasing a tiny sound of satisfaction that he swallowed deep inside himself. His fingers went for her hair, the silken strands overflowing in his hands.

They strained against each other awkwardly, side by side on the squabs, trying to touch more, taste more. Frustrated, unable to get enough of her, he wrapped an arm around her waist and pulled her onto his lap. Her legs straddled him, knees coming down on either side of his hips on the seat. His hands closed on her thighs and pulled her closer until he felt the heat of her through her skirts.

He tore his lips from her. "Is your leg all right this way?"

"Yes," she gasped, her eyes bright and wild in the shadowy interior of the carriage. "Don't stop." She pulled his head roughly back down to hers. Their lips collided fiercely. Her hands tangled in his hair.

He gripped her hips, guiding her into a rocking motion against him. His hands skimmed over her waist to her rib cage. He cupped her breasts, relishing the sound of her muffled cry against his lips.

He felt the aroused beads of her nipples through the fabric of her gown. Her hands clenched in his hair as he dragged his thumbs across them.

Pulling back, he watched her tremble on his lap, head thrown back, lovely throat arched. Smiling, he chafed and plucked at her nipples until she shuddered over him, grinding down on his hardness with a keening cry.

Groaning, he dove a hand into her hair and hauled her back, kissing her harshly. She whimpered into his mouth and he softened his kiss, tracing her mouth with his tongue. He loved that sound. Could spend nights listening to it, to all the sounds she made as he explored her body.

He dragged his lips to her jaw, trailing his tongue down over the stretched cords until he came to her hammering pulse. He gently nipped there at her neck and then followed with his tongue, licking and sucking until she trembled against him. All the while the delicious weight of her breasts filled his palms.

Anna pulled back this time, staring down at him with eyes that glowed, lit from a fire within.

Her hair spilled loose all around her, and he reached up, burying his hands in it, trying to pull her back down to him, eager to taste her again.

She withheld herself, staring at him with those eyes that reached inside him and touched some forgotten part. "Owen."

His name brushed over him like a caress. He trailed his thumb over her lips, tracing the lush shape, imagining the sweet torment of her mouth roaming over him.

She kissed his thumb, open-mouthed. Her moist breath fanned the pad of his finger, and he couldn't stop himself from sliding his thumb inside the warm cavity of her mouth. She took him in, sucked, and his gut tightened.

She pulled back slightly, his thumb resting on her bottom lip. "I need you."

Her words jarred something inside him, doused him in cold reality. Because while she might want him, he was the last thing she *needed*.

He expelled a ragged breath. Closing his hands around her waist, he set her on the seat across from him.

She blinked. "Owen?" Her voice vibrated with bewilderment.

"I can't do this, Anna." He couldn't take her inside a carriage like she was some wench accustomed to a quick, meaningless tup.

She began to hastily tidy her hair, pulling the mass into a clumsy knot. "I understand."

He wanted to ask precisely what she understood, but she babbled ahead without waiting for a reply.

"'Twas a moment's madness. Nothing more."

Is that what she thought? That they had suffered some fleeting lapse in control? That he had not wanted her yesterday? That he still did not? That he would not tomorrow?

He bit back an ugly oath. He wanted her so desperately his body shook from the near pain of it. He closed his eyes in one hard blink and managed to speak in an even voice.

"Yes. Nothing more."

Chapter Twenty

Annalise hesitated before the door to the dress shop. She looked up and down the sidewalk, grateful at the dearth of shoppers this early in the day yet. It wasn't Bond Street, thankfully. She wouldn't have allowed herself to be seen there, but this shop seemed obscure enough. The risk of bumping into someone who knew her would not be too great at this shop. Not that Bloodsworth would be strolling about anywhere so early in the day. He rarely rose before noon.

A bell chimed as Owen opened the door for her.

She glanced at him. "Why are we doing this again?"

"Come now." He motioned to her ill-fitting gown. "The least we can do is procure clothes for you that properly fit. Yes?"

She grasped a handful of burgundy skirts. The gown was too large, like all her rest. She couldn't ever recall finding a dress too large before. The fabric sagged around her waist and torso and the skirts were much too voluminous. Mrs. Kirkpatrick had fetched a maid to hem the bottom, to save herself from tripping, but Annalise knew she could have done better work herself. The hem was uneven and sloppy. All in all, she looked a bit of a mess. A fact Owen had clearly noticed.

He gestured her inside. The proprietress moved forward expectantly, eager to serve.

Annalise hesitated in the threshold. "You needn't put yourself to such trouble."

He looked down at her, his expression once again stoic. He failed in any way to resemble the man who had kissed her so passionately in the carriage yesterday. In those moments, his eyes had been full of brightness, of life. Hunger for her.

When he looked at her now, there was nothing there. He scanned her perfunctorily. "I'd say perhaps any trouble would be worth it. Necessary, even."

Cheeks burning, she managed a nod. "Very well." It would be nice to make a fresh start with clothes tailored for her.

With a hand at the small of her back, he guided her inside.

The proprietress took one look at Annalise and clapped her hands together sharply before rushing her. Apparently no explanation was necessary.

"Welcome, welcome." She motioned to several dresses on display. "We have several gowns already made for your lady. We are happy to make any necessary alterations."

Annalise's cheeks burned hotter at the implication that she was somehow Owen's lady. Nothing could be further from the truth. Even if she wanted to be. Even if *he* wanted her to be. She was married to a wretch of a man.

"Very good." Owen nodded as though he were half listening. "I have an errand at the cobbler's down the street. I'll return shortly." He handed the dressmaker his card. "See she has anything she needs."

The dressmaker's eyes widened. She bobbed her head happily, her fingers stroking over the card.

His attention returned to Annalise. His gaze skimmed her quickly, and, as if recalling how utterly lacking her wardrobe was, he added, "Which should be about everything."

That said, he left her alone with the eager dressmaker.

She stood awkwardly for a moment until the

dressmaker ushered her forward. Soon she was lost in a sea of dresses, undergarments, stockings, slippers, shoes. A girl emerged from the back to assist, and Annalise couldn't help seeing herself in the downcast eyes and hurried movements, each movement deliberate, eager to please.

"Really," she spit out as a muslin gown was pulled over her head—a gown she had no notion where she would wear. Once she left here she would have no fine parties and teas to attend. She would be returning to a simple life.

"I honestly don't need—" The words were muffled in a sea of tulle and lace, before she received—was that an elbow?—a sturdy poke to the side.

The air escaped her in a huff of pain.

"If a man as handsome as that one offered to buy me a new wardrobe, I wouldn't be refusing."

She settled a cold glare on the dressmaker once the sea of petticoats swept free of her head. She wanted to bite out that nothing came free in this life. Because it certainly never had for her.

She held her tongue and suffered the last of the dressmaker's prodding, refusing an enormous ball gown of red silk. Where on earth would she wear that monstrosity? Clearly the woman was ready to take full advantage of Owen's generosity.

Ready to be rid of the dressmaker, she put on a new walking dress of satin brocade—the dressmaker refused to let her again don her ill-fitting gown—and moved toward the front door. "I'll find Lord McDowell myself."

"Very well. Shall we send everything to the earl's residence? Or perhaps another?" She glanced at the small card that appeared as if by magic in her hand. Speculation brimmed in her eyes. Annalise had never explained their relationship, and she knew the woman was beyond curious. Clearly she was not Owen's wife or he would have introduced her as such.

She met the woman's inquisitive stare and suppressed a smile at the dressmaker's blatant attempt to learn who she was. "Yes. The earl's address, please."

Even having lived with Jack, she was not quite accustomed to giving directives. Especially not to people who would not have spoken two sentences to her unless it was to unceremoniously order her about.

She stepped outside and took a gulp of air, glad to be free of the shop that reminded her too much of the place she had spent years loathing in Yorkshire.

Glancing left and right along the sidewalk, she tried to determine the direction to the cobbler. She identified the wooden sign hanging perpendicular to the building several stores down and started toward it with decisive steps, her slippered feet falling silently.

A body emerged from the door of a tobacconist's. The gentleman stopped himself short of colliding into her, bracing a hand on her arm to halt his momentum.

The moment she felt the hand on her skin, she knew.

A tremor rippled out from that point of contact and coursed through her. Cold fear washed over her. Everything slowed, pulling to a near stop. She slid her arm free and lifted her gaze to the well-dressed man, confirming what she had already sensed.

"My apologies." His gaze flicked over her, barely looking at her as he moved to step around her, but then jerked to a hard halt.

She froze, almost as though she could make herself invisible if she simply held herself still.

He turned slowly to fully face her.

She watched, her eyes wide and unblinking, aching in her face. In one glance she took in his well-appointed attire. Groomed impeccably, as always. No black for mourning. In fact, he was dressed quite cheerfully in his green velvet jacket and striped cravat the color of apricots. His hair was styled and crisp, swept back from his forehead.

This was the man she had thought to spend the rest of her life with. Now she could only stare at him with dread and terror rising swiftly inside her, threatening to consume her, while marveling that she had ever thought his smile charming.

He stared at her as though he were seeing a ghost.

Her husband seemed somehow *less*. Less handsome. Less tall. For the first time, she noticed the weakness of his jaw. The flatness of his gaze.

"Annalise?" His voice sounded faraway, like a distant echo.

She shook her head, everything firing to life inside her.

She lurched back several steps. Bloodsworth grabbed her arm, his fingers hard and digging.

She swallowed her cry and forced a tremulous smile. "You mistake me for someone else," she lied, desperation making her say anything in that moment.

He gazed at her, studying her face as if he wished to see something there that proved her ridiculous claim that he was not staring at his wife.

"Annalise," he repeated after a stretched silence. "It is you." Those dark, cruel eyes swept over her again. "Much improved, I see. And did my eyes deceive or are you minus a limp now? How did that little miracle come about?"

Fed by indignation, she spit out, "I broke my leg when I nearly drowned in the river. It was properly set this time."

He shrugged. "Oh, then I did you a favor, it would seem."

"You tried to murder me," she hissed.

His eyes roamed her face and body appreciatively. "You're full of fire now, aren't you? I might have had a taste of you before tossing you overboard had you looked this appealing before."

Her stomach heaved at his words, at the notion of him touching her. Her free hand lashed out and slapped him across the face.

Instantly, his jovial air vanished. The imprint of her hand stood out starkly against his cheek. His eyes looked murderous . . . an all too familiar expression. One that had haunted her those first few nights when she woke in the wagon. The nightmares had only faded over the last few weeks. She was certain Owen had something to do with that. But now . . . face-to-face with Bloodsworth again, she recalled the terror she had fought so hard to forget.

He glanced around them, and the reminder crashed down on her acutely that they were not alone. Not like last time. He couldn't attack her. There were witnesses. A couple across the street paused and stared at them before hurrying along.

He yanked her to his side and began walking. "That was very brave of you . . . and stupid."

She dug in her heels. "Let me go or I shall scream."

"Go ahead. And then I will tell them you are quite mad. I'm a duke. A member of the House of Lords. Respected by all. I have the ear of the Queen. Who do you think they will believe?"

He paused with her in front of one of the many shops lining the street. She stared at him in horror, her breath coming in sharp pants.

He was right, of course. It was her worst fear. She looked around desperately. They had moved farther from the cobbler's shop, but she knew Owen would appear any moment, and that filled her with equal parts dread and relief.

"Let me go," she whispered, her gaze darting back to his face.

He laughed harshly. "Too late for that. You should have disappeared while you had the chance. I wish you had." He nodded. "I've plans now. Things in the works with Lady Joanna. Remember her? She was quite disappointed when I married you . . . and quite delighted over your demise. I'll not have you ruin things."

Yes. She should have vanished. She knew that now. She was a fool to have remained in Town. She should have taken her leave after they returned yesterday, only she couldn't. She let herself get caught up in Owen. She could admit that now. He had come to mean something to her. He had trapped her in his web. Oh, she knew he had not intended for it to happen. On the contrary, he would be horrified to know she felt any manner of attachment for him.

"I can disappear now," she volunteered, knowing she had to persuade him to believe that. She had to get away from him . . . because she saw the truth in his eyes. If he took her from this street, it was over. She was truly dead.

He would finish what he started on their honeymoon barge. She'd never make it to his home in Mayfair. He would never tell the world that he'd found his wife.

She would never see Owen again. That realization was perhaps the most bitter to accept. Owen would not know what happened to her. He'd simply think she'd run away.

She studied Bloodsworth's perfectly neutral expression, knowing what it masked. If he dragged her inside his carriage, that would be the end of her. If anyone could get away with it, he could.

She could hear Owen's voice in her ear. *Trust your instincts.*

Letting that fortify her, she pressed, "You don't

have to dirty your hands with killing me." Her gaze skimmed past him, around him, stalling.

"So you are suggesting that I just let you go . . ."

The idea clearly did not sit well with him.

His look turned speculative, assessing. He eyed her again, his gaze skimming her new dress. "Where have you been all this time, Annalise? Someone is clearly keeping and caring for you. A man?"

He must have seen something in her face. He smiled slowly, although there was no mirth in the curve of his lips. If anything, possession burned there. And something else. Something that made her feel even more threatened.

"Yes. Of course, it's a man." His free hand reached out. He ran one finger along the frilled edge of her heart-shaped bodice, dipping beneath the fabric. She jerked at the scrape of his nail against the top of her breast.

"Is he teaching you things?" His hand on her arm softened, his fingers stirring against her flesh in small circles that made her skin crawl.

She shook her head and looked away, revolted by the suggestive gleam in his eyes.

With the gentlest touch, he pulled her closer to his side and murmured in her ear, "You are mine . . . I can do with you anything I see fit."

"You're a monster," she ground out.

He responded with a short laugh. "Suddenly I'm regretting that I did not sample what lies beneath your skirts . . ."

And yet he did not regret trying to kill her. Bile rose up in the back of her throat.

"Anna." Owen's voice rang out, and everything inside her seized.

Chapter Twenty-one

Relief, dread. Both sentiments washed over her.

Bloodsworth's hand tightened on her arm again. "Is that him?" he demanded in a low voice.

She nodded and then stopped, catching herself. She did not know *how* to respond. She had never imagined this—Owen and Bloodsworth face-to-face. Of all the worst case scenarios, this was one she had not anticipated.

"Ah. I see that it is he. And from the lovely pink to your cheeks, I gather that you care for him. I imagine that it would hurt a great deal to be the sole reason for his demise."

All the warmth bled out from her face as his meaning sank in. "You wouldn't . . ."

He angled his head. "Truly? You think not? I

would not even have to dirty my hands this time. I could simply hire some miscreant to dispatch him for me." He uttered this as though he were remarking on the weather.

She quickly glanced at Owen and back to Bloodsworth again. She knew he spoke the truth. He'd suffer no compunction ending Owen's life. Owen, who had only ever tried to help her, who tolerated her intrusion and demands on his life. He didn't deserve such a fate. Especially after all he'd been through. He hadn't survived a war to come home and be killed by the likes of Bloodsworth.

Her stomach rolled. She pressed a hand to her lips, fearing she might be ill. Swallowing back the tide of bile, she dropped her hand. Her fingers curled into fists at her sides. The sudden urge to inflict violence upon Bloodsworth overcame her. He would not harm Owen. She must see to that. *She would.*

"Leave. Him. Be."

The duke smiled. "Ah, such fire in your eyes. If looks could kill, I think I'd perish where I stand. Is this love then, my pet? Touching. And so tragic if he should die because you don't know how to make yourself scarce. Because you didn't know how to die like a good girl should."

She flinched at this.

He tsked his tongue and shook his head as

though she were a misbehaving child. "You should have never shown your face in Town. Really very unwise."

"Promise not to harm him, and I'll disappear." She spoke quickly, her voice a feverish rush. "I'll bury myself in some small corner of the country. In years, no one will even recall my face. I am quite forgettable. No one will remember you were ever even married to me."

He scrutinized her, weighing her words, searching for the truth in her eyes. His gaze flicked to Owen, moving in their direction, before returning to her. "I believe you mean that." And yet there was something in his words . . . a lingering distrust. Still, he nodded in agreement. "Very well. Know that if you surface, I will kill him. As soon as we part ways, I will follow you. I shall have his name and know where he lives. His life is in your hands." His fingers tightened on her arm. "Understand?"

She nodded, a relieved breath escaping her. Owen's fate was in her hands, and she would make certain he was not hurt.

At that moment Owen caught sight of her standing with Bloodsworth and paused. Everything about him tensed. It was imperceptible. And yet she saw it. She knew.

He flicked an imaginary piece of lint off the front of his jacket, but his gaze never left Bloodsworth. To the casual observer, he would appear nonchalant in manner, but she had made a study of Owen from the moment she opened her eyes to him in the back of Mirela's wagon. She recognized the unwavering intensity of that gaze.

She well remembered his pose. The squared shoulders slightly pulled back. The tension feathering his clenched jaw. She had seen him like this before, on their picnic outside the fair when those two ruffians harassed them. And of course she had not forgotten what he did to those men with such ease and finesse.

Owen looked at her and then back to Bloodsworth, assessing, and she knew he was trying to correctly read the situation. Was Bloodsworth a stranger? Or someone she knew? A friend?

A quick glance revealed that Bloodsworth wore one of his artful smiles. The one she had always thought conveyed polite interest, but now she knew the darkest of thoughts lurked behind it.

Anxiety ribboned through her. Her hand pressed against her side, fingers curling, fisting the fabric of her skirts.

"Come. You have my word. Leave now," she urged, hoping to avoid a confrontation between the two men.

"I should like to meet your lover," he mused, clearly enjoying her misery.

"As yourself?" she hissed. "That will only complicate matters."

He shrugged, neither agreeing or disagreeing.

"Please, stop toying with me," she murmured. "I'll leave Town this very night. Just . . . *go.*"

She couldn't bear to watch Owen turn from her once he knew she was this man's wife—and surely he would. She only had this last day with him . . . she did not want it full of ugliness.

Her husband cocked his head thoughtfully as Owen, who had paused slightly, now advanced on them, his strides swift and sure, his face cast in its usual blandness.

"Please, he will be upon us any moment." She tugged at her arm, but Bloodsworth held fast.

"Anna." Just the sound of that false name made her shiver. Not for the first time she wished Owen knew her real name. "Who is this?"

Bloodsworth cocked his head, surveying Owen.

"I—I—" She looked to her husband, the truth sticking in her throat.

Owen didn't wait for her to answer, though. Or perhaps her hesitation was the only answer he needed. His gaze locked on Bloodsworth. "Take your hand off her."

Her husband stiffened at her side, and she was quite certain this was the first time in his life anyone had issued him a command. He pulled back his shoulders, and she knew whatever his intent, he would reveal his identity now. "Do you know who I am?"

"I don't need to know."

"Oh, I think you do."

She sucked in a breath, the tightness in her chest a physical ache.

This had become worse than facing Bloodsworth and falling into his clutches again. Owen turning his back on her—losing him. That was the worst part of all this. Even if she had to leave him.

She did not acknowledge the fact that she had never *had* Owen in the first place. Somehow she had felt bonded to him since the beginning. She had fooled herself into feeling safe with him. Absurd, when she was married to a man who would rather kill her than have her for a wife. She should have never been lulled into a sense of safety.

Owen was not hers. Never had that been clearer than now.

She blinked hard and long, waiting in dread for Bloodsworth to declare her his wife and for Owen to walk away. Except Bloodsworth didn't say anything. He didn't have the chance.

Opening her eyes, it was to find that Owen had moved with startling suddenness.

She gasped softly as his hand closed around

Bloodsworth's throat. "I can promise that if you don't unhand her, you will know only pain." He spoke slowly, succinctly, angling his head. "I've spent years learning how to inflict pain on men much more imposing than you. It will be an easy matter."

There was something in his face, a steeliness in his eyes, a flatness in his voice, that guaranteed he meant every word.

The color leeched out of Bloodsworth's face. Apparently he believed Owen.

His hand loosened but did not completely fall away from her arm. His tongue darted out over his lips. "You dare touch me? Threaten me?"

Annalise almost did not recognize his voice. Gone was the arrogant, lofty tone.

Owen nodded once. "Unless you want me to spill your blood all over this pretty jacket of yours, let her go." The way his lip curled over the words told her he thought nothing of Bloodsworth's fine attire. His knuckles whitened at Bloodsworth's throat and she knew he was exerting more pressure.

Her husband's face reddened as Owen continued, his voice a deep, ominous rumble. "It's amazing how much blood is in the human face. It's the head, really, I suppose. Those injuries always bleed the most."

Bloodsworth's eyes bulged. His hand trembled on her arm, and, as though he noticed the shameful tremor, he finally let her go.

Almost instantly Owen released him.

Annalise looked with astonishment at Bloodsworth. He was shaken, one hand rubbing at his throat as he took several steps back. This man whose memory had terrified her for so long was *afraid*. It dawned on her then that he was the veriest of cowards. One who bullied those weaker—such as an unsuspecting bride on her wedding night.

He glared at Owen as he backed farther away, lips pressed into a hard, cruel line.

A part of her should have been comforted at the ease in which Owen overpowered Bloodsworth, but she knew it did not matter. In his mind, he was calculating that he would have to hire multiple miscreants to kill Owen should she not follow through with her promise and vanish into obscurity.

"Anna," Owen said, motioning her to his side, his gaze never straying from Bloodsworth. She moved in closer, allowing herself to take comfort in his nearness even though she knew it was fleeting. He could not protect her. Only she could protect him.

Her husband's gaze slid to her and the threat she read there made her throat seize. He would relish hurting Owen. Or rather, *having* him hurt. She sent him a single nod that she hoped conveyed that she was as well as gone. He could count on that. Anything to keep Owen safe.

Bloodsworth held her gaze a beat longer and then turned abruptly, fleeing in the opposite direction. Air expelled from her lungs.

Owen's hand settled at the small of her back. "Come," he instructed. A quick glance revealed the rigid set to his jaw. He was not happy, and she intuitively knew it wasn't just with Bloodsworth, the stranger who refused to unhand her. Indeed not. Much of the ire she felt radiating off him was aimed at *her*.

His hand on her back turned her and guided her down the sidewalk. She looked several times over her shoulder, almost as though she expected to see her husband give chase. Unnecessary, of course. He would follow them. He'd said as much, but he would be discreet. Especially after Owen nearly choked the life out of him.

Despite herself, she felt satisfaction curl deeply through her. That would be something she would take with her to warm her heart in whatever obscure location she buried herself.

She quickened her pace. Owen's hand dropped away from her back. She spotted their carriage at the end of the street. The groom descended when he saw them, pulling open the door. A quick glance over her shoulder revealed no sight of Bloodsworth. All the same, she knew he was out there. Forever close. It was her task to make certain close never became too close again.

Falling back on the velvet squabs, she released a shuddery breath, grateful to be free of her husband. Now she simply had to say good-bye to Owen.

A lump formed in her throat that she couldn't fathom. It was incomprehensible. She always knew they would part ways. There had never been an expectation otherwise. She gripped the edge of the seat and squeezed the cushion until her fingers ached.

She forced a tremulous smile and lifted her gaze to Owen, prepared to offer some dismissive remark about overly forward gentlemen. When they arrived home would be soon enough to explain she was leaving. After she packed. Perhaps on her way out the front door. She winced. *Such a coward.*

Any words she intended to speak died on her lips the moment she met his formidable gaze. His eyes gleamed almost black in the shadowed confines of the rocking carriage.

"Enough games." His lips barely moved as they formed the words. "Who are you really?"

Chapter Twenty-two

Silence fell between them the moment Owen uttered the question. If possible, her hands tightened even more against the squabs. Even in the shadows he could detect the whitening of her knuckles.

His hands opened and closed at his sides with suppressed fury. He would like nothing more than to turn around and chase after that bastard who had bled all the color from Anna's face and left her trembling across from him in the carriage.

He had never seen her like this before. Even with all his churlish and rough ways, she had never once appeared as she did now . . . *afraid*.

The carriage hit a rut. She reached for the wall to steady herself. "Wh-What do you mean?"

"Damn it, Anna. No more games."

Her eyes widened. The fear was still there, writ all over her round face, but not for him. Not because of him. She was still back there on that street.

She met his gaze directly. The paleness of her cheeks made her eyes even more prominent, the brown bright as a chestnut mare he'd once had as a lad. His father had bought it for him on his eighth birthday. His brothers were jealous, and he had been so proud of that horse. He'd loved and tended her himself. No groom had a hand in it. She had been all his and he doted on her.

He'd wept when she broke a foreleg. He put the creature down himself because his father said that's what a man did. For some reason the memory of that horse as he stared at Anna brought forth a host of uncomfortable emotions. The same helplessness he'd felt as a boy faced with a doomed horse returned to him.

"We've carried this on long enough." Her voice was small and hurried, scarcely filling the space between them. "It's time I leave."

He moved across the carriage and landed beside her on the seat, crowding her. Her eyes flared, the velvety brown melting something inside him.

She inched away, her back bumping the wall

of the carriage, her hand reaching for the strap above her head, as though she needed something to cling to.

"Leave where?" he demanded.

"I can manage on my own."

"Indeed? This time you won't end up half dead on some riverbank."

She gasped. "That's not fair."

"No. It wasn't, but you are so certain that it won't happen again. It almost makes me think you recall what happened . . . if you can be so certain it won't happen again."

She shook her head from side to side. "What do you want from me? I know you never wanted the burden of me. I appreciate everything you've done, but it's time for me to move on."

"Oh. Where will you go? Do you even know? Is there a destination in mind? Have you a plan?"

Her gaze beseeched him. "It doesn't matter, Owen—"

"It matters. It matters to me." His chest lifted high with a ragged breath as they gazed at one another, hearing what it was he wasn't saying—*you* matter to me. At least he assumed she heard it. The realization thundered through him like artillery cannon.

She closed her eyes as if his nearness—or his words—caused her physical pain. He knew not which, but that only infuriated him. Why should she hide from him? Hide and evade and *lie.*

He inched his face closer. So close he could actually smell the soap on her skin, the lemon in her hair. "You can trust me."

The carriage rolled to a hard stop and the door was pulled open before she could respond. If she even intended to.

They sat still, gazing at one another for a heavy moment, sunlight pouring into the carriage from the open door. She slid her gaze away and scooted around him, taking the groom's proffered hand to descend.

He followed her inside, tension knotting his shoulders. Once in the foyer, he seized her hand and led her up the stairs. He evened his pace, still mindful of her leg. She, however, appeared to have no difficulty keeping up with him.

"Where are we going?" she asked.

"Where we can continue our discussion in private."

She stalled outside the door to his bedchamber, taking her bottom lip between her teeth and worrying the flesh. "This is unseemly."

He arched a brow and snorted. "We've been sharing adjoining rooms. Shall you enter through your door and I enter through mine and we meet in the middle?"

She scowled at him but made no objection when he pulled his door open and waved her inside. But when she stepped in, she moved far across the room, a careful distance from him.

He advanced and circled her slowly.

She chafed her arms. "Stop doing that."

"What?"

"Stalking me," she snapped, her eyes flashing.

He stopped and surveyed her with only one thought riding in his mind. "The man today. Who was he?"

She strode to the window, her skirts swishing at her ankles. Presenting him with her back, she peered out the damask drapes.

He studied the rigid set to her spine as she answered him, "Simply some boorish fellow."

He crossed the room and grasped her arm to force her around. "You lie abominably. I suggest you quit altogether and try for the truth. For once."

Her chin lifted. "I haven't lied . . ."

A quiver of something else hung in her voice. Perhaps she hadn't outright lied, but she had not been forthcoming with him. "Evaded. Omitted. It's semantics, Anna."

"It's neither here nor there, Owen." She tried to twist his hand off her arm, to no avail. "I'm leaving, so you needn't feel responsible for me anymore. It's no longer necessary."

He growled, "Woman, you are maddening."

"I should think you would be relieved," she charged, bright splotches of color flaming her cheeks. "I'm ready to continue on with my life and free you of your responsibility."

"And what life is that? The one you suddenly remember? The one that has to do with that bastard we just left?"

Her lips pressed stubbornly shut.

"What are you so afraid of?" he pressed.

That chin flew higher and her eyes burned. "I am not afraid."

He stepped closer. "Sweetheart, everything about you drips fear."

She stilled, her eyes horrified.

"That's not true!" She renewed her efforts to escape his hold, struggling wildly, her words choked and angry. He'd clearly hit a nerve.

With a growl, he flung his hands free of her.

She staggered back.

"Fine. Go. Will you need the funds I promised?" He bit out a laugh. "Of course you do. I wouldn't want you to perish after going through the trouble of nursing you to health. That would be a tragic bit of irony." He dove into his jacket and dangled several notes before her.

She slapped at his hand furiously, her face stricken. "I don't want your money. Keep it."

"Oh, unnecessary, is it? Have you a destination in mind, then? A protector waiting eagerly for your return?"

Something dark and ugly twisted inside him at the notion. He dropped the notes, watching briefly as they fluttered to the floor before his gaze tore back to her. "In any case, they are yours, Anna."

She staggered back several steps, her wild-eyed gaze fastened on him. "You wretch!"

Unable to look at her another moment, not trusting his hands to remain at his sides, he turned and moved to the window that had held her rapt attention only moments before.

Rage and desperation simmered inside him as he sensed her moving away. As her soft tread made for the adjoining door, a sinking sensation came over him.

She was really leaving.

"Good-bye, Anna," he uttered so quietly he was not certain she heard him.

He heard a whisper of fabric, a slight intake of breath, and realized she had not fled the room. In fact, she sounded quite close behind him.

Turning, he caught only a blur of her as she launched herself at him. The instant her curves tumbled into him, he caught hold of her—soft, pliant female overflowing in his arms.

Her hands came up to his face, her palms holding his cheeks as if he were something she must memorize through touch.

Sensation overwhelmed him. Her hands on his face. The abundance of curves against his hardness. The sudden rising of his cock.

He scarcely registered her hoarse whisper. "My name is Annalise."

Chapter Twenty-three

Owen stared down at her intensely. "Your name isn't Anna?"

She shook her head, aware with that single admission she stripped away every barrier between them.

"Annalise," he breathed near her lips, stimulating the already over-sensitive flesh.

The mere sound of her name, at last, on his lips, sent a shiver through her. Her name had never sounded like that. Never so guttural, thick with promises of wicked things that happened in the dark.

His head dipped, almost kissing her, but for some reason she jerked back, arching away. She craved him with her every fiber, but perhaps it was that very thing that frightened her so much. Her need. Her hunger for him.

Nothing had changed with his whisper of her name. Bloodsworth was still out there, the threat of him very real. And not just to her, but to Owen. Her gaze skimmed his face, savoring the square jaw and strong lines. Surrendering to her desire for him would not change the fact that she had to leave.

Her arms relaxed, palms lifting away from the planes of his face.

Just as she was about to take a step back, his arms wrapped tightly around her and hauled her close.

Her cry of surprise was swallowed up by his lips in a kiss that robbed her of the last of her will. With a muffled sob, she wrapped her arms around his neck.

Exhilaration ripped through her when he lifted her off the floor. He held her tightly, bodies pressed flush as his mouth devoured hers. He turned her in a small circle, walking her backward to the bed. Her slippers did not so much as graze the floor as he carried her.

"Aren't you tired of carrying me about?" He had done it enough since they first met. "I can walk, you know."

He released her lips from their feverish kiss.

"Sweetheart, I'm not taking any chances. There's only one place you're headed right now."

A shiver chased over her flesh as his meaning sank in. When he lowered her to the center of the thick mattress, she had no doubt.

She propped herself up on her elbows, watching as he stood at the side of the bed, hurriedly stripping off his jacket, vest, and shirt. All the while his eyes consumed her. Even though she did nothing more than watch him, he stared at her with fiery intent, the promise of everything to come burning sinfully in his eyes.

Whatever qualms he'd held earlier about keeping her at arm's length had fled him. As much as she wanted to know what had happened to change his mind, she dared not ask for fear that he might change his mind back again.

She wanted this—him. Even just once. It would be something she would have to take with her.

His boots hit the floor with a thud, and then he was crawling toward her like some manner of jungle cat—all flexing muscle and sinew. Her mouth dried and watered alternately.

He straddled her with his knees on either side of her hips.

"And you, Annalise, have entirely too much clothes on your person."

She wet her lips and arched her throat, holding his gaze, a deep languor coming over her—with the exception to a low tug in her belly that demanded relief. "Then rectify that matter."

His hand deftly worked the tiny buttons lining the front of her gown. "There are entirely too many of these," he muttered before finally parting her bodice. She lifted up for him as he shoved her gown off her shoulders and pulled it the rest of the way down her hips, leaving her only in her undergarments.

As he focused his attention to the ribbons at the front of her corset, she ran a hand down his chest, reveling in the sensation of bare skin against her palm. A light matting of hair covered the top of his chest, tapering down in a thin, nearly nonexistent ribbon that disappeared inside his breeches.

Her gaze followed, lowering to the definable bulge of his erection. She had felt it earlier, the growing hardness pressing against her belly. As though it were still there, that place between her legs clenched.

Her breath hitched as she imagined him freeing himself from his breeches and putting himself inside her. Nothing about it alarmed her. On the contrary, the throb between her legs grew.

His knuckles skimmed the top flesh of her breasts as he freed her from her corset. Next came her petticoat and drawers . . . all else until she wore only her simple shift and stockings.

At the first touch of his hand on her bare thigh, she gasped.

He pulled his hand back. "Did I hurt you? Your leg . . ."

Shaking her head, she grabbed his wrist and placed his hand back on her thigh. With her eyes locked on his face, she guided his hand up her thigh. Instinct drove her. A desperate urge for him to relieve the ache he had started.

Her lips parted on a sigh as she moved his hand higher, his fingers skimming over the inside of her thigh.

A low growl escaped him. "Your skin is like silk."

She parted her thighs wider. Her shift fell back to her hips and she felt cool air wash over the exposed core of her. Heat fired her face as his gaze followed suit, roaming over that most secret place.

She stopped his hand's ascent, holding him still where her thigh almost met with the very heat of her.

"Annalise."

She shuddered at the sound of her name. Her gaze flew to his.

"Don't stop. Show me where you want me."

Her breath falling short and hard, she nodded.

The ache between her legs was no less intense. Bared before his gaze, it had only deepened. Still holding his wrist, she guided him to her, settling his hand over her heat.

He closed his eyes and brought his forehead to hers. She could feel the very pulse of him there, fused to the core of her. He didn't even move, but the burning imprint of his hand, his palm and fingers against her, made her gasp.

"So wet, Annalise."

She whimpered. Her hips lifted, thrusting against his palm with a will . . . a knowledge that she did not yet understand, even as her body knew, and sought.

He lowered his mouth to hers, whispering the words, "So eager." As his palm moved, burrowed against her in a way that had her arching against him in sudden response, her fingernails dug into his bare shoulders.

"You like that?"

"Again," she choked, nodding furiously.

He rotated his wrist and found the spot, did it again, grinding on her in a way that made her want to fly from her skin.

She cried out and bucked against his hand. "What . . . are you . . . doing?" she panted against his ear.

She had never heard of anything like this happening before. Not with a mere touch. Agathe's and Sally's indiscreet whisperings had never revealed anything so shattering was even possible.

Then suddenly the pressure was gone, his fingers parting her slick folds, sliding shockingly against her with a finger, searching, hunting, at last unerringly finding that tiny pearl of pleasure. Her mouth opened wide on a silent cry as he circled it with his thumb, pushing and rolling until she shuddered in his arms.

His lips pressed against her throat, his words vibrating on her skin, "There, love."

Just as ripples of sensation eased over her and she began to feel satiated, he eased a finger into her channel.

She moaned, arching, fingers digging anew into his shoulders. Everything within her tightened and twisted once again as his fingers stretched her, sinking deeper and deeper.

He burrowed his head in the crook of her neck. "God, Annalise, you're so tight . . . so wet . . . I can't wait."

Wait? She didn't want him to wait. The burn was back, throbbing and tormenting. She wanted it fed.

She let out a small mewl of frustration and slipped her hand between them, caressing him through his breeches, her gaze locking on his. "Then don't wait."

Chapter Twenty-four

With a groan, he brushed her hand aside and freed himself from his trousers. Anticipation coursed through her. He cursed as he kicked them off, leaving her for a moment. Cool air wafted over her, making her shiver.

But then he was back. Every delicious inch of him, silk on steel. The weight of him settled between her legs. It was exciting and a bit frightening, the lean hips, muscled thighs sprinkled lightly with crisp hair chafing at her tender thighs. It was intimate and raw and totally unlike anything she had ever felt.

"Look at my face. I want to watch you."

Her gaze snapped to his eyes, the blue deep and mesmerizing.

His finger stroked beside the corner of her eye, inching up to glide over her eyebrow. "So beautiful."

Heat flamed her face, but she stopped herself from contradicting him. "So are you."

His warm chuckle was his response.

He was unlike anything she had ever known. Even as she squirmed in anticipation, he stared at her as if he were memorizing her, as if he had all the time in the world. He reached down and pulled her shift up her torso and over her head.

"Much better."

She fought to ignore the fact that she was exposed before him with all her imperfections. The way his eyes roamed in appreciation, he didn't find fault in her.

"Now?" she asked shakily. His manhood pressed heavily along the inside of her thigh and it was hard to think of anything else.

"You're nervous." He smiled seductively, his well-carved lips curling slowly.

"I'm not," she protested, but the tremor to her voice betrayed her. She was beyond thought, beyond speech. There was only sensation.

"It's fine . . . we'll relax you again." Leaning down, he pressed his mouth to hers in a wet, open-mouthed kiss. His tongue slid inside to taste her again and again until she was a mass of pudding beneath him. Her bones softened, her muscles liquefying.

She slid her hand around him, down the slope of his back. The sensation of his bare, taut buttock against her palm excited her. His flesh tightened and flexed in her hand, filling her with a heady sense of power. He growled when she squeezed him.

He ground his manhood against her, the long length of him slipping against her wet folds, creating a delicious friction. She panted, thrusting her hips until her sex felt swollen and hot, weeping in need of him.

He still kissed her, but she was now moaning into his mouth, quivering and overcome. When his hand found her breast, she lurched at the contact. He watched her beneath heavy lids as he lowered his head, still smiling that wicked smile even as his mouth parted, descending on her nipple.

She tensed in anticipation as his mouth closed over the tip of her breast. She released a breathy sigh as he pulled her nipple deep into his mouth, the velvet feel of his tongue rasping around the peak in languid strokes. The hot lave sent her over the edge. She was lost, her head writhing against the bed.

"That's it, Annalise."

The sound of her name on his lips was like an elixir. She seized his buttocks in both her hands and lifted her knees.

It was all the invitation he needed.

He lifted his mouth from her breast, and the hard length of him ceased its delicious friction. The head of him found her entrance and his shaft speared her in one deep plunge. She felt impaled.

She screamed, her nails digging into his flesh. He was too much. She couldn't take him.

He cupped her face, holding her gaze. "Annalise, I'm sorry. It will ease. Sssh." He rained kisses over her face. The corner of her lips, her mouth, her cheeks.

He remained lodged within her, the fullness of him becoming less invasive. The sting dulled to a vague burn. He thrust again slowly, carefully, again and again, building friction, stoking that fire back to life.

His pumps grew deeper, but still restrained, tempered. His body trembled over her, his buttocks taut beneath her palms.

He breathed harshly in her ear. "Forgive me, I must move . . ."

His strokes quickened then. She gasped at the sensation. Each one seemed to reach all the way to her womb. His force matched his speed. He slammed into her, his hands sliding under her.

He cupped her derriere in both of his large hands, lifting her, better positioning her for his hard thrusting.

Something tightened inside her again, coiling and squeezing. With no deliberation, her inner muscles clenched and clung to him as he delved deep in the core of her. He groaned, clearly appreciating her efforts. His hands slid into her hair, pulling her face close to his. He burrowed his lips in the crook of her neck, his teeth lightly scoring the flesh.

The entire act stunned her. She made tiny gasping sounds that she couldn't stop if she wished it. It was scandalous and shocking . . . more intimate than anything she had ever imagined. She had never felt so close, so exposed . . . so connected to another person.

She turned her face and pressed several openmouthed kisses to his shoulder. He growled again, catching her mouth up in his again.

He kissed her like he could never have enough. Even as he continued to pump his hips, the hard length of him sliding into her, his lips clung to hers.

She opened her mouth against his in a silent cry as he worked over her, his sleek body so very big, and male, and beautiful. A sharp yelp escaped her as something inside her snapped. Sensation flooded her, rippling to every nerve ending. Her vision blurred. She became incapable of holding up her legs. They slipped down on either side of his hips on the bed as he took one final, shuddering plunge inside her.

He covered her, the weight of him wondrous and not the least bit cumbersome . . . even if her lungs did struggle to expand from the pressure of his significant form.

Apparently, he did not miss the wheeze of her breath. He lifted himself up on his elbows. His eyes gleamed down at her tenderly. "Sorry. Better?" He brushed loose strands back from her forehead.

She nodded, knowing she must look like a besotted fool grinning up at him. "I've never been quite as perfect as I am in this moment."

She felt him pulse inside her, reminding her that he was still lodged there, joining them together. Her cheeks burned at still experiencing him there . . . feeling him so deeply when not in the act of lovemaking. It was somehow more intimate.

His gaze skimmed her, a physical touch. Her face felt hotter as his eyes traveled over her bare breasts. "I'd have to agree that you are pretty perfect right now . . ."

He rolled to the side, sliding from her body and

taking her with him, tucking her against himself. His hand stroked her bare arm. "You were a virgin."

She was relieved he could not see her face, knowing she must be impossibly bright now. "Yes. Are you . . . surprised?"

He didn't answer for some moments, but his fingers continued to draw small, electric circles on her skin, comforting her. "No. I think I knew. Or rather, I suspected."

How? She bit back the question. It would have opened all manner of discussions revolving around who she was and what happened to her leading up to the moment he found her. That was the one subject she needed to avoid with him.

Owen was an honorable man. If she told him about Bloodsworth, he would insist on protecting her. And he couldn't. Not without risking himself. And she wouldn't have that.

"Annalise," he murmured as though testing the sound of her name. "It suits you."

She smiled against his chest, turning her face so that her lips brushed his smooth, warm flesh.

He continued, his voice deep and sober, compelling. "You've been hiding more than your name from me."

Her smile evaporated. "I have." No sense denying what was obvious anymore.

"Will you tell me what happened now?"

Her fingers lightly drummed over his chest. "Yes." She closed her eyes against the lie. "But can we have this for right now? Just a while longer? Must we spoil it so soon with talk of me and my less than savory history?"

"Very well." His circling fingers stilled, his hand settling over her arm, clasping her gently, each finger a warm imprint. "We will have time enough later for full explanations."

Only they wouldn't have time later.

She had to see to that. She had used up the last bit of her time with him. As much as it pained her, she needed to be gone this day—as soon as possible. Before Bloodsworth decided that she wasn't honoring her promise and acted.

He expelled a breath. She tensed, waiting for him to continue interrogating her.

"You're going to be one of those," he said.

"Those what?"

"One of those females who require time to bask in the aftermath of lovemaking."

Her smile returned, relieved at his teasing tone. He was granting her a reprieve. "That's done then, is it?"

"Hm-mm."

"Then I suppose you may relegate me to that category of female . . . although I don't care to think about the long line of females who've basked in the aftermath of your lovemaking." She swatted playfully at his chest. She imagined with his prowess, she was one of several.

His fingers sifted through her hair. "I confess memories of anyone else are rather vague at the moment."

She propped her chin on his chest and gazed into his eyes. The darker ring of blue circling the iris seemed more prominent, almost black. "You don't have to do that."

"What?"

"Say things like . . . that. I know you're experienced . . . that this is simply . . ." Her voice faded away. Her face grew miserably hot.

"This is simply what?" he pressed.

She floundered before settling on a word. "Nice."

He grinned, his arms wrapping around her to gather her closer against him. "You are remarkably adept at the art of the understatement. I think we both know this is more than nice, Annalise."

A shiver chased over her skin. At his deep voice pronouncing her name, still so new to her ears. At his insinuation that he seemed to think *this*—what had just transpired between them—meant something. That it could be more than a simple tryst.

When she knew it could not.

It could not mean anything beyond the moment.

As his breathing deepened, she knew he was falling asleep. His body relaxed beneath her, lethargic and unsuspecting in her arms. A quick glance revealed his eyes had closed.

She felt the pull of sleep as well . . . her muscles soft and satiated. It would be so very easy to fall asleep in his arms.

She sighed and the sound captured all her longing. For a moment she allowed the notion of sleeping the day away with him to tempt her. To dream and ignore, forgetting the specter of Bloodsworth, lured her.

It was an impossible dream. She had never been one to run from reality. She must do the right thing even if that meant leaving this man who had come to mean something to her . . . *everything*. Even if it meant leaving someone who, unbelievable as it seemed, appeared to want her in turn.

Her eyes burned. She blinked them rapidly, hoping to dispel the sting. She'd never had that. She had fooled herself into thinking she would have such a thing with Bloodsworth, but deep in her bones she'd known it wasn't real. He did not want her.

With great care, she lifted Owen's arm from where it draped around her, pausing to look down at him, her heart aching. She watched him for several moments, assuring herself that he well and truly slept, but also memorizing him for the stretch of lonely days ahead.

She pressed her hand to the bed gently and scooted away, careful not to use so much pressure that he would notice the dip in the mattress. Easing from the bed, she stepped down to the floor, keeping a cautious eye on him. Nothing. He slept on, looking more innocent and vulnerable than she had ever seen him. Almost happy. Peaceful. Perhaps it was the lovemaking.

Perhaps it was you. Perhaps you gave him this.

She shoved aside the arrogant thought. Even if it were true, she could not let herself stay and risk him. What kind of woman would that make her? No doubt there were countless women eager to fill his bed. She was no better than any of them. One of them would make him happy and bring him peace and contentment.

One of them would give to him what she could not.

Owen woke to shadows, his head light and surprisingly clear, free from the echoes of nightmares he had long accepted as his penance.

He held himself still, listening, probing deep within himself. Nothing lurked there. He smiled slowly, cautiously grateful for the rare rest he'd been granted.

He did not have to wonder why. Of course it was her doing. Annalise. The female he had wanted to be rid of. The very one he had considered a burden. Astonishingly, she had turned out to be the antidote to all that had ailed him and kept him from peaceful slumber.

Grinning, he shook his head and rubbed his eyes awake. A bit fanciful, he knew. Perhaps not *all*, not everything, but there was no doubt she gave him other things to consider.

His body tightened in anticipation of taking her again, sliding himself into her heat. That would have to wait, of course, until she gave him some answers. Starting with who that bastard had been today to put such fear in her eyes.

The day had turned to dusk. Thin gray light filtered in between the part in the drapes. His arms stretched out beside him, reaching for her. Not finding her, he frowned and lifted his head. She was not in the vast bed.

Assuming she had left him to his sleep, he rose. No doubt she had wanted to bathe and refresh herself. A deep sense of satisfaction spread through his chest. He had introduced her body into the carnal act. His cock hardened at the memory of how sweet she had been.

He rose in one swift motion, his frown returning as his gaze swept over the bedchamber. He did not care for waking to find her gone. The experience left a strange hollowness inside him. A foul taste rose to coat his mouth.

He would have to correct the matter of separate rooms. He wanted her in his room, in his bed—in his life. He couldn't fathom that he had ever wanted or expected her to leave. The man he had been when he first returned home . . . the dead shell that had faced his brother and Paget was a distant thing. He felt alive. As though he had woken from a deep sleep. She had filled the hollow places inside him again. Sensations, emotion, flooded him.

He wanted, *needed,* to be able to reach for her in the middle of the night. To sink into her softness. To feel her thighs wrap around him as her nails scored his skin.

As untried as she was, she had satisfied him like never before . . . like no other. She had dispelled his demons. Her sweet body bewitched him.

Sliding his trousers on, he ignored the twinge of skepticism his thoughts elicited. He sounded like a romantic, and he had never been that. Even before the rebellion, he'd been more practical in nature. He had assumed he would marry Paget because he liked her, loved her even. Not because she burned a fire in his belly. It had never been this for him before.

He fastened his trousers, eager to find her and resume where they left off. He didn't bother donning his shirt. He strode bare-chested to the adjoining door, opening it without a knock. The room was empty. He entered and glanced about before starting for the door leading into the corridor, ready to locate her within the house. However, he paused, the open door of her armoire catching his notice. Scowling, he moved forward and yanked the door wider, revealing . . . nothing inside.

The few garments Mrs. Kirkpatrick had obtained for her were missing. Gone.

His stomach sank, and he knew. Her clothes weren't the only thing missing.

She was gone, too.

Chapter Twenty-five

It was pouring when she arrived at the inn. A boy rushed out to take her valise from the coachman. She knew the hour to be late. Her body ached from sitting long hours on a less than comfortable seat cushion.

Even as wearied as she was from a long day crammed into a coach with other passengers, she hurried to the building in the rain-shrouded night, her feet swift and eager to reach the hulking shape.

She lifted her skirts and avoided the worst of the puddles, but was still quite drenched by the time she entered the taproom.

The innkeeper's wife greeted them, offering them warm, spiced wine and a place before the fire as their rooms were prepared.

Shivering, Annalise stared into the flickering flames and half listened to Mrs. Felham chatting merrily about the cousin she was journeying to see in the North country. She knew quite a great deal about Margaret Penderplast and her solicitor husband (who frequently missed church) and their twins: Rose (with the unfortunate lisp) and John (who terrorized Cook by hiding creepy crawling things throughout the kitchen).

Mr. Felham snored where he sat beside his wife, his head nodding upon his neck—much as he had since they departed Town.

Annalise had met the couple upon boarding the coach. Mrs. Felham declared that a young and unchaperoned lady was clearly in need of her vigilant eye. Annalise didn't object. Especially when the other occupant of their coach, Mr. Snyder, spent a good portion of his time brushing against her. A fact Mrs. Felham noted with a deep frown.

"Mr. Snyder, be so good as to keep your person on your side of the carriage or I will have words with the driver."

Mr. Snyder had glowered at the matron, angry color staining his pock-pitted cheeks. He muttered unintelligible words beneath his breath, but stayed on his side of the carriage. It seemed even busybodies served a purpose.

Last night Annalise had found a room to rent

near the coaching station in Town. Not that she had slept a wink. She was quite certain her eyes were red from a combination of tears and lack of sleep. She was exhausted. Yet she could not stop her thoughts from returning to Owen. What had he thought when he woke to find her gone? He could never know how hard it had been for her to leave him—or that she had done it *for* him.

She had taken the notes he dropped on the floor. The measure felt mercenary, but she could see no other way to leave Town. A necessary sin to keep Owen safe. The funds would see her far from Bloodsworth. She did not have a specific destination in mind. She would simply travel north until she found someplace that *felt* right. Somewhere she could call home, hidden enough so Bloodsworth would never find her.

"Sleep well, my dear," Mrs. Felham trilled as she was led from the room. "We'll see you in the morning."

Annalise could hardly keep her eyes open as she followed the innkeeper's wife upstairs.

She nodded absently as she was shown to a small spartan room with a single bed, chair, and washstand. A narrow window overlooked the yard and washstand. It could have been a broom closet for all she cared. As long as she could be alone and catch a few hours of sleep.

Left alone, she did not bother to undress. She simply removed her boots and fell onto the bed, instantly falling into a dreamless sleep.

Owen rode hard through the night. Heedless of rain and the mud-filled ruts in the winding road. He could think only of Annalise. Of reaching her and holding her. And wringing her neck. He was not certain which urge was strongest.

He would not allow himself to consider that he would never see her again. That she had somehow slipped from his world as suddenly as she dropped into it. His stomach rolled at that unthinkable notion and he dug in his heels.

Of course, tracking her couldn't have been a simple matter. He'd had more luck hunting rebels through inhospitable terrain.

A woman fitting her description had taken a coach last evening heading south to the coast. He had given pursuit, only to catch up with a female several years older and bearing little resemblance to Annalise aside from possessing brown hair. At that point he backtracked to Town and returned to the coaching station, where he learned that another woman of her description had taken a northbound coach earlier that morning. Since she had fled last evening, he had assumed she would catch the first conveyance out of town. His mistake. Apparently she had stayed the night somewhere.

Now he rode with a vengeance, trying to catch up with the northbound coach, hoping she had not gotten off at one of the posting inns along the way and gone in a different direction from there.

If that were the case, her trail was hopelessly lost to him. His only hope was to catch up with the coach that had a half day lead on him. If she wasn't on it, then perhaps someone on it remembered her and even knew where she was headed next.

One thing was for certain.

He would not give up.

Annalise was still groggy from slumber when she woke to a room that had grown much colder than when she first entered it. For some reason, she resisted burrowing deeper into the small bed. An instinctual wariness held her motionless.

It took her a moment to recall where she was in the dark. The room was as black as when she dropped onto the bed earlier in the night. Her body still felt as heavy as stone. Her muscles dead weight.

She held herself still, unmoving, on the bed. And not simply because she was exhausted. Something else kept her immobile.

A voice whispered across her mind. Owen's deep familiar voice counseling her. *Trust your instincts.*

Awareness zipped along her nerves. She listened, tensing. A floorboard creaked to her left and she knew she was right. Her instincts were right. She woke for a reason, and it wasn't simply the cold.

Her limbs tightened in readiness. It was impossibly dark. If she could not see with ease, then neither could the individual who had dared to invade her room.

Her mind raced, calculating what his next move could be. He wouldn't simply grab her. He couldn't clearly see her position on the bed. He would need to reach out and *feel* his way toward her. That was when she would have her chance.

She braced herself, waiting, her heart hammering wildly in her too-tight chest.

And then it came. A slight sinking of the bed to her left.

She took her chance. Shot her fist through the dark and struck him. She was awarded a grunt. Rolling to her right, she sprang to her feet and skirted the bed, determined to reach the door before he regained his wits enough to catch her.

Her fingers closed around the latch the moment a hand seized her, clutching a handful of her dress. "Come on now," he rasped as he yanked her hard enough to send her tumbling into him. She smacked back into his wiry frame with a muffled cry.

"Now don't fight it, love. It will go easier." She instantly recognized the nasal sound of Mr. Snyder's voice in her ear, ruffling her hair. "Nothing personal, but I got to do what I was hired for. That rich bloke paid me well."

Hired. Instantly she knew. "Bloodsworth sent you?"

"Don't know the gent's name. Don't matter. All I need to know is he's going to pay me double when the job is done."

She felt such the fool. Snyder must have followed her when she left the town house.

Bloodsworth had never intended to let her go. She should have known he wouldn't honor his word.

She whirled around and crashed her fist into the side of his head, making contact with his ear.

He howled and she flew back to the door, yanking it open. She plunged into the corridor and ran into a hard wall. A body. Arms came up to close around her.

She cried out, struggling wildly.

"Annalise!"

The sound of her name stilled her. She lifted

wide eyes to the man holding her, then blinked as though her eyes deceived her.

"Owen?"

He couldn't be here. He shouldn't.

He opened his mouth, starting to say something, but his gaze lifted beyond her shoulder.

She followed his gaze, looking behind her at Snyder standing in the threshold, eyeing them both warily.

She opened her mouth to explain but never had the chance.

Snyder slipped his hand inside his jacket and yanked out a knife. A leer took over his pock-pitted face as he brandished the blade in front of him. "I was hoping this wouldn't get messy." He shrugged one shoulder. "No help for that now."

Owen shoved her behind him and launched himself at Bloodsworth's hired man, moving so quickly she hardly registered his movements.

The two men lost themselves in the gaping darkness of her bedchamber. She rushed ahead and peered into the gloom, trying to see what was happening. She heard powerful thwacks and pained grunts.

"Owen!" Her eyes strained for a glimpse of him, praying the knife had not found him. She looked left and right down the corridor, considering pounding a door for help but was also afraid to step away for even a moment . . . as if in that moment he would somehow need her.

Suddenly they quieted. The only sounds that of their ragged breaths.

"Owen?" she whispered, her heart hammering wildly in her chest as she stood silhouetted in the doorway.

A light flared to life within the room. Owen stood over the lamp, only slightly worse for wear, the knife, clean of blood, in his hand.

Snyder was curled into a ball on the floor, clutching his ribs, panting as though he couldn't catch his breath.

She stepped inside the room, her gaze returning to Owen. "Are you hurt?"

He shook his head.

"How did you find me?"

He slid the back of his hand against his bottom lip, wiping the thin ribbon of blood clean. "You forget. There was a time when I hunted people. I was particularly good at it."

She nodded, a lump forming in her throat. "Of course." Of course, indeed. How foolish of her.

Steps sounded in the hall. Mr. Felham appeared in a dressing robe, his wife peering over his shoulder, clutching his arm with both hands.

"Oh!" she sputtered when she took in the scene. Her wild-eyed gaze landed on Snyder. "Oh, that wretch! I knew he was up to no good, sniffing about you. Are you injured, dear?"

Before Annalise could answer, Mrs. Felham's gaze swung to Owen. "Who is this man?" Her eyes narrowed distrustfully. "Mr. Felham, send for the constable at once!"

"Mrs. Felham, he's a friend! He came to my assistance."

Mrs. Felham sniffed, mollified.

"I shall alert the innkeeper to send for a constable." Mr. Felham nodded in Snyder's direction. "Come, Mrs. Felham. I think the young lady is quite safe now." He nodded at Owen before guiding his wife from the room.

Safe. The word echoed hollowly through her. She would never be safe. Not as long as she was married to the Duke of Bloodsworth and he preferred her dead.

The couple shuffled off down the hall. She stared after them for a moment before looking back at Owen, stark resignation filling her heart.

Just the sight of him made her ache. All the feelings were still there. Stronger. Leaving, saying good-bye in her mind, hadn't put him away from her thoughts . . . her heart. He was there, etched indelibly into her soul.

Regret consumed her that she had ever met him. That her heart had even known what it was like to be held and kissed and loved by someone so extraordinary. Someone who could make her shiver with a look. Whose touch could reduce her to a quivering, breathless, boneless mass.

No. She had to have something. Had to know passion, love. She deserved that, at least, didn't she? Her life shouldn't have all been longing. Longing with no actual satisfaction. At least she'd tasted desire, even if only fleetingly.

Owen motioned to Snyder, who was trying to rise. He failed, crumpling back into his pathetic ball. "What is this?" he asked her.

She struggled to swallow the lump, knowing she couldn't hide the truth from him anymore. She wouldn't pretend ignorance. "I woke to him in the room . . ." She stopped, the thickness in her throat getting the better of her. And there was the realization that the truth meant explaining to him why this man had been there, and who had sent him.

Owen's face drained of all color. He was before her in two strides, his hands on her arms, then sliding up to frame her face. "What did he do to you?"

She shook his head.

"Did he hurt you?"

"No. I escaped into the hall and collided with you before he could."

Some of the color returned to his face, but something else remained there. A muscle feathered the flesh of his cheek, and she knew his control was hard-won. He looked down at Snyder like he wanted to return to him and hurt him all over again.

"Owen," she said, turning his face back to her.

His eyes narrowed, focusing on her with an intensity that practically burned. "Why did you leave?"

To keep us safe. *To keep you safe.*

She inhaled deeply. "I'll go back to Town with you."

There was no reason to keep running now. Bloodsworth would scour the country until he found her and made certain she was dead. She couldn't run from him. She saw that now. Snyder might not be the only one he even sent after her. There would be more. Others to come. She knew it. She inhaled thinly through her nose.

And another realization hit her. Hard and ugly. She bit her lip until she tasted the coppery tang of blood.

As long as she ran, she hadn't changed. She was the same broken girl who had washed ashore. The girl she had vowed to never be again.

Owen lifted his hand and brushed her lips gently, his fingers coaxing her to ease her bite. His expression intense, he studied her like she was some manner of riddle he must solve. "What are you doing?" he murmured with a slight shake of his head, and she knew he meant more than hurting herself. He meant everything. All her secrets and half-truths. Giving herself to him and then disappearing into the night.

"I'll tell you everything."

He smiled crookedly, ruefully—still so handsome that her heart ached—and she knew he did not quite believe her.

She would go back to Town with him. She would tell him everything. Every ugly truth. Starting with the fact that she was another man's wife.

And then she would do the only thing she could to keep Owen safe—and possibly even herself, too. Although keeping Owen safe took precedence. She had dragged him into danger. She would see him out of it. He might have been able to handle Snyder tonight, but Bloodsworth was evil. He was capable of anything.

Her eyes suddenly blurred. She blinked the burning sensation back and stared at Owen as though her world were not ending.

As if she would not be returning to her husband.

Chapter Twenty-six

Owen watched her sleep as they traversed through the streets of London. She listed to the side, her cheek pushed against the carriage wall, her lips parted slightly as she breathed deeply.

She'd fallen asleep almost instantly. By the time he'd finished overseeing the securing of his mount to the back of the carriage and joined her inside, she was fast asleep. Explanations could wait. They had waited this long. He'd let her rest.

The carriage stopped and he opened the door before any of the grooms could reach it. Turning, he reached inside for her and settled her in his arms. She murmured unintelligible words and burrowed into his arms. Her hair fell loose over his hand, the tendrils soft and silky.

Dawn suffused the sky with gentle shades of pink and orange, washing out the lingering gray of twilight as he carried her up the steps of his town house.

Mrs. Kirkpatrick emerged, poised to greet them. He shook his head at her, indicating for her to hold silent and not wake Annalise. She stepped aside for him.

He took the steps two at a time. Once in his bed-chamber, he kicked the door shut softly behind them. He lowered her to his bed and carefully slipped off her cloak. Next came her boots.

Finished, he took two steps back and watched her, mesmerized at the unguarded view of her. She sighed and curled onto her side, her hand slipping beneath her cheek. She looked so innocent. Sweet and peaceful and beautiful in his bed. He never wanted her to leave. He wanted her in his bed every night.

He glanced over his shoulder to the door. It was morning. There were things he needed to do, but weariness tugged at him. He couldn't recall the last time he had slept.

Bending down, he tugged off his boots. Next came his cravat and jacket. He eased down on the bed beside her, studying her as she slept, appreciating the dark fan of her eyelashes on her creamy cheeks. He knew when she woke she was going to tell him what had scared her into running away, but that didn't scare him.

He closed a hand over the one that lay limply between them.

He laced his fingers with her slighter ones. Even smaller than his, the fit was so right. *Perfect.*

He marveled at the tightness in his chest, the warmth that pervaded him just staring at her. She did this to him. No one or nothing else had since he'd left home for India over four years ago. He wasn't going to lose this feeling again.

He wasn't going to lose her.

When he woke, it was hours later. A thin thread of light glowed from around the edges of the damask drapes. He quickly glanced to his side, almost as though he feared she had left him again.

But she was still here. His breathing instantly eased.

She'd moved onto her back. One arm was flung above her head, the other stretched out to her side. She slept like she did not have a care in the world. He smiled.

She sighed and her breasts pushed enticingly against her bodice. The slight stiffness of his cock became an insistent throb. Rolling to his side, he ran a finger along her jaw, savoring the skin that he knew to be soft.

His hand moved, drifting unerringly to the hem of her dress, which had risen to her knees in sleep. He tugged it upward, meeting her stocking-clad knee. He teased the inside of her knee there.

She released a small breathy sigh and parted her legs wider in unspoken invitation. He sat up, watching her face closely as his fingers moved along the inside of her thigh toward the slit in her drawers.

Her features loosened, her lips parting in a low moan as he cupped his hand over the very core of her. The heat of her filled his palm. She thrust her pelvis, pushing herself into his touch.

He eased a finger inside her, reveling in the sweet warmth of her surrounding him, tightening around him. He ached at the thought of his cock there, buried in her.

Her fingers clenched the counterpane and her spine arched off the bed, her legs widening even farther.

Her eyes fluttered open, glazed with a desire that fed his own, stoking the fires low in his gut. The rich brown gleamed like pools of dark chocolate. He came over her to lose himself in her eyes as his fingers plied her soft folds, adding another finger to plunge in and out of her slick heat.

"Owen," she breathed, her hands coming up to grip his shoulders.

"Annalise," he rasped a beat before he kissed her. She tasted of lemons and that indescribable taste that was hers alone. Her fingers dug into his shoulders as his tongue parried with hers.

He groaned, his hand moving for his breeches, never breaking their kiss as he anxiously freed himself. She cried out against his mouth as he drove into her. She lifted her legs to take him in deeper.

He slid his hands to cup the rounded swell of her bottom, holding her for his penetrating thrusts. She quivered beneath him and he knew she was close.

"Come, follow me, sweetheart," he encouraged, not wishing to reach his climax before she achieved her own.

Her head came off the bed, her hair wild and dark all around her. Just as her eyes. So very deep and dark, they pulled at him and spoke to his very soul.

He reached between them, finding her pleasure spot, the tiny sensitive nub buried in her woman's folds. She whimpered at his first touch. He pressed harder, rolling the sweet, little pearl as he drove into her.

Her arms came around him, her mouth open and arousing as hell against his neck as she released a sharp cry.

He groaned, spilling himself deep inside her. He collapsed over her, satisfied in a way he had never felt before.

"I'm crushing you," he muttered, pushing himself up on his elbows on either side of her.

"I don't mind," she whispered, her hands coming up to frame his face, holding him, pinning him with her mesmerizing eyes.

"Annalise?" He smiled down at her, feeling that familiar tightness in his chest.

She held his gaze. A curtain fell over her eyes. Something he couldn't decipher.

Wariness filled him. He started to pull away, but her hands tightened on his face.

"I—" Her voice broke suddenly, and that stark emotion in her eyes . . .

He suddenly understood it. She was afraid.

"What, Annalise?"

"I'm married."

Everything inside him froze, revolted. She wasn't married. She couldn't be.

"No." The word dropped like a stone between them. "You were a virgin—"

"The marriage wasn't consummated," she was quick to reply.

"Obviously," he growled, her words sinking in. A dark terrible fury rose up in him. He climbed off her and dropped down on the bed beside her.

She rose to her knees, smoothing her rumpled skirts down. "Owen, please . . ."

"When were you going to tell me this, Annalise?"

She's not yours. She can never be yours. It was the only thought that rushed through him. Dark and clawing and deep.

She shook her head, and offered up the lame excuse, "I don't want him . . . If I could go back and undo it . . ."

"But you can't," he said harshly, as much to remind her as to confirm it for himself.

Moisture gleamed in her eyes. "You are right. I can't go back and unmarry him. I can't change how naive and trusting I was. So desperate for love and approval that I could believe a man wanted me for more than my immense dowry."

He had wanted her. Owen blinked hard, demanding, "Is that your plan, then? Commit adultery so that he will grant you a divorce?"

"What? No." She shook her head, looking genuinely surprised. "Nothing about this, about us, has been a manipulation. You are the only thing real, the only good thing that I have ever had."

He snorted. "Nothing you say can be trusted." Bile rose up inside his throat as the knowledge sank in that she was not free to be with him. She belonged to another. He forced the foul taste back down and turned, walking a hard line across the room.

"There's more . . ."

"More?" He stopped and released a harsh, ugly laugh.

She nodded. "I'm the Duchess of Bloodsworth." He watched her throat work. "He was the man you saw me with on the street."

He closed his eyes in a hard blink, opening them to look at her, perhaps seeing her for the first time. He didn't know her at all.

"The Duke of Bloodsworth? And yet he permitted you to leave with me?" The bile was back. "What game are you two playing at?" He shook his head, swallowing down the bitter taste. Coldness washed over him, numbness. "You certainly lowered your standards to let me in your bed."

"No. Don't say that." She shook her head, her eyes enormous and pleading, almost reminding him of a child. Since the start, he knew she was hiding something, but he had not imagined this.

He had not imagined she was hiding the one thing that would keep her from ever being his.

Turning, he strode from the room.

"Owen!"

He continued down the corridor, the sound of his name on her lips like a knife to his back.

Chapter Twenty-seven

Annalise watched him go, a burning sob rising in her throat. She brought her knees to her chest and covered her mouth with both hands as if she could stop the sound from spilling out. She rolled to her side and buried her face in the bed. A mistake. His scent was everywhere.

Tears rolled hotly down her cheeks unchecked, their salty taste finding a way beneath her hands to her lips. She couldn't help herself. She turned her face into the bed and breathed him in, desperate to memorize this last smell of him.

It was better this way. Better that she hadn't told him everything. He'd been too shocked to press her for more details. She had seen that in his face. Perhaps he would hate her now. Hate her and put her from his mind.

If he knew all of it, that Bloodsworth had tried to kill her . . . that he was the one responsible for sending Snyder after her, he would be duty-bound to keep her safe. Again. His honor would demand it. He'd never let her return to her husband. But now he would.

She was another man's wife. She had kept that all-important fact from him and that's all he could see at the moment.

Fighting back tears, she pushed up from the bed. She moved mechanically, changing clothes, using the basin of water to clean herself. She splashed water again and again on her face, as if that would somehow wash away the pain.

Staring at herself in the looking glass, water dripping from her chin and nose, she marveled at how different she looked from the girl who had wed Bloodsworth months ago. No longer so frightened. There was strength in the lines of her face. Resolve in her brown eyes. She would not return to her husband as the vulnerable girl he had tossed into the water and left for dead.

Dressed in fresh clothes, she moved toward the vanity. Sinking down on a stool, she tidied her hair, sweeping the brown mass into a simple knot.

This time she wouldn't bring anything with

her. The clothes she had here didn't belong to her. Nothing here belonged to her. Claiming her cloak from where Owen tossed it to the floor, she swept it around her and departed the room.

The door to the library was cracked and she heard the clink of a glass inside. She paused outside of it, envisioning Owen sipping from a glass of brandy. She longed to go to him, but the memory of his face, so stricken and horrified when she told him she was married, gave her pause. This was better. No need for him to glimpse her face. He might see the truth.

She loved him.

Totally. Completely. Unapologetically.

She could go to Bloodsworth because of him. Because she knew love. Her love for him made her stronger. Better. Strong enough to confront Bloodsworth. Strong enough to stop hiding. Especially since doing so would keep Owen safe. The risk would be hers alone. As it should be. She alone would confront her husband. Looking away, she hurried past the library door.

On the bottom floor one of the grooms stepped forward to intercept her as she opened the front door. "Miss Anna? Do you need the carriage brought around?"

She hesitated only a moment. "Yes, please."

Why not? It was no secret she was going . . . and no secret *where.*

In moments she was moving across Town. The streets were crowded with conveyances—members of the *ton* out for an evening of diversion. By the time she reached the duke's Mayfair residence, dusk had fallen. The house was ablaze with lights, and she surmised her husband was entertaining for the night.

She didn't knock.

One should not knock at the door of her own home, after all. A groom turned, startled, as she entered the vast foyer.

"See here—" he began.

She held up a hand, angling her chin just so. "Do you not recognize me?"

Even before their nuptials, she had visited the house countless times.

The servant frowned, scrutinizing her. Then he gaped, recognition lighting his face. "Miss Hadley? I m-mean, Your Grace?"

"Where's my husband?"

The groom motioned vaguely. "He's in the dining room. He and his guests only just sat down."

She nodded. "Very good. Thank you."

"Shall I escort you, You Grace?"

"I know the way." She walked past him with sure strides straight into the proverbial lion's den.

She has left again. I thought you should like to know, my lord."

Owen looked up from his glass of brandy. "Thank you for that report, Mrs. Kirkpatrick." He did not even bother to keep the withering sarcasm from his tone. He was in a foul mood and she approached him at her own peril.

"Edmond drove her to the Duke of Bloodsworth residence in Mayfair," the housekeeper added, unfazed as she stared at him with such expectation. As if she was waiting for him to rise and *do* something. Go after her, he supposed.

"Again, thank you, Mrs. Kirkpatrick. That will be all."

Pursing her lips, she nodded and swept back out of his library.

He finished his brandy in one long swallow. Annalise had wasted little time returning to her husband. As was right, he grudgingly acknowledged. She belonged to Bloodsworth. Standing, he sent his glass crashing into the wall. It exploded into a thousand pieces.

She should be with her husband. The man who had wed her before God. Who had lost her . . .

and let her end up broken along the shore of a river.

And now Annalise was back in his hands. *Bloody hell. No. No, she was not.*

Not if he had anything to say about it.

Charging from the room, he stormed out of the house, suddenly not caring what was right or wrong. He only knew she belonged with him.

Chapter Twenty-eight

The voices grew louder as she approached the dining room. She knew before she pushed the door open that he was entertaining a large group. Splendid. She couldn't have hoped for a better scenario. There would be several witnesses And not just *any* witnesses. His friends. Peerage. He could not be rid of her so easily again.

Stepping inside the narrow wood-paneled room, no one noticed her at first. She was able to observe Bloodsworth with his two dozen guests undetected. Candlelight played over the ladies in their shining jewels and fine satins and brocades. Even the gentlemen were resplendent in their rich jackets and colorful cravats.

She recognized many of them. They had attended her wedding. The duke sat at the head of the table. She watched with a detached sense of bemusement as he chatted with Joanna, seated to his left. The quintessential English rose with her corn silk ringlets bouncing on either side of her head. She giggled at something Bloodsworth said. Her rosy pink lips curved in the most delighted of smiles.

Dimly, Annalise recalled that he had been charming. Attentive and kind. Now Joanna was the recipient of his attentions. How ecstatic she must be to have finally won him.

One by one gazes drifted her way. The Marchioness of Ridgefield's gaze landed on her and she screamed, dropping a spoon into her bowl with a resounding clatter. She fell against the back of her chair in a near swoon. Her husband quickly grasped her shoulder to keep her from falling to the floor.

The duke swiveled around in his seat.

Everyone stared at her now. A hush fell over the room.

Her husband pushed to his feet, his eyes wide. His lips worked and she knew he did not know what to say. He did not know what *she* would say. What aspersions she might cast upon him.

His shock filled her with immense satisfaction. She felt in utter control of the moment—of *him*. It was a heady thing.

He had not expected for her to stroll back into his world. He thought he had effectively silenced her. Terrified her into running until one of his underlings caught up with her and finished what he had started on their wedding night.

"Annalise!" Joanna cried, rising to her feet. She stepped closer to Bloodsworth, her lovely blue gaze full of panic. She reached for his arm, her fingers grasping the cuff of his jacket as if desperate to maintain some form of contact with him.

The duke lightly shook her hand off, casting her a rather helpless look. "Joanna . . ."

Ah. She recalled Bloodsworth mentioned he had plans in the works. Apparently those plans had involved Joanna. Plans her return had just thwarted.

The duke returned his gaze to her. Only she could see the venom in his eyes as he proclaimed, "Annalise, you're alive! My prayers have been answered."

To her credit, she did not laugh. With a brittle smile, she replied, "As have mine."

She managed not to cringe as he stepped forward to press a kiss to her cheek. His hands held her shoulders. Only she felt the dig of his fingers bruise her through her cloak. Stepping back, he demanded, "But where have you been?"

"A kind farmer and his family took me in. I must have slipped and fell over the boat—"

"Just as everyone suspected," Bloodsworth declared a bit too loudly. "The wedding champagne had been flowing too freely that night, I fear." He cupped her cheek. "Dear girl, you were quite unaccustomed to such revelry."

"Indeed, I could not remember myself at first." She brushed her head. "I injured my head."

The duke's eyes locked with hers as understanding passed between them. She was not denouncing him as a murderer. At least not yet.

Bloodsworth was all action then, making his apologizes to his guests as he ushered her toward the door, eager, presumably, to be alone with his long-lost bride.

"Forgive me. I'm sure my wife is quite spent."

Everyone murmured understanding remarks, even as their eyes told a different tale. They would all long to hear more of Annalise's misfortunes.

Only Joanna stood silent, her face varying shades of green. Her father strode forward and seized Bloodsworth's arm, demanding, "My lord, what of us? My daughter—"

The duke clapped him once on the shoulder. "Please. You are my guests. We shall discuss matters in the morning."

The older gentleman sniffed, clearly still affronted. He turned his gaze on Annalise, raking her scornfully, obviously annoyed that she had the presumption to be alive.

"Come," Bloodsworth cajoled. "Do not leave, my friend. You and your daughter have my highest regard."

A long moment passed before Joanna's father nodded.

"Very good." Nodding in satisfaction, the duke led her from the dining room. The instant they cleared the room, his hand on her arm became hard and bruising.

"Quite a spectacle, wife. I did not even credit you with such stupidity."

"Truly? I think me ingenious."

"And how do you imagine that?" His feet pounded out his ire as he dragged her up the stairs with him.

"You cannot kill me again after I've very publicly returned from the dead, now can you?"

"I'm the Duke of Bloodsworth. I can do whatever I bloody hell want." He thrust her ahead of him into a bedchamber. She nearly lost her footing from the force of his shove.

She rounded to face him, bracing herself to again be alone with a man who wanted her dead.

He shut the door after them and advanced on her. She held her ground.

"You should have kept your word and disappeared—"

"As you kept your word? You hired someone to kill me."

One side of his mouth twisted. "He failed, I see. I suppose if you want something done properly, you best see to it yourself." He brought a hand to her neck. His fingers gently circled her throat, grazing lightly, making her skin crawl.

"Only you did try to do it yourself. And you failed, too."

The flesh near his eye jumped at her taunting reminder. The only sign that she had annoyed him. "What of your lover?" he asked, the hand still on her neck. "He seemed a rather possessive sort."

Her chest tightened at the mention of Owen. "He tired of me," she lied, hoping he believed her. She needed him to forget about Owen.

He angled his head, considering her. His hand skimmed down her neck, flattening over her heart. "Indeed? A shame he took what was rightfully mine."

Revulsion swamped her. She lifted her chin defiantly. "The opportunity for that has passed, Your Grace."

He laughed bitterly. "True. Even assuming I could stomach staying married to you . . ." He surveyed her. "You're still a lowborn bastard."

"So let us rectify matters." Her gaze narrowed on him. "*Without* killing me."

He laughed. "I confess I find you much more intriguing. You aren't quite the dull object I married months ago. And your looks are much improved."

"I'm suggesting a divorce," she snapped, recalling Owen's earlier words.

"Impossible. We haven't grounds for divorce—"

"Adultery."

He blinked. Lifting the back of his hand to his mouth, he laughed.

She had surprised him. She angled her head and pushed her advantage. "That would qualify as grounds for divorce, would it not? *And* the shame would be mine." She held her breath, waiting.

He considered her for a long moment, no doubt contemplating that a divorce on the grounds of adultery would place the shame on her and make him the sympathetic party. She did not care one whit for her reputation as long as she was free of him.

"There would still be a scandal." He tsked his tongue. "Much too ugly. It would ruin my chances with Joanna."

Annalise cocked her head. "Joanna has always been enamored of you. She would overlook it."

"I'm not concerned with her. The chit is thoroughly mine . . . of that I have no doubt. Her father is quite another story."

"Agree to a divorce or I shall walk out of this room and announce to everyone that you tried to kill me. That would likely cause a greater stir and send Lady Joanna's father running."

His hand was suddenly at her neck again, tightening around her throat. "You dare threaten me, you little bitch. I'm the Duke of Bloodsworth. What are you but a lowborn upstart? Any tale you spin will be discounted."

"Oh, but the gossip," she wheezed. "How you should hate that." She scratched at his hand until he eased his grip.

He pushed his face close to hers. Spittle flew onto her cheek. "You think yourself so clever?"

"It's a question of which scandal you prefer. At least a divorce gets you rid of me."

His face twisted into something feral and desperate. Eyes glittering with a malice that sent a bolt of fear down her spine, he pressed closer, his cheek brushing against hers. "I think I shall keep you. There's pleasure to be had in torturing you for all the trouble you've caused."

She went cold and felt the blood leech from her face.

His voice slithered around her. "I might not

be able to kill you, but there are fates worse than death, you know. Abuse and punishments. Shall I show you?"

She didn't have a chance to react.

He forced her back until she collided with the bed. He shoved her down and straddled her. It was all horrifically familiar. She scratched fiercely at his hand. Her breath escaped in hard, desperate pants as her nails scored him, but it was as though he didn't even feel her.

He looked down at her, his lips curling back from his handsome face. "Go ahead. I like the fight."

From the flare of his nostrils, she knew he spoke the truth. He wanted her resisting him.

But she couldn't simply surrender. She saw Owen's face in her mind. Tears burned her eyes. He would want her to fight. She couldn't *not* fight.

With a choked sob, she struck him across the face. The sharp crack rang out in the room.

He grabbed both her wrists, securing them and pinning them above her head with one hand. His other hand caressed her face, drifting down her throat. Reaching her breast, he fondled her roughly through her gown.

She snarled and snapped her teeth at him. He jerked his face aside, chuckling. "No worry. I shan't leave a mark on you. At least not where anyone can see. There will be no talk. You shall look quite presentable in the morning."

He lifted the hand from her breast for the barest moment before his knuckles crashed into her side.

She cried out, the air expelling from her lungs in a great, pained whoosh.

He grabbed the front of her gown and yanked. The rip of her dress was an ugly and obscene sound on the air. His eyes glittered wildly down at her, his lips curved in a cruel smile as he fumbled at her skirts.

Dazed from the blow to her ribs, she struggled to recover . . . to move, to fight. She kicked, thrashing her legs. It did no good.

He wedged himself between her thighs. His hand slid up her stocking-clad thigh and his breath came harder, faster, in her ear. "You feel good, Annalise."

"No," she growled, wrenching her hand free. This would *not* happen to her. She clawed his face, grunting in satisfaction at the bloody scratches welling on his cheek.

He laughed, his eyes wild, and that's when she knew he was truly unhinged. It would take more than her fingernails to his face. She slammed the base of her palm into his nose. He howled, blood spurting, showering her. His hands flew to his nose.

She squirmed out from under him. On her feet, she turned for the door, stopping when she came face-to-face with Joanna.

The girl looked from Annalise to the duke, her eyes taking in everything. "Bloodsworth!"

He whirled around at the sound of his name.

"What are you doing?" she demanded.

He stumbled up from the bed, hands still pressed to his bleeding nose. "Joanna, darling. What are you doing in here?"

Joanna pointed at her. Annalise attempted to cover herself, but her gown hung in tatters in front of her. She gave up and clutched at the bedpost.

"You told me you never wanted her . . . that you had to marry her."

"I did." Bloodsworth waved his blood-smeared hands soothingly. "What are you doing here? We'll talk in the morning."

"I came to hear for myself that this will change nothing between us." Suddenly, one of Joanna's hands flew up from the voluminous folds of her gown. She clasped a revolver that looked absurdly large in her small hand. She aimed it somewhere in the vicinity of Bloodsworth.

He jumped back. "Gor, Joanna, watch where you're pointing! Where did you get that?"

She set her chin at a petulant angle. "It's Papa's."

Annalise tucked herself behind the bedpost as

if that might protect her from a stray ball. Clearly these two were perfect for each other.

"Put that thing down. Nothing has changed between us. I still love you," he assured her, waving his hands and eyeing the revolver nervously.

"I don't believe you," she cried, jabbing the weapon in the air at him. "Why is her gown ripped?" Tears spilled down her cheeks. "I thought you loved me! How could you even touch her?"

Annalise cringed, waiting for the crack of the revolver.

Bloodsworth backed up several steps. "Joanna, my love! What are you doing?"

She panted, her breath falling hard and fast. "I'm not going to let her ruin this." She then swung the revolver on Annalise. "Why did you not just stay dead, you stupid cow? He doesn't love you. He never loved you!"

Panic surged inside her as she stared down the barrel, trying to shrink behind the post. Was this it, then? How she would die?

She moistened her lips and spoke quickly, her words a jumbled rush. "Wait. If you shoot me, you won't have him. The house is full of people. They will swarm in here the moment you fire. Think, Joanna. What will happen to you then? Don't let him ruin your life."

Joanna charged forward another few steps. "You are the one ruining everything!"

Annalise risked a glance at her husband. He had ceased to back away. In fact, he inched closer to Joanna, a slow smile forming on his face. Of course. If Joanna killed her, it would be the end of all his problems. The end to her.

He crooned so low, Annalise had to strain to hear him, "If she were gone, then I would be free to marry."

"He'll be free to marry," she said, "but it won't be to you. You'll be in prison!"

Uncertainty flickered across Joanna's face. The revolver wobbled, lowering a fraction in her hand. A sob spilled from her lips. "I don't know what I'm doing . . ."

Annalise's shoulders sagged in relief, now that the revolver was no longer pointing at her.

The door burst open then, and Owen stood there, legs braced, shoulders squared.

Her heart leapt to her throat. She released her clutch on the bedpost and stepped forward. "Owen . . ." His name trembled from her lips. His presence both thrilled and frightened her. He shouldn't be here. And yet he was.

Another man's wife or not, he'd come for her.

Dimly, she noticed one of the grooms in the doorway behind him, clutching a bloodied nose to match Bloodsworth's. It did not require much imagination to deduce who was responsible for that.

Owen's gaze swept over the bedchamber, missing nothing. Including her state of dishabille. His eyes scoured her, taking in her mussed hair and ripped gown.

Something flashed in his eyes then. A rage she had never seen. Especially from him. He'd always been so in control of himself. So calm and steady. Hot color burned his swarthy cheeks.

His gaze shot to Bloodsworth, and a moment later he launched himself across the room at the duke. They tumbled to the floor, rolling and crashing into a small side table. Glass shattered.

Joanna yelped and danced out of the way, brandishing the revolver in a wide arc. It was a wonder the thing didn't go off.

Owen's arms sawed through the air. His shoulders pulled powerfully at his jacket as his fists met the duke's face with loud, crunching smacks.

"Stop! Stop it!" Joanna screeched, wildly waving the revolver.

"Shoot him!" the duke bellowed, angling his face away from Owen's brutal punches to get the words out.

Joanna pointed the revolver at the men.

"Joanna, no!" Annalise dove forward, arm stretched out.

A loud shot cracked the air.

The smell of smoke stung her nostrils as she froze, staring at the two men. Blood spattered Owen's face and chest.

She flung a hand over her mouth to stifle her scream. Her legs wobbled, ready to give out beneath her.

"Owen?" she croaked. The blood rushed to her head, filling her ears with a numbing roar.

His wide gaze locked with hers. He shook his head as if he did not quite know what had happened.

Action fired her limbs, carrying her to his side. If he was hurt, he'd need assistance immediately. There was no time for her to gawk and wring her hands. "Did she shoot you?"

"No . . . It's not my blood." He glanced down at himself, patting his blood-soaked front as if verifying his own words.

She released the breath she had been holding.

Joanna began to scream then. A shrill screech that reverberated off the walls. She dropped to her knees beside Bloodsworth, the revolver thudding to the floor. She rolled him from his side to his back, which was when Annalise saw the nasty wound in the side of his head.

She averted her eyes, her stomach churning.

Owen quickly pulled her away. They rose to their feet, giving Joanna and the body a wide berth.

The groom in the doorway rushed closer to see and made an odd bleating sound before racing back out of the room.

"He's dead," Annalise muttered numbly, shaking her head in disbelief. Bloodsworth was a wretch who had tried to murder her, but she didn't relish the sight of his corpse.

Joanna's screams quieted, turning into a low, keening wail. Her hands pounded at the duke as if she could somehow revive him with the force of her fists.

Then everything blurred as people flooded into the room. Joanna's father barreled in and swept her into his hold. The watch arrived, no doubt fetched by the zealous groom. Soon more uniformed men from the local constabulary arrived. Joanna's cries only grew louder as she was led away.

Annalise was ushered from the chamber after answering a series of questions, leaving Owen behind. A quick glance revealed him in deep conversation with one of the constabulary.

The butler led Annalise belowstairs into the vast library. She fidgeted anxiously. Her hands shook so badly she sat on them in attempt to still them. Owen soon joined her. He had changed from his bloodstained clothing. Dressed in a shirt that fit him too tightly, he sat beside her on the settee.

He tugged her hands free and folded them into his own. He chafed them gently, his dark eyes peering at her intently. "Annalise? Are you . . . are you well?"

She nodded jerkily.

His gaze skimmed over her. A blanket hid the evidence of her ripped, bloodied gown, but he'd seen that earlier. He hadn't forgotten. "Are you hurt?"

She shook her head as she glanced down. "I stopped him before he could hurt me. The blood is his, not mine."

A slow smile spread across his face. "You did that to his nose?"

She nodded.

"You're amazing." He brushed his lips close to her ear, his hands chafing warmth back into her fingers. His smile faded. Cold realization settled into the dark blue of his eyes. "He was the one. He hurt you. He put you in that river."

"Yes."

"And you went back to him?"

"He would have hurt you. That's what he threatened to do the day I saw him in Town."

Sighing, he ran a hand through his hair, sending the dark blond strands flying in every direction. He leveled a tormented stare on her. "You were looking out for me?"

She moistened her lips. "Yes."

"Don't—you shouldn't—" He stopped and closed his eyes in a long blink. He inched his face closer to hers, his voice a rough whisper as he said, "My life is not worth more than yours."

"I could not let anything happen to you."

He threw back his head, gazing unseeingly at the ceiling. His hands clenched around her still trembling ones. "Of course, you did not consider that it would destroy me if I lost you."

At this announcement, her hands only shook more. She sucked in a breath that felt too raw and sharp going down.

After a moment he returned his gaze to her face. "You're safe now, Annalise. You're free."

Her gaze held his, those words rattling inside her head. *Free.*

"She'll be fine once we get her some warm tea and up to bed," the housekeeper volunteered, intruding on their little exchange.

Annalise's gaze snapped to the housekeeper. She glanced around the vast library. This was Bloodsworth's home. Not hers. She had no desire to stay another moment beneath this roof. "I'm not sleeping here," she announced. "In this house." The very idea made her shiver.

Owen brushed a tendril of hair back from her cheek. It was tender, but she inadvertently flinched. He frowned and pulled back, his eyes flickering over her. There was something unreadable in his gaze.

A great commotion outside the library drew her attention. Jack Hadley burst inside the room. Someone must have sent for him. She rose unsteadily to her feet, uncertain.

His gaze landed on her, his eyes wide and so like her own. Beyond him stood Marguerite and her husband.

"Annalise," her father choked.

Marguerite rushed past him to embrace her. "We thought you were dead."

Guilt stabbed at her. She had dismissed returning to her family after Bloodsworth tried to murder her. Jack had neglected her all her life until a year ago, and as fond as she was of her sisters, she saw them only infrequently. She did not think any of them really cared about her. Apparently she had underestimated them.

Her chest ached as she felt her sister's tears against her own cheek, evidence of how much she cared.

Jack's hand trembled as he caressed her head.

"I'm so sorry, Annalise. I pushed you into marrying Bloodsworth." His voice faded and he closed his eyes in a pained blink.

"Come, Annalise. Let us go home." Marguerite looped her arm around Annalise's waist and started to lead her from the room.

Annalise stopped, her gaze moving back to the settee where Owen had been sitting.

Only he wasn't there now.

Frowning, she looked around the library, searching. Her gaze flew over Jack and Marguerite to the housekeeper, "Where is . . ."

"Lord McDowell?" The housekeeper motioned behind her. "Oh, he just slipped out."

Her heart squeezed. Her gazed skipped wildly around the room, desperate, hopeful, as if she might have somehow overlooked him before.

"Come, Annalise." Marguerite squeezed her waist. "We'll get you home and soon all of this will be but a dim memory."

Annalise nodded numbly even as she still looked, still hunted for the sight of him.

He was gone.

Chapter Twenty-nine

Owen knocked on the door to Jack Hadley's Mayfair mansion. He glanced down the street. One block over sat Bloodsworth's mansion. She had lived so close to that bastard. He closed his eyes in a pained blink, recalling how close he had come to losing her.

Owen exhaled. The man was dead. He'd not give him another thought. He had enough demons in his past. Bloodsworth would not be added to their numbers. His only thoughts were for Annalise now. For being strong, good enough for her. For both of them. If she would let him.

He'd told himself to stay away. Her father and sister had swept in, and he just slipped from the room. What did she need him for anymore? Bloodsworth was dead. She had her family. Her freedom.

He'd told himself this for the last three days. He'd told himself to stay away. That he was nothing she deserved. That he couldn't be the kind of man she needed. He might not be Bloodsworth, but neither was he good enough for her.

She'd placed herself in danger. For him. He didn't want that kind of sacrifice from her, but she had gone and done it anyway. That kind of goodness and—he hoped—love, flowed through her. He would not be a fool to let her depart his life.

The front door opened and he presented his card. The butler led him to the drawing room. He waited impatiently for her, sitting for only a moment before rising and pacing the length of the room.

"Owen?"

He swung around. She stood in the doorway, garbed in a gown that once again did not fit her properly.

He couldn't help smiling. "I should have sent your new wardrobe over."

Her expression clouded over and he immediately regretted the words. He didn't want to send her clothes here. He wanted them to stay in his house. Just as he wanted *her* in his house.

Her chin lifted a notch. "Is that why you came? To discuss my clothes?"

He dragged a hand through his hair. He was fumbling this. "I came to see how you are faring."

"I've been home three days. You are only concerned with my welfare now?"

"I knew you were out of danger."

She nodded and advanced into the room. Lowering herself to a settee, she smoothed her hand over her lap. "Yes. I am quite safe now. Thank you, Lord McDowell."

He stiffened at the proper use of his title. He did not want that chilly reserve between them.

In two strides he was beside her. "Owen," he growled, taking her hands from her lap and folding them in his own.

With wide eyes, she tried to pull them free. He clung tightly.

"Why are you here?" she demanded, her brown eyes gleaming with anger.

His gaze devoured her face. "I'm here for you."

She ceased tugging her hands away. She moistened her lips. "I appreciate your concern," she began, her voice trembling. "It would have been more timely three days ago, but it's nice to know you care." She uttered this last with such derision that he knew she did not believe he cared.

Her hands slid free then and she was on her feet, moving for the drawing room doors. "You can find your way out."

He reached her in two strides, grabbing her arms and swinging her around, his voice rough as gravel even to his own ears. "Damn it, I'm not going anywhere until you listen to me."

Annalise blinked up at him, quite certain if she stood before him another moment and endured his extended sympathies she would break down and cry.

Three days. Three days had passed and he had not come. She had wept herself to sleep. It seemed absurd now that she had vowed to never be vulnerable again because she'd never in her whole life felt like this. And it was because she loved this man. She was raw and exposed before him, her heart in his hands, and he did not even realize . . . did not even care. Did not even want her.

She jerked her arms, trying to pull free, almost panicked to escape him before he realized how utterly at his mercy she was . . . that her heart was already his hostage.

"Let me go!"

"Annalise," he growled, wrapping his arms around her and hauling her close. "Why won't you listen to me?"

She shook her head, feeling the desperate burn of tears in her eyes. "No."

"I can't let you go . . ."

"Why?" she choked.

Something akin to panic crossed his face. She had never seen that look before. "Because I'm in love with you."

She stilled, her mouth sagging in a small O of surprise.

"God knows I've tried to let you go ever since I found you," he said hoarsely. "I can't. God, I can't. I don't want to." He dropped his forehead to rest against hers. "But if you ask it, I will."

His strong body shuddered against hers with the release of his confession. She brought her hands up to frame his face, holding him as if he were some bit of magic that might vanish into air.

She pressed her open mouth to his. He sighed, and she slid her tongue to meet his, kissing him greedily until they were both panting. Until his hardness prodded at her belly.

He lifted his lips. "I love you, Annalise." The words fanned her lips and her heart lifted, swelled until it ached.

"You . . ."

"I love you," he repeated. "I want to marry you. Today. I know that's not possible, but we can have the banns posted within the week." He stopped for breath, searching her face. "Say something." He drew a ragged breath. "Say *yes*."

She wrapped her arms around his neck. "Yes!"

He crushed her in a hug and lifted her off her feet.

"I love you, Owen."

His hand smoothed over the hair at the back of her head.

"Just promise me no honeymoon cruises in the country," she added with a gasping laugh, trapped in the tightness of his hug.

"Oh, Annalise, we won't be leaving our bedchamber for a great long time." His voice rumbled huskily beside her ear. "I might keep you there for the rest of your life, in fact."

She giggled as he pressed a kiss to her neck. "Indeed. That will be adventure enough."

Author's Note

A few years ago I was reading from a book of fairytales to my daughter when we came across the Chinese fairy tale, *The Beggar Princess*. In this story, the Beggar King's daughter marries a penniless young man with high social ambitions. Greedy for the money she brings to their union but embarrassed by his low-bred wife, he throws her overboard. Sound familiar? The Beggar Princess survives, of course. At this point in the story my daughter and I were breathless with anticipation to see the Beggar Princess overcome such a tragic turn, claim her happily ever after, and—fingers crossed!—watch as the wretched husband got his comeuppance. As I continued reading, that expectation was dashed.

The Beggar Princess and her husband eventually meet again. To make a long story short, he apologizes, she forgives him and they live happily ever after. The end. I was horrified . . . and left struggling to explain to my four-year-old daughter that women do not live happily ever with men who attempt to murder them.

Needless to say, the story of *The Beggar Princess* stuck with me all these years. It inspired the idea for the Forgotten Princesses series, and nothing is more fitting than concluding this series with Annalise's story. She is *my* Beggar Princess—the way the story should have been told. I hope you agree and enjoyed reading it as much as I enjoyed writing it.

Happy reading,
Sophie

TEN THINGS I LOVE ABOUT YOU

978-0-06-149189-4

If the elderly Earl of Newbury dies without an heir, his detested nephew Sebastian inherits everything. Newbury decides that Annabel Winslow is the answer to his problems. But the thought of marrying the earl makes Annabel's skin crawl, even though the union would save her family from ruin. Perhaps the earl's machinations will leave him out in the cold and spur a love match instead?

JUST LIKE HEAVEN

978-0-06-149190-0

Marcus Holroyd has promised his best friend, David Smythe-Smith, that he'll look out for David's sister, Honoria. Not an easy task when Honoria sets off for Cambridge determined to marry by the end of the season. When her advances are spurned can Marcus swoop in and steal her heart?

A NIGHT LIKE THIS

978-0-06-207290-0

Daniel Smythe-Smith vows to pursue the mysterious young governess Anne Wynter, even if that means spending his days with a ten-year-old who thinks she's a unicorn. And after years of dodging unwanted advances, the oh-so-dashing Earl of Winstead is the first man to truly tempt Anne.

Give in to your Impulses!

These unforgettable stories only take a second to buy and give you hours of reading pleasure!

Go to ***www.AvonImpulse.com*** and see what we have to offer.

Available wherever e-books are sold.